THE BIG SQUEEZE

Also by the author

The Kiss Off

The Come On

THE BIG SQUEEZE

JIM CIRNI

SOHO

Copyright ©1991 by James N. Cirnigliaro.

Published by
Soho Press, Inc.
853 Broadway
New York, NY 10003

Library of Congress Cataloging-in-Publication Data

Cirni, Jim, 1937–
The big squeeze / Jim Cirni. — 1st ed.
p. cm.
ISBN 1-56947-058-8
I. Title.
PS3553.I76B54   1991
813'.54—dc20   90-19851
CIP

Manufactured in the United States

For the Inzettas, Rose and Jim;
Bruce and Sharon; Mark, Michelle, Margo and Mallory.

With special thanks to Elsa Lewin,
Tonita Gardner, Eric Kocher and Willa Morris—the Group.

Lu mortu e mortu
pinsamu a lu vivu

THE BIG SQUEEZE

CHAPTER ONE

They didn't have to say anything to each other. They'd pulled this a hundred times before: stand around, blanket the room with hard looks and soft threats. Then hold out your hand and get paid. Simple as that. Except on occasion when they had to lean on the sucker. But that was rare.

Dip rang the bell. A woman answered, frizzy blonde with tired eyes peering out from behind the door. Early forties from what Dip could see of her; lines around the mouth and the corners of her eyes. But not bad, not bad at all.

"You Mrs. Gruber?"

"Don't remind me," she said.

"Your husband home?"

"Is the Pope a Jew? No, he's not home. Who the hell are you guys, anyway? You're not cops, I know that much."

Prize stepped forward, gave the door a gentle shove. "We're collectors from Goodwill."

The blonde looked him over, raised an eyebrow and said, "I get it."

Prize said, "No, *we* get it."

"Look," she said, "I already told you. He's not home."

"How do we know?" Prize said. "We just met you. I know broads a year don't tell the truth. Could be he's in there now, okay? Watchin' soaps maybe."

"You wanna come in, is that it? Wanna look around?"

"Beats standin' out here," Prize said.

While Gruber's wife was thinking it over, Dip said, "We're not gonna hurt you. Just wanna wait a bit."

She stepped out from behind the door, filling the frame with a sheer pink dressing gown, white legs peeking out from a short nightie underneath, boobs you could see pretty clear under two layers of frills.

Dip glanced over at Prize, caught the look on his face, eyes fixed on two dark circles, chest high.

"Well?" she said. "You gonna gape or come in?"

"Both," said Prize. "Nice place you got here," he told her.

"Sure," she said, "if you like motel rooms."

Dip looked around: walnut furniture, thin cushions on a bony couch, beige carpet stained and worn, end tables littered with magazines and used coffee cups. Near the window was an open ironing board with a basket of whites underneath. A game show was blasting on a black-and-white TV, some chick from Tacoma, screaming, jumping around like a hundred cans of tuna fish was something she'd always wanted.

Gruber's wife lowered the sound and positioned herself in front of the window. Her nightgown disappeared in the back light. "Bedroom's in there," she said, jerking her head to one side. "Go on, look. You won't find him."

"Check it out," Dip said to Prize.

"You check it out. I wanna talk to Mrs. Gruber, okay?"

"Helen," she said. "Call me Helen. What about you? You got names?"

"I'm Cisco," said Prize.

"Don't tell me," she said. "He's Pancho. Right?"

"I'm pissed," Dip said. "Look, if he ain't here, where is he?"

4

"Don't know," she said. "Haven't seen him in weeks."

"Why the hell didn't you say that in the first place?"

"Come on," she said, "don't get mad. Can I get you something? A drink? Coffee?"

"You got two grand lyin' around, we'll take that."

"You're gonna bust him up, aren't you?"

"Not if he pays."

She eyed Dip for a moment, then Prize. Dip was frowning, Prize was smiling. The choice was simple.

She glided toward Prize and said, "All right, so we got a situation here. What you call a conflict of interest. I mean you want his money, right?"

Prize winked. "Correctamundo!"

"That's the point," she said. "So do I."

"Life's a bitch," Prize said.

She smirked. "Tell me about it."

Meanwhile, Dip cruised the apartment, kitchen first, then the bedroom. No Gruber. He opened the closet and the dresser drawers, saw what he wanted, then covered the bathroom to confirm it.

He went back inside to hear some more lies, Helen Gruber saying, "Believe me, I wish I knew where he was."

"Wish harder," he said. "Haven't seen 'im in weeks, huh? What's he using for clothes? Inside, a closet fulla suits, shirts."

"He leaves them here. I mean it—really."

"His laundry, too? There's shorts in your hamper, T-shirts. What's he do, drop 'em off once a week?"

"My God," Helen said. "What are you, a skivvies freak? Get off on smells? Jesus."

Prize laughed but Dip knew he'd caught the message: same old story, wife helping a husband who didn't deserve help on his best day.

"Tell you what," Prize said. He pointed a finger at the laundry basket. "I find his BVD's in there, you eat 'em, okay?"

Helen Gruber closed her eyes real tight, aimed her nose at the ceiling like she was running it through her mind, the plus and minus of giving him over. A few seconds, then her eyes popped open, the hard face went soft and she cleared her throat.

Here it comes, Dip thought: proposition number one.

"Come on, you guys, don't do this to me." She spread the gown to show her legs, twisting one to give them a rear view. "Look at this calf, the veins. Six nights a week on my feet waiting tables, breaking my ass for rent money."

"We don't want *your* money," Dip said. "It's your husband's we want, givin' back what he owes."

"Two thousand dollars?"

"Yeah," Prize said. "Includin' carryin' costs. So tell us, where's he at?"

"Look," she said, "I mean, be reasonable. How's he gonna pay if you cripple him up? I need the money same as you. More, even."

"Where is he?"

"I need a cigarette," she said.

Prize gave her one of his Kools, lit it for her. "Where?"

She inhaled the smoke like it was country air on a spring day. "Where else?" she said, letting it out. "The track."

Dip said, "For that he's got money, eh?"

She shrugged.

"We'll wait," Prize said. "Go on, finish your ironing. We'll just watch."

She started to gripe but clammed up when Prize raised his hand. "You won't even know we're here, okay?" He put a cigarette in his mouth and parked himself on the couch. Dip took a chair near the door.

They waited.

Ten minutes later they heard the lock tumble. The door opened and Gruber sailed in. "I nailed 'em, babe! You shoulda been there. I—" He cut it short when he saw Prize. Prize, sitting there, looking casual, smiling at Gruber under a halo of cigarette smoke.

6

Gruber raised his chin. "Who the fuck are you?"

"How much you win?" Prize said.

Gruber said, "Look, pal, I don't know who you are but you better get outta here."

Dip got up quietly, moved in behind him. "Or what," he said.

Gruber spun around. "What the—"

Dip hit him. A short chopping punch to the solar plexus. Gruber gasped, doubled over and went down.

"Oh my God!" cried Helen. She ran out from behind the ironing board. Prize grabbed her, held her close.

Dip said, "I was you, I'd stay quiet."

"Yeah," Prize said. "'Less you wanna be layin' there next to 'im." He cocked his head, gazed at the fallen man. "Gotta admit, he looks kinda lonely. Don't he, Pancho?"

"Yeah," Dip said. "Real lonely. Like he ain't got a friend in the world."

Gruber turned himself over, started squirming. Dip looked down at him. A disgusting sight, Gruber crawling around with his red face, eyes leaking water. Another small-time shaker, rolling high on someone else's dough. He wanted to kick him but held back. The guy was too easy. One punch and he's ready to open up, like a flower on a spring morning.

"My friend asked you a question," Dip said.

Gruber shook his head. "Question? What question?"

Prize said, "Kick 'im in the nuts!" Dip cocked his leg. Gruber curled up in a ball.

"For God's sake," Helen wailed. "Give him a chance!"

"Hear that, Gruber?" Prize said. "She cares about you."

"Bastards!" Helen hissed.

Prize said, "Just two bastards and a no-good sonofabitch."

Gruber said, "I got your money."

Prize pushed Helen away. "See? See how easy it is. Next time *you* belt 'im, okay? Guaranteed he'll treat you better."

"All right," Dip said to Gruber. "Two large. You got it or don'tcha?"

7

"Two grand?" Gruber said. "I only borrowed one."

"That was six months ago," Dip said. "You ain't paid shit in three and you ain't been around to reason with. Whadaya do for a living, Gruber? Besides bein' a welsher."

"I'm a salesman," Gruber said. "Office supplies."

"Pay good?"

"For Chrissake," Prize said. "Take the bread, okay? I got a date in ten minutes."

It took only seconds for Gruber to count it out. Two thousand in small bills, handing it over like he should have done in the first place.

Patty's Restorante. Hardwood floor, tables without cloths, ladder-back chairs, ceiling of corrugated tin; light bulbs here and there, so dark you could barely see across the room. Not that anyone cared to, nothing to see but shady characters. Prize swaggered in, Dip following.

"The Prize is here," Eddie Jack announced, as if the Prize ever needed to be announced. Prize, lighting up the dingy place with his broad smile, that little hop in his walk, one hand at his crotch, tugging. The local joy boy.

"I'm buyin', Eddie," Prize hollered to the barman. "The Prize made a score today."

"Whadya hit?" Louie Lips said.

"Yeah, whadya hit? A triple? Bet it's a triple."

"Not what," Prize said. "Who!"

Louie waved a hand at him. "You and them broads. They'll bury you one day."

Prize wormed his way between Louie and the man called Phillie Fruits. Dip took a seat at the short end of the bar by the door. Diesel and Paulie Jr. walked in. Prize made a face and said under his breath, "Just what I need, Goofy and Pluto. Friggin' Paulie. Guy can smell money all the way from Queens."

Paulie went to a table while Diesel grabbed a stool beside

Phillie Fruits. "Over here," Paulie said, beckoning to Dip, then Prize. They nodded and walked over. "How'd you make out?" Paulie said.

"I'm fine, Paulie," Prize said. "How are you?"

They took chairs and sat, Paulie between them. "I'll ask *you*," he said to Dip. "How'd you make out?"

"I'm fine, too," Dip said. "The back's kinda stiff but—"

"Cut the shit! You find that prick or didn't ya?"

Prize took the money from his pocket and gave it over. "Two grand, Paulie. As ordered."

Paulie Jr. was a big, heavyset guy whose muscles had turned to flab about twenty years ago. His broad chest had sunk all the way to his beltline, and that iron jaw of his was nothing any-more, layers of loose flesh that hung and shook from his face like an old hunting dog. He was a fat mess in a chair but still as tough as they come, a rugged old warhorse. Definitely no guy to mess around with.

Dip watched as Paulie went to work. He was waiting for a change in expression, for the lights to go on in Paulie's eyes, like, "Okay, boys, you had your fun." But counting two grand in hundred-dollar bills was a major effort for Paulie Jr. His lips moved as he made the tally, licking his thumb, rolling back each bill with slow deliberation.

They could hear him now as he closed out the count: "Fifteen hun'red, sixteen hun'red,"—*lick*—"seventeen hun'red, eighteen hun'red,"—*lick*—"nineteen, twenty." And here came the light, like a rheostat behind Paulie's eyes.

Dip wasn't sure what made Paulie happier: getting his money or hitting the count on the first try. Whichever it was had made him happy enough to wink, peel off some bills and place them on the table. "Your cut," he said.

Prize said, "Gee, thanks, Dad. Just think, Dip. Now we can go to the movies, okay?"

Paulie lowered his chins into his chest. He clutched his over-sized belly and made a noise that sounded very much like laugh-

9

ter: a choking, rumbling sound mixed with a hack that shook his jowls and brought water to his eyes.

Prize lifted a single brow and aimed it at Dip. "That's an eighteen-hundred-dollar laugh you're hearin', Dipster."

Dip said, "Good thing it ain't more. He'd choke himself to death."

"You guys . . . ha, ha, ha . . . you fuckin' guys . . . ha, ha . . . you . . . ha, ha . . . crack me up . . . ha, ha, ha."

Diesel was standing there all of a sudden, looking down while Paulie looked up.

"What."

"Phillie Fruits," Diesel said. "He might have a line on that guy we're lookin' for. Better hear 'im out."

"Yeah, yeah, okay. Be right there. But these guys . . . ever talk to these guys? They'll crack ya up, Deez."

Diesel shrugged. He went back to the bar and Paulie Jr. began to crank himself up, his thin calves like a Volkswagen jack under a sixteen-wheeler. "You did good today, fellas," he said, breathing heavy from the lift. "But don't let up on 'im. Hit 'im again next week, all right?"

He started his turn then stopped. "Oh, almost forgot. Tony wants to see ya, Dip. At the funeral home tonight—before the wake."

"What's he want?"

Paulie Jr. jerked his round shoulders. "What's the difference?"

Dip arrived at Petrillo's Funeral Home in his brand-new suit: a double-breasted navy blue import with pleated pants and a starched white shirt. In respect for the dead he wore a black tie and carried an oversized mass card which he'd immediately offered to Tony Montello, holding it out in his left hand while extending his right hand for the shake it never got.

"Sorry for your trouble," Dip said.

"Yeah," Tony said. "Tough break."

Dip looked down at his hand. It wasn't that Tony was deliberately ignoring him. He was talking serious shit to his underboss, Sal "Trick" Tricari, and Dip's timing had been way off.

Without a word, he placed the card on the podium outside the slumber room where Louise Montello was in temporary residence.

He considered going inside to rattle off a few Hail Marys. But he thought better of it when he glimpsed the crowd. There had to be two hundred guys in there and not one of them was saying a word about the dearly departed. So he scribbled *Jack Dippolito* in the visitors' register and headed off for a smoke.

"Yo, Dip! Hold up a sec!" It was Tony, no doubt coming back for that handshake.

Once again Dip held out his hand. Tony pumped it limply. "I want you to do me a favor, Dip."

"Name it," Dip said. "You know I really feel bad about Louise. I mean, she was a good woman. Least that's what I hear."

"Yeah," Tony said. "Come with me, Dip. I wanna talk."

With more than a little pride, Dip followed his don back up the corridor toward the front entrance and directly into Charlie Petrillo's office, a glass box with a big desk, cabinets, and a few chairs. The chairs were lined up along a paneled wall that sported a half dozen plaques praising Charlie for his outstanding achievements in the neighborhood. Dip had known the Petrillos for years. If Charlie had achieved anything, it was for patching and painting stiffs blown apart in gang wars.

Tony closed the door, parked his ass on the edge of Charlie's desk and said, "There's gonna be headaches tonight, Dip."

Dip waited for an explanation of the trouble. From the way Tony's eyebrows were bunching up it had to be heavy-duty.

"It's my asshole brother-in-law," Tony said.

"Uh-oh," Dip said.

"Yeah. Imagine the balls on that guy. Wants to make peace with his sister. Eight years he made like she was dead. Now that she is, he wants 'ta talk it out."

"He's not comin' here?"

"You don't know Joey Cara. He'll do anything to stick it up my ass." The phone rang and Tony snapped it up. "Yeah."

Dip knew all about Joey Cara. If you lived in Brooklyn you knew Cara and you knew Montello, the childhood rivals who, as bosses, had cut the borough in half ten years earlier and battled one another from then on. The only break in the contest was the shaky truce Louise, Cara's sister, had insisted on during her two-year illness. Even Joey couldn't turn his back on his dying sister's request. But the truce had passed with her.

Louise was gone now, and from what Dip could see, all bets were off. Tony hung up.

Dip said, "I can't believe he'll show. Not here. I mean Jesus, Tony, Joey's not that crazy. There's gotta be a hundred guns here tonight. Including mine."

He raised a trouser leg over his ankle, showing Tony the holstered .32-caliber snubnose he'd inherited from his brother, Nickie. Dip had never used the gun. He only carried it to shake up the deadbeats who wouldn't pay their debts no matter how hard you hit them or how many arms you broke. It wasn't what he wanted to do for Tony Montello, but it beat the hell out of shooting people.

Tony waved his hand in Dip's face. "Cover it up before you blow your toes off. I got enough guys for that kinda shit."

"I don't get it," Dip said. "Whadaya want me to do?"

"It's my kid," Tony said. "I want you to watch 'im. Keep 'im here in the office, amuse 'im. Tell 'im war stories about your brother and me. Tell 'im anything you want but keep his ass outta the way. I don't know what Joey Cara's got in mind. Could be a lotta bullshit, could be trouble. You never know. But Jimmy's a weird kid. Got delusions. You know how it is, eh, Dip?"

How what is? Dip wanted to say. But he nodded and said, "Sure, Tony."

"Okay," Tony said, and left. Then in came his kid wearing an eight-hundred-dollar suit and a hundred-dollar tie. A steady flow of traffic passed by the glass in Petrillo's office. What had to be ten dozen guys—guys he didn't know by sight, but would have known

by name (had he been out in the hall where he wanted to be) —
streamed by. He should have been alongside Diesel and Paulie Jr.,
and Trick, who was doing the introductions, especially with Joey
Cara coming. The kid looked just like his old man at that age and
dressed like his Uncle Joey.

Tony Montello had spent the better part of his life battling Joe
Cara. As little kids from the same neighborhood they'd fought
each other, each with his own gang, scrapling over territory.
There had never been a clear winner. Not in all those years. The
rivalry just went on. For thirty-five years they had fought one
another.

When they were twenty, they joined separate Families, Joey in
Bensonhurst, Tony in Greenpoint. As Tony moved up, so did Joey.
By the time they were forty, they'd each reached the top and war
was imminent in the streets of Brooklyn. It was only a matter of
time. Then Louise got involved.

Joey Cara knew that his feelings for his sister went beyond
anything normal, but he didn't care. Whatever she wanted, Joey
would give her. "I want Tony Montello," she told him. She'd been
seeing Montello on the sneak. He had been widowed a year
earlier. He had proposed and she had accepted. Joey was crushed.
Louise felt bad for her brother but she wouldn't let it go. She
wanted what she wanted.

"I want your word," she said. "Say you'll never hurt Tony. Swear
it to me."

To Joey, making that vow was anguish. But he took her hand and
granted her betrothal wish.

Joey had never gone back on his word although he had been
tempted. He'd taken shit from Montello. Publicly Joey Cara
blamed the Council: they wouldn't condone a hit on Montello. It
saved face for Joey, but everyone knew the situation was eating at
him. Now she was dead, her stepson was nineteen, and the feud
was about to reignite.

More men arrived to pay their respects.

"Fuck me," Dip said under his breath.

"And the horse you rode in on," said the kid. They were the first words he had spoken.

Dip looked at him. Tall, rangy kid; good looking, with thick black hair, like his old man's, but down to his shoulders.

"Whadya say?"

"You heard me."

Jimmy unfolded his legs, fished a pack of Camels from his pocket. "Gimme a light."

"How old are you?"

"Twenty."

"You're nineteen."

"Oh, man, gimme a break."

"I'd love to," Dip said, "but you wouldn't like it."

Jimmy put a cigarette in his mouth. He kept it there, unlit. "I know all about you, Dippolito," he said. The cigarette bounced around, a real tough look. "You ain't even a made guy. You're a flunkie, for Chrissake. You want the truth, it's goddamn embarrassin'."

"How do you think *I* feel?" Dip said.

"I bleed for you. You got a light or don'tcha?"

Without a word Dip handed him a book of matches. Jimmy opened it with one hand, turned down a match and lit it with his thumb. "Thanks," he said, snorting blue smoke out of his nostrils.

Dip smirked and shook his head. Jimmy caught it. "What's your problem, man?"

"Who's tougher?" Dip said. "You or your father?"

"What the hell does that mean?"

"Forget it."

"No, you started it."

"Skip it," Dip said. "You wouldn't understand anyway."

"I understand more than you think," Jimmy said. "More than *he* thinks, too."

"Your old man's no jerk, kid. He didn't get where he is by acting tough."

"How the fuck would you know?"

"You work for a guy twenty years, you get to know 'im. He doesn't act tough because he doesn't have to. He *is* tough. Actin' and bein' is two different things."

"Jesus," Jimmy said. "Twenty years. I was you I'd go to night school. This job ain't workin' out."

"I been to night school," Dip said.

Jimmy took a drag, blew it out. "Now I know you're an asshole. I'm quittin' school pretty soon. I ain't gonna waste my time learnin' shit I'll never use. I don't have to."

Dip thought it over. Kid had a point. With Tony on top, his future was set. He wouldn't have to sweat for the small change. Not like me, Dip reminded himself.

"That's what I thought when I was your age," he said. "Look where it got me."

"Hey," Jimmy said, "tell it to Sweeney, eh? I got my own problems."

"Yeah," Dip said. "You got it rough."

Jimmy went mute and Dip went back to watching the mourners outside the glass partition. Ten o'clock and no Cara. Maybe the guy wasn't crazy after all.

"So what's the story?" Jimmy said, looking down at his gold Omega.

"What story?"

"Joey Cara. Think he'll show?"

Dip shrugged.

"That's right," Jimmy said. "What the hell would you know? I'll tell you this though. He puts a move on my old man, I'm goin' out there, kick some ass."

"You're goin' nowhere," Dip said. "Case you forgot, kid, you're at a wake. That's your mother inside. So show a little respect and do like your old man says. Stay outta trouble."

"She ain't my mother," Jimmy said. "My mother died when I was ten."

"I know that," Dip said. "But Louise took care of you, didn't she? Gave you meals, cleaned your clothes?"

"Big deal," Jimmy said. "She never gave a shit about me. Only thing she ever cared about was my old man's money."

"How do *you* know?" Dip said. "From what I hear she loved your father. She stuck it to Joey, didn't she? Her own brother? And they were close, too. He had a fit when she married Tony, disowned her, for Chrissake."

"I'm glad she's dead," Jimmy said.

"Hey, look," Dip said, "why don't you shut your mouth?"

"Why don't *you*? You want the truth?"

"About what?"

"Louise and my old man."

"I don't wanna hear it," Dip said.

"He's been foolin' around on her. How's that grab ya?"

"By the balls. And you're tellin' *me* about it? You got a lot to learn, buddy."

"Shit," Jimmy said. "Who you gonna tell? Word gets back, I never said nothin'. Yeah. He fooled around and I told her. That's what killed her. And that's the truth."

"Jesus," Dip said. He heard the commotion before he saw it, knew it was Joey Cara. The guy had a voice like Wolfman Jack, and it was bouncing along the halls, shaking the glass walls of Petrillo's office. Not even the plush wallpaper absorbed the volume.

"I came here alone!" Joey Cara shouted. He was short and dumpy, had a round face, flat nose, and a pencil mustache over thin lips.

"Good," Tony said. "You can leave the same way."

"I wanna talk to my sister."

"That's what prayers are for."

"Outta my way! I'm gonna see Louise."

Joey Cara took a few steps along the crowded corridor toward the visitation room. Dip couldn't see him anymore, but he had a clear view of Trick and Paulie Jr. Trick nodded at Paulie. Paulie motioned down the hall and Diesel appeared at his side, pressed against the glass of the office wall.

Jimmy popped out of his chair. "C'mon, let's get out there!"

"Siddown," Dip said.

Jimmy hesitated, then went for the door. Dip grabbed his arm. "Stay put!"

Jimmy struggled. He was a big kid, well-developed in the chest and shoulders, but no match for Dip. At six-three, there weren't too many guys he couldn't handle. He pulled the kid back and put a bear hug on him.

"Be cool," he said. "He's got enough help."

Dip didn't see the first punch, didn't know who threw it. But Diesel fell backward against the glass and the next thing he saw was a half dozen guys doing swan dives at Joey Cara.

"I'm gonna flatten that guy!" Jimmy hollered.

"You're gonna watch," Dip said. "Like me."

They took Joey with little trouble, held his arms and had him pressed against the far wall as Tony walked up to him.

Tony said, "It's only for Louise I'm gonna let you walk outta here." He was so close to Joey, they were touching noses. "I'll ask you one more time. You gonna leave like a gentleman or ain'tcha?"

"And I'm askin' you, scumbag: Do I see Louise or don't I?"

"Get 'im outta here," Tony said.

They dragged Joey toward the front door. "You've had it, Montello! You're finished!"

"Go on," Tony said, now standing in the doorway to the office, "go see who you gotta see."

"You're dead! *Morta!*"

Tony waved him off. "We'll see who's dead."

"Great," Dip muttered. "Now we're in for it." He waited until they'd hustled Cara out before releasing Jimmy.

"Thanks for nothin', you gutless bastard," Jimmy said, his face flushed. "I'm gonna tell 'im what you did."

"Don't be a jerk," Dip said.

"We'll see who's a jerk." The kid went to his father. "You all right, Dad?"

"Get inside," Tony said.

"Yeah, but—"

"Get in there!"

Trick and Tony came in and closed the door. The two of them settled into chairs.

"He wouldn't lemme help you," Jimmy said. "I wanted to help but he wouldn't lemme go."

"Shut up!"

"Shit," Jimmy said. He plunged his hands deep in his pockets and plopped on a chair. "I never do nothin'."

The scowl that Tony had for Jimmy began to fade, replaced by a warm smile which he now directed at Dip. "You did good, Dip. This kid'a mine . . ." He shook his head. "I don't know."

"He's all right," Dip said. "He'll be okay. A little wired, that's all."

Jimmy flicked his head. "Who the hell asked you, Dippolito?"

Tony said, "He did what I asked 'im to do. That's more than I'll say for you. Better wise up, Jimmy. I'm tellin' you, ya better learn."

"I'll learn," Jimmy said, "when you teach me."

"Get 'im outta here, Trick," Tony said. "Take 'im inside, let 'im pray for his mother."

"She ain't my mother."

Dip had always thought he owned the fastest hands in Greenpoint, until he saw Tony's. His arm shot out—*smack*—and Jimmy's face jerked to one side. Trick flinched and went for the gun inside his jacket. An open palm had left a bright red imprint on the kid's cheek.

Jimmy's eyes filled up but he didn't cry. He just sat there looking up at his father. There was no defiance in his look, or any other expression Dip could read. He'd swallowed his pride and was accepting humiliation without a whimper. The kid had shown something here and Dip wondered if his old man had picked up on it as the wake ended abruptly and they all stepped into the hall.

"So whadaya think?" Trick said.

In the hallway they prepared to leave: Trick, Diesel, Paulie Jr., and Dip surrounding Tony Montello, Jimmy edging toward the room where the body was laid out for viewing.

"We got an army outside," Paulie was saying. "He'd be nuts to pull a stunt tonight."

"That's the headache," Trick said. "We know Joey's nuts."

"Well," Tony said, "we better get used to it. From now on nobody's safe." He turned to Paulie. "I want you to take my kid home. Take Dip with you."

Paulie made a face. "What good's he gonna do?"

"Don't worry about Dip," Tony said. "He's all right. Besides, Jimmy likes 'im." He motioned Dip closer. "Ain't that right, Dip?"

"I don't know," Dip said. "He don't seem to like anybody."

"Don't let 'im fool you. I know the kid. Believe you me, he likes you."

Dip had his doubts, about a lot of things. He didn't believe for a minute that Tony knew shit about his kid. He also didn't believe Joey Cara would put a move on Tony. Not yet, anyway. He'd wait for a better time, a better place. Still, he thought, you never know.

Meanwhile, the last thing in the world he wanted to do was hold hands with Jimmy Montello while the rest of the crew held a shootout in front of Petrillo's. He'd never live it down, for Chrissake. The whole thing with the guys was image.

Petrillo's funeral home increasingly resembled a military outpost. It was a frigging arsenal. Guys checking their guns, spinning the chambers, buffing the finish on their sleeves. Christ, what assholes! Dip thought.

"All right," Tony said, "here's what we do. Diesel, you get the car, bring it around. Trick, you go out first, looks okay, gimme the sign. If Joey's out there he's gonna see me. He'll make his move or follow me. That'll clear it for you, Paulie. Dip, you keep the kid close. Give us five, ten minutes, then move out."

"Right," said Paulie.

"Right," Diesel echoed.

"Oughta work," Trick said. "One thing for sure. He pulls an act and the whole fuckin' city's gonna know it was him."

Tony said, "Find my son, Dip. Tell 'im we're leavin'."

Dip nodded and went to get the kid. He found him in the viewing room.

"What the fuck?" Jimmy said. "How come I gotta go with you?"

"Because your father says so."

"Ah, man, what a drag."

"Why?" said Dip. "'Cause he wants your ass in one piece? He's worried about you. I'd be too, you were my kid."

"Shit," Jimmy said. "This 'kid' shit sucks."

Dip smiled. "Think it's bad now, wait'll you grow up."

From where he stood behind the glass door, looking out at the street, Dip couldn't imagine anyone getting cute. There were ten guys out there, milling around, just waiting.

"Looks okay to me," he told Paulie Jr., standing next to him.

Paulie grunted.

"There's Diesel," Tony said as a white El Dorado eased up to the curb. "Okay, Trick, check it out."

Trick opened the door and a gust of wind blew in. It was cold as a bitch out there but nobody wore a hat or coat.

Styles had changed, Dip thought. He flashed to Nickie and the way he looked the last time he'd seen him. Twelve years ago, January. A big-ass overcoat and a gray fedora worn low over his eyes. Robert Mitchum! Nickie never left the house without his goddamn fedora. They'd found it thirty feet from his body. Dip had claimed it along with the rest of Nickie's stuff. He still had it up in his closet, Nickie's gray fedora, stained with blood from the shot that blew his head apart.

Jimmy was getting antsy, bouncing around while they waited behind the door. Outside, Trick was leaning against the Caddie, talking it over with Diesel.

"Lemme go with you," Jimmy said.

Tony ignored him.

"Nothin's gonna happen," Jimmy said. "C'mon, lemme go."

Dip put his hand on Jimmy's shoulder. "Relax, kid. He knows what he's doin'."

"Okay," Tony said. "There's the sign. Let's go."

He hurried out and started down the steps toward Trick. Jimmy bolted after him. Dip lunged, but too late; the kid had already caught up. Tony whirled and, at that moment, Dip saw a car across the street, smoke purring from the exhaust, tinted windows open a crack on the driver's side.

"Heads up!" he hollered, pushing Paulie aside, running after Jimmy.

"It's a hit!" someone yelled.

Tony dropped to his knees. He tried to haul Jimmy down but the kid pulled away. He stood there pointing, the car burning rubber, the barrel of a gun jutting from its window.

Shots cracked.

Dip threw his body at the kid. They hit the ground with Jimmy mostly underneath.

"He's pullin' out! Get 'im, nail the sonofabitch!"

Dip couldn't see a damn thing. His head was buried in Jimmy's chest, his arms around him, holding tight. From a distance, tires screeched, faded away.

"Forget it," Paulie said. "He's outta here."

Tony was on his feet. "Jimmy! Where's Jimmy?"

"Right here," Paulie said. "Dip's got 'im."

Dip hadn't moved. The kid was still under him, pinned to the ground.

"Get offa me, you ape!"

Tony leaned over. "You okay, Jimmy? You hurt?"

Dip felt a hand on his shoulder. "Good work, Dip. All right, let 'im up."

Dip rolled over, pushed by Jimmy who was scrambling to his feet. Tony said, "Jesus, Jimmy's hit. There's blood all over 'im."

Jimmy had a large bloodstain down the front of his jacket.

"I'm all right," Jimmy said.

Dip tried to get up, too, but a sudden pain shot up his arm.

"He's hit," Paulie said. "It's Dip. They got 'im."

Dip looked down at his new suit. The front was covered with blood. He moaned. Three hundred dollars shot to shit.

By now Dip was surrounded by Trick's crew, staring down at him like they'd never seen anyone shot before. Pretty funny, except Dip was in no mood to laugh. A dozen guys and he's the one that gets nailed.

He didn't know where he'd been shot or how serious it was. The only bright spot was the location of the pain: in his arm, not his chest. He figured he'd live.

Tony hunkered low, put a hand under Dip's head, raised it off the ground. Somebody shoved a balled-up overcoat underneath for a pillow. "How bad?"

"They wrecked my suit," Dip said.

Tony laughed. "He's all right. Get 'im inside. I'll have Charlie look at 'im."

"Thanks," Dip said, "but I ain't ready for Charlie. Not yet I ain't."

They brought him inside. Jimmy tagged along. Charlie Petrillo seemed to know what he was doing. He peeled the shirt off Dip's back and poked around with soft, pudgy fingers.

"It's clean, Tony. Just a graze. You're a lucky man, Dippolito. Another inch or two, you'd be downstairs on one of my tables."

Dip pictured himself, cold and blue, with Charlie Petrillo sticking tubes in him, draining his blood, humming along with Tony Bennett on the Make-Believe Ballroom.

"That's a lotta blood for a graze," Trick said.

"Looks bad," Charlie said, "but it's not. I'll paste him up for now." He pulled a card from his wallet, gave it to Dip and said, "Go see this guy tomorrow. He'll square it away."

Dip examined the card: Dr. Renzo Garella. It wasn't major medical but it was just as good. Better in fact. With Garella there'd be no forms to fill out and no report filed with the P.D.

Tony sent Jimmy outside with Diesel and Paulie Jr. While

Charlie cleaned the wound, Trick and Tony lit their cigars. Along with the smoke, they blew ideas around Charlie's office.

"Had'a be Cara," Trick said.

"I don't know." Tony squinted. "I'd like to believe it. I mean I got a hardon for this guy won't quit. But I don't know. It's not his kinda move. Too sloppy, the whole thing was a mess."

"You saw 'im when he left," Trick said.

Tony shook his head. "The whole joint saw 'im, heard 'im. He was pissed enough to take me out right here. But I know Joey Cara. He blows hot but he's cool underneath. He's a real planner, Joey is."

"I ain't sayin' it was him out there," Trick said. "He had time for a call. Five minutes, all it takes to get a button."

Tony moved closer to Dip and Charlie. He seemed fascinated with the way Dip's arm was getting wrapped. "You're an artist, Petrillo, a real master. I didn't tell you before but you did a beautiful job on Louise. That cancer ate her up. What the hell was she? Ninety pounds?" He looked back at Trick. "I hear you, Trick. But I'm still not convinced. I'll get Joey or he'll get me. But not like this, the way it happened tonight."

"That's it," Charlie said, closing his first aid kit with a sharp click. "All set."

"Thanks, Charlie," Tony said. "Give us a minute, will ya? You too, Trick. I wanna talk with Dip."

Dip wasn't feeling very well, his arm hurt more than he was letting on. He just wanted to go home. But that would have to wait. Tony was lining him up for a bullshit story and all he could do was hear him out.

He wasn't comfortable being alone with Tony Montello. He didn't mind the personal attention, but it was something he should have gotten years ago. Not now, because he'd caught a bullet. What he did tonight was instinct. He saw trouble and he reacted. Hell, he'd been doing that his whole life and no one, especially Tony, had ever said a word about it.

"How's it feel?" Tony said.

Dip touched his arm. "No big deal."

"I owe you, Dip. You hadn't jumped the kid, mighta been him got hit."

"No sweat," Dip said.

Tony nodded, rubbed his chin and said, "I got nobody else, Dip. No brothers, no wife. Most of all, I got no other kids. Don't ever tell 'im, but I got big plans for that little sonofabitch. Oh, I know what you're thinkin'. But I don't kid myself. He might catch it one day. Though if that happens, God forbid, I don't wanna be around to see it."

Dip watched him grab a chair and slide it over.

"I never told you this, Dip," Tony said, "but I liked your brother. He was a stand-up guy. It hurt like hell when he got it."

"Hurt me, too, Tony. Hurt a lot."

"Yeah," Tony said. "I guess it was my fault in a way. I'm the one sent 'im. That Dempsey character. Shoulda known he wouldn't go down easy. Crummy little bar like that. The guy shoulda rolled over, paid us the few lousy dollars and gone about his business. But no. Crazy Irish bastard, had to play it hard."

Dip felt his eyes welling up. Tony'd better shut his face. "Nickie knew the risk," Dip said. "He wouldn't'a blamed you any more than I do."

"Jackie Dippolito," Tony said. "I shoulda done more, ya know? For you and your mother. How is she, anyway?"

"She died. Three years ago."

Tony's eyes popped. "You shittin' me? Oh, Christ. Jesus. Why didn't you tell me? Sonofabitch. I woulda done somethin', Dip. Sent money, flowers. Goddamn!"

Dip was really squirming now. All this humble, nice-guy shit just wasn't holding up. If Tony honestly cared, he would have asked about his mother right after Nickie was killed. Instead, what she got was a few grand and a promise to pay off the house.

He put a cigarette in his mouth. Tony lit it for him.

"Can I say somethin'?" Dip asked.

"Sure," Tony said, like: You're the king, Dip. Say anything you want, it's okay—for tonight.

Dip said, "You don't owe me anything. Not for what happened to Nickie. And definitely not for tonight. I'm glad your son's okay but it's not because of me. I do my job and you pay me for it. Simple as that."

Tony pursed his lips. His head bounced up and down like he agreed wholeheartedly with what he'd just heard. It's what he wanted to hear and Dip knew it.

"I like you, Dip. Trouble is I'm too far from guys like you. I oughta get out more, talk to my guys, let 'em know I care. Whadaya doin' these days?"

Dip had a hard time concealing his shock. Was it possible he didn't know? More likely he didn't give a shit.

"So what is it?" Tony said. "You workin' the phones?"

"I haven't done that for ten years. I'm a collector now. For Diesel and Paulie Jr."

"Right," Tony said quickly. "Sure. I forget sometimes." He got up. "Well, look. I ain't gonna forget what happened tonight. I'm gonna think about it, talk it over with Trick. Could be we'll move you up, find a better spot. How'd that be, eh?"

"You're the boss," Dip said.

CHAPTER TWO

Dip had a bad night. His arm kept him awake; his talk with Tony, the uncertainty of a new job.

Moving up in the organization was something he'd always wanted. Now that he had a promise, he wasn't sure anymore. A better job meant greater risk. Especially now. The smell of war was so thick he could taste it. Regardless of what Tony said last night, Dip knew they'd be going after Cara. The thought of a war made him shudder as he watched the morning sun cut a pattern on his bedroom wall. He didn't feature ending up the way Nickie had.

And Robin. What about Robin? Could he really expect her to live with something like that? No fucking way.

So what's the alternative? Cut her loose? Sure. And do what? He was tired of bouncing around with Prize. He'd had his fill of bimbos, dates at the Copa and the one-night-stands. He was thirty-five. Time to pull it together, give a little.

Ease off, Dip. You're tired, the mind's on overdrive. Hit the shower, scramble an egg, pop a few Excedrin. You made the choice so live with it.

The phone rang.

He didn't answer. If it wasn't Robin it had to be Prize. He didn't know anyone else who would ever use the phone. The only friends he had were connected guys, and every one of them was too paranoid to dial. They spent all their time driving over when they could easier drop a coin and save the gas.

It kept ringing.

Robin or Prize? Not that it mattered. Robin lived right upstairs and Prize had a place around the corner. Whichever it was, they'd be at his door soon enough.

He let it ring. When it stopped, he hauled himself out of bed, cursing the pain and thanking God at the same time that it wasn't his right arm.

He had a routine he followed every morning. Coffee first, then a shower and a large, hot breakfast. He loved to cook and was proud of the skill he had in the kitchen. He'd learned it all from his mother. He'd watch her put the meals together, then try it himself the following week. Except for breakfast. His mother was never big on breakfast. That was something he'd picked up on his own.

The kitchen was in the back, overlooking the yard. Even for Greenpoint it wasn't much of a yard: about thirty feet of hard dirt, a small cement patio buckling in the middle and cracked around the edges. He used to play back there as a kid, he and Prize, sneaking up from the cellar where old man Vincenzo made the wine that stunk out the joint. They were tenants then, top floor right, rooms no different than the ones he had now. Except now he owned the place. Thanks to Nickie, who'd bought it for their mother after their father died in '58.

Jack Dippolito, land baron. Five rent-paying tenants at four-fifty a pop. Not bad for a dropout with a high school equivalency diploma. But not good, either. He wasn't tied to his roots. He *was* a root. Like his neighbors whose families had lived and died on the same block for three generations.

Toughest thing about change, Dip thought, is not being part of it. The whole country's flipping out: crooks in the White House, creeps burning the flag, fags marching down Fifth Avenue. He felt out of it, a stranger in a city he knew like the back of his hand.

He put up a pot of coffee. It took longer to make with one hand, but he got it done and was heading for the shower when Robin knocked on the door. He knew it was her by the knock: two quick raps, like she didn't want to bother him, wasn't sure she'd be welcome. Not that he blamed her. For almost a year he'd been running hot and cold, driving her nuts with his own uncertainty. He wasn't used to "commitments," as she called them. He'd never been this close to a woman, never let himself. Robin had opened a door in his life and he'd been trying to close it ever since.

He hooked his arm in the sling Charlie had made for him, went to the door and stood behind it. Because of his arm, he was in no rush to face Robin. He wasn't sure what he'd tell her, which is why he hadn't called her last night. Put off today what you can do tomorrow. He should have learned by now that tomorrow comes too fast and nothing ever changes when it does. Oh, well.

He opened the door and stood there in nothing more than his shorts, and the sling he hoped would conceal the wound.

"Hi," he said. "Want some breakfast?"

"My God!" she said. "What happened to you?"

He stepped aside to let her in.

She stood about five-four. Which made her look about four-five next to Dip. She had long black hair she kept straight and clean and parted down the middle. Her eyes were pale gray. She had full lips, white teeth, and high cheekbones that had caught Dip's eye the first moment he'd met her.

"So what happened?" she said.

"I'll tell you later. I need a shower. There's coffee on the stove."

"Just a *minute,* Mr. Dippolito!"

He turned and faced her. Her cheeks were flushed.

"You going to tell me or not?" she said.

"C'mon," he said. "It's nothin'. A small accident."

"Is that why you didn't call last night? I heard you come in. Who were those men with you?"

"A few guys from Patty's. Forget it, it's nothin'."

She went to him, pulled the sling aside and peeked in. "Accident, huh? You're lying, Dip. I always know when you're lying. What happened?"

He pulled away. "See what I mean? I told you, I can't tell you things. You gotta stop with the questions, Robin. I mean it."

"Hey, I'm not your priest. I *know* what you do."

"You don't know shit," he said. "And that's how it oughta be."

"That's *not* how it ought to be. Besides," she said, "I know enough. You forget what you say when I'm making love to you."

"That ain't fair," he said.

"Oh, come off it. You haven't worked a day since I've known you. You spend all your time at Patty's, you and Prize. Think I don't know it's a hangout for gangsters?"

"Oh, man."

"Don't 'man' me! We've talked about this till we're blue in the face. When are you going to shake those bums out of your life?"

"And do what? I don't have a job, remember? I never promised anything."

"Sure," she said. Then she aped him, hunching over like a gorilla, knuckles dragging: " 'I'll get out one day, Robin. I swear I will.' "

"One day ain't now," he said. "I'll quit when I'm ready. Besides, I'm gettin' a new job."

She gave him a look, like: I-don't-have-to-be-a-farmer-to-know-cowshit. She said, "What *kind* of job?"

"Whadaya mean, 'what kinda job?' Sellin' ice cream cones to starvin' Eskimos! You want me to change, I'm changin'. Now let's can the crap for a while, okay? I'm all grungy, need a shower."

He gave her a second to come back at him. What he got was a soft smile. She pointed at the sling. "You'll need help," she said. "Come on, let me help you."

"Ouch! Take it easy, eh?"

"Then stop squirming."

29

They were in the shower, Robin under the water, Dip just out of the flow, standing sideways with his left arm toward the wall. She'd been trying to sneak a look at the wound. So far he'd kept her off.

"This half's clean," she said, patting his rump. "Turn. Unless you want to smell on one side."

"How about the front?" he said. "You didn't do *that* yet."

"Oh, no? Then how come he's standing tall? Come on, turn around. All or nothing, that's the deal."

She pressed her chest against his good arm, then rocked her shoulders.

"I take it back," he said.

"What."

"You. You don't look Irish after all." He placed his finger on the end of her nose. It was small and straight with a slight bob at the tip. "The nose looks Irish," he said. "But these tits are definitely Jewish."

"How would you know? I thought you only dated Italians."

He bent down and kissed her nipples, the hot spray bouncing off his back. She moaned and threw her head up. She had wide hips that made her waist seem smaller than it was. He liked to tease her about the hips, that she needed them for balance. "You better stop," she said, her voice low, throaty.

"Mmmm," he said, painting circles with his tongue.

"Your arm. You'll hurt yourself."

He squinted up at her, through the water. "I'll chance it."

It was an old claw-footed tub, large enough for both of them to sit in, or play in. He reached behind her, shut the tap and turned her around. Without a word she spread her legs and placed her hands on the wall, leaning forward like a suspect in a shakedown.

He'd always been klutzy with women, awkward. He'd never been told but then he'd never stuck around long enough. It was different with Robin. He wanted to please her and she wasn't too proud to show him how. Like what he was doing now to the back of her neck, brushing his lips across her skin.

He parted her wet hair and blew lightly behind her ears. She shivered and he pulled away, watching her shoulders turn into goose flesh. "More," she said.

He took his time, using his tongue like a feather, up and down, side to side, over the nape of her neck. He nipped her ear lobes and she shivered again.

She cleared her throat but it didn't matter. Her voice was still deep and raspy. "You're getting better at this, Dippolito."

"I been studyin'," he said.

She arched her back a little more. "Show me what you've learned," she whispered hoarsely.

He had to bend his knees. She felt him probing and pressed against him. "Oh, God," she said. "Slow, Dip. Please, do it slow. God."

He did it slowly at first. It didn't help. He was too hot to hold back. She sensed his urgency and changed up. "Fast, Dip. Do it fast!"

He moved quickly but carefully, trying to be gentle. He felt her shudder and he tensed. "Let it go, Dip," she said.

He wanted to stop but he was too close to the edge.

Robin said, "It's all right, hon, it's okay."

Forgetting his wound, he wrapped her in his arms, pulled her close and let himself go.

Robin cried out.

"Shit," he said.

She waited for him to release her. He pulled away and suddenly felt his head going light, the steamy room closing in.

"Too hot," he said.

She spun around. "Dip, you're bleeding!"

"I'm all right," he said. "Just get me outta here."

Back in the living room, he flopped on the couch.

"It's my fault," she said.

Dip on the couch, his arm across his chest, felt the room had finally stopped spinning.

"What're you blamin' yourself for? You can't help it you're the sexiest broad in Brooklyn."

"Let me look at it."

"Forget the arm. It's all right."

She came toward him. He slid over to make room. "How'd it happen, Dip? You still haven't told me."

"Don't be a pain in the ass," he said.

"Why? I'm an intelligent, upper-middle-class Jewish female. It's my God-given right to be a pain in the ass. Besides, who else is going to care about you?"

"I got friends."

"Oh, sure. They're lined up in the street, can't wait to see how you feel. You've got one other friend, Dippolito. Speaking of which, where is that prize package of yours?"

"He had a funeral today. Don't worry, he'll be around."

"Don't hold your breath."

"I thought you liked Prize."

"I do. I just don't like what he stands for."

"What the hell's that mean?"

She got up and began pacing again, her breasts swinging free under one of Dip's sweatshirts, bunched at the hips, white panties peeking out. She made a U-turn and went to the window, split the blinds and peered out.

"Looks cold."

"Yeah," he said, wondering if she'd finished and gotten off the soapbox. He couldn't defend Prize any more than himself. They were two of a kind.

She wasn't finished. "Do you think Prize will ever settle down?" she said.

"You mean like me?"

"Cute, Dip. But it is time, wouldn't you say? I mean, you're both pushing forty."

"Mid-thirties," Dip said. "Don't rush it."

"Oh, *I* can wait," she said. "But I'm not so sure about Mother Nature. The day's coming when even Prize will have to slow down."

"Never happen," Dip said.

"I don't know," she said. "You ask me, I think he's a bad influence."

He said, "My whole life's a bad influence."

"Then change it," she said, an over-the-shoulder shot.

"What the hell you want me to do, Robin? Wash cars? Sell hot dogs on the corner? I'm a punk, for Chrissake."

She came back to him. "You're not a punk, Dip. You're too sensitive."

"Christ," he said. "Don't ever say that in Patty's."

"God forbid. Not Patty's. That's one helluva sandbox, Patty's."

Dip said, "What you want is a guy who's straight, Robin."

"I had one, remember?"

"Gary? That creep? Least I admit what I am. You got a rank taste in men, s'all I gotta say."

That did it. She got quiet and went back to the window.

Best way to shut her up was to mention Gary. That sleazy son of a bitch. They'd been married for a year when they took the rooms upstairs. Robin, quiet, letting big-mouth do all the talking. "I'm a promoter," he said, walking the rooms, running his hands over the walls, looking for cracks and a new paint job. A promoter moving to Greenpoint. The only thing Gary ever promoted was himself.

For six months Dip had kept his mouth shut, hearing the fights, Robin crying, pleading with him to stop. He'd catch her the following morning on her way to work, eyes swollen, arms bruised. A real sweetheart, Gary.

"How's it goin'?" Dip would ask, casual, his glance avoiding her shame.

She'd lower her face and say, "Fine," like nothing happened.

"Hey, look. It's none of my business. But you ever need help, just clang the radiator."

A week later he heard it. The walls shook, heavy footsteps overhead. They'd been going at it for hours, the fight reaching him through the ceiling, their floor. It was bad enough she had to pay the bills by herself; beating up on her in a major way, that was the last straw. The last for Dip, too. A wife-beating junkie? In his house? He couldn't wait to get his hands on him. Low-life mother-fucker. He took the stairs three at a time and didn't bother to knock when he reached the door.

Robin was on the floor, arms over her face, while Gary, big-ass promoter, threw punches.

"What the hell *you* want? Get outta here!"

The guy was a six-footer, wiry but out of shape and high on shit. Dip could have handled him with a virus and a hundred-two temp, even with the candlestick the guy was menacing him with.

He looked at Robin, unsure if she approved. Broads were funny that way, unpredictable. A guy treats them like dirt, but they're the first to yell "foul" when you try to help them out.

"Get him out of here!" she said. "Please. Get him out. I never want to see him again."

"You heard," Dip said. He pointed toward the door. "Get out! 'Less you wanna spend your life with a candlestick up your ass."

Gary didn't squawk. He raised his hands and said, "Okay, okay, I'm goin'." He craned his neck, looking for Robin. "Thanks for nothin', bitch!"

Dip walked him down the stairs, out to the stoop. He turned Gary around. "Listen to me, hotshot. I'll tell you this one time. Don't matter if she wants you back. You step one foot in this house the state'll have to support ya. Got it?"

"Here he comes," Robin said, fussing with the blinds.

"Prize? Told you he'd come."

"Look at him grinning," she said, her head tilted, tracking Prize up the front steps. "Must have been some funeral, a million laughs."

Dip pictured his best friend, those long legs and that bebop walk; music on the brain, rhythm and blues, rock'n roll, headful of funky sounds. A couple of grand in caps and the eternal smile to show them off. Lenny Bustamente, alias Prize. Greenpoint's original up-guy.

He hadn't even knocked on the door and already Dip felt his mood changing, getting lighter. It's the way it was from the time they were kids. It always would be.

"I'd better get dressed," Robin said.

She headed for the bedroom. Dip held out his arms. "Gimme a kiss."

"Oh, sure. Now you're happy. You ought to let *him* give you a shower. Most women have women for competition. I've got Prize."

"I like 'im," Dip said, "but I don't love 'im."

"Huh," Robin said. "You shouldn't love *me* as much."

Doors were slamming, front and vestibule. Dip had never known Prize to make a quiet entrance.

"Hey! Big Dipper! You in there? It's your main man."

Robin shook her head. "Go on, 'Big Dipper,' answer the door."

"It's open," Jack Dippolito called.

The door flew open and Prize stepped in, alligator shoes under gray flannel slacks, black blazer, and a paisley tie.

He pulled a cigarette from his mouth. "My man, Dipster," he said. "Look at'cha. Layin' warm on the couch while the rest of us freeze our nuts. Do me a favor, Dip. I buy the farm, don't put me in no cemetery. It's too fuckin' cold, okay?"

He snapped his head just in time to catch Robin closing the bedroom door. "I caught'cha!" he called to her. "I'd know that ass anywhere. Hey! Robin, tweet-tweet! Your daddy know you're playin' house with a ginzo?"

Behind the door, Robin hollered, "Up yours, Prize!"

"One time, Robin baby. Just one time."

"Shut up, Prize," Dip said.

Prize stretched his grin. "I love that chick. Fuckin' hips." He hugged his waist with his right arm, held his left in the air and began dancing. "Fly me to the moon, let me sit upon a star—hey, man, check this." He swayed to his own music, rocked forward then back on his right foot, his left leg held way out. He rolled his neck and gazed up at the ceiling. "A dip for the Dip," he said. "How about that, eh?"

35

"Terrific," Dip said. "A real Arthur Murray. Even look like 'im."

Prize straightened up, cigarette back in his mouth. He'd lost the grin, brown eyes squinting through curling smoke.

"I heard what happened. You okay? Christ, Dip, like I'm sorry, man. I shoulda been there."

"Yeah, sure. Like you woulda saved me, right? Where the hell were you, anyway?"

He grabbed his crotch. "Duty called, you know? But you're okay, eh? Seen Garella? Great doctor, man. I had piles once. Tied 'em up in a fuckin' rubber band and snapped 'em all the way to fuckin' Jersey. What he say? You all right?"

"You're as bad as her. Forget about it. So, how was the funeral?"

"You kiddin'? Didn't know better I'd think it was Marilyn Monroe they were buryin' out there. Christ, talk about limos. Far as the eye could see, nothin' but limos, okay? Fuckin' Montello. Guy's got class, I'll say that for 'im."

"Look," Dip said. "Don't say nothin' about this to her. I don't want her nervous."

"Nervous about what?" Robin said, zipping her jeans, marching toward them. "All right, Dip. Tell me."

"Your boyfriend's a hero," Prize said. "He saved the king. Long live the fuckin' king."

"I saved the prince," Dip said.

Prize raised a finger. "For which the king will be forever grateful. Made a ton-load'a points last night, Dipperoo. Word's out you're goin' places."

"So am I," Robin said, heading for the door.

"Where you goin'?" Dip said.

"Work."

"Thought you called in sick?"

"C'mon, Tweets," Prize said, "stick around. We'll have lunch, okay? What's on the menu, Dip?"

Robin grimaced. "How can you stand this man? You're hurt and he expects you to make him lunch."

Prize laughed. "Takes more than a bullet to stop the Dipster."

"Bullet! *Bullet!* Oh, that's great. Wonderful!"

"Damn it, Prize."

"What? What'd I say? You're in love, ain'tcha? For better or worse?"

"Fuck," Robin said. "You're a real prize."

Prize turned to Dip. "What's wrong with her? She on the rag or what?"

"You're disgusting," Robin said.

"Jesus, Dip, help me out here. She's killin' me."

Dip wasn't thrilled with the way it was going. He didn't mind them teasing each other, he was used to it. But this kind of shit, if he didn't step in, would lead to a grudge. He didn't want that. He cared too much for both of them.

"C'mon you guys, knock it off. Tell her you're sorry, Lenny."

"Hey, you kiddin' or what? I love this chick." He dropped to his knees, spread his arms and said, "Forgive me, Tweets. You gotta forgive me or I'll die on the spot." Then he clutched his chest and fell on the floor. "Oh, God, she don't love me no more. Call the doctor, Dip. Tell 'im I'm sinkin' fast." He groaned, threw his legs in the air and let them fall.

Robin went over to him and looked down. "Get up, you damn fool."

"Kiss," he moaned. "I need a kiss."

She looked at Dip, who only laughed. She sighed, bent down and kissed him lightly on the cheek. Suddenly Prize reached out, grabbed her by the waist and pulled her down, rolled her over and kissed her hard on the lips. They wrestled around for a moment before Prize released her.

"Forget the doctor," he exclaimed. "Call the morgue. Tell 'em I just died and went to heaven."

They were in Tony's kitchen—Trick, Diesel and Paulie Jr., standing around with thumbs up their asses, filling the room with smoke and dumb looks.

Tony Montello was hot. Nobody'd heard a damn thing about

37

who had taken the shot at the funeral home. Not one fucking word. Joey Cara was laying low and nobody had a clue.

"Gimme somethin', Trick. You better gimme somethin'."

"We been tryin'," Trick said. "Nobody's talkin'."

"That's right," Paulie said. "We shmeared a few guys but nobody's talkin'."

Tony said, "You guys are good at spendin' money. Used to be guys didn't talk we gave 'em knuckles. I wanna know who pulled the trigger."

"Was Joey all right," Trick said. "Had'a be."

"Had'a be? We start a war 'cause of *had'a be?* Come on, Tricari, earn your fuckin' money. Gimme somethin' to go on."

Diesel coughed on his cigarette.

"What about you, Deez?"

Diesel knitted his brow. "Ain't sure. Maybe nothin'."

"Maybe nothin' he says. You got somethin' or don'tcha?"

"Ain't sure." Diesel scratched his chin. "Down at Patty's last night, a few guys flappin' their gums." He shrugged. "I don't know, prob'ly nothin'."

Tony spread his arms, palms up, eyed Trick like "what's with this guy?"

Trick said, "You like Buffalo?"

"The city?"

"No, the meat!"

Diesel worked on it. "Never been there," he said.

"That's where you're goin'," Trick said. "Now spit it out, for Chrissake! We got farts in the wind over here, this guy playin' games."

"All right already," Diesel said. "I'm at the bar, 'bout two in the morning. Boppy—you know 'im, small guy, beady eyes, owes more to shys than he'll make in his life?"

"Yeah," said Tony. "What about 'im?"

Diesel shrugged. "He's down the end, battin' the shit with Phillie Fruits. 'Joey this and Joey that,' you know?"

"S'all right, Deez, take your time. We got all fuckin' day."

"Nothin', Jeez, no big deal. I go down there. Boppy's half in the tank, Phillie's so loaded can't see straight, lookin' up at the Schlitz sign, one eye covered, tryin' to focus. I say, 'What's the word, Bop? You got a line on Joey we should know?' He fucks around with a stirrer like he don't wanna talk. I say, 'Hey, numbhead, you know somethin' or don'tcha?'"

Diesel stopped and looked around, Tony first, then Trick.

Trick said, "Do we order a pizza or what? Come on, for fucksake, what'd he say?"

"He got a cousin knows a guy in one'a Joey's crews. Out in Bensonhurst. They're gumbas or somethin'. Anyways, the cousin said . . ." Diesel stopped, took a deep pull on his smoke.

"I'm gonna kill this guy," Trick said.

"After me," said Paulie.

"The guy said Joey ain't lookin' for war. He's plenty sore at you, Tony. But a war he don't want."

"That's it?" Tony said. "You bust our guts for this? If Joey's plenty sore he's not gonna sit around callin' me names."

"I know," Diesel said. "He wants to get you legal. The guy told the cousin—"

"Fuck the cousin!"

"Let 'im finish."

"I'm gettin' old," Paulie said.

"You wanna hear this or not?" said Diesel.

"All right, Diesel. Whadaya mean, 'legal'?"

"Like he nails you on somethin' and takes it to the Council."

Tony's face lit up. "Yeah. Sure. Smart piece'a shit, Joey is. He's up to somethin'. Knows he can't beat me in a war so he plays the angles. I like it, like it a lot."

"You like it?" Trick said. "Guy wants 'ta close you out and you like it? Christ, Tony. I mean—"

"Let's off 'im," Paulie Jr. said. "Get it the fuck over with."

Tony waved him off. "He'd like us to try. Don't you see? That's why he messed it up at Charlie's place."

Paulie wrinkled his nose. "I don't get it."

"Me neither," said Diesel.

Trick nodded at Tony.

Tony said, "We're surrounded with morons. Look, he wants me to go after 'im. I make the first move, he goes to the Council. Yaps a storm—Montello's fuckin' up. We can't fight 'em all, Paulie. No way."

"So whada we do? Sit around, wait for the scam?"

"Relax, Trick. No. First I gotta be sure." He turned to Diesel. "Diesel . . ."

"That's all he said, Tony."

"You did good. Now shut up and listen. Find Boppy, bring 'im in. We'll get a line on this guy from Bensonhurst. Cara wants 'ta be cute, okay. So can I."

"I don't like it," Trick said. "I think we oughta blast 'im."

"We got time, Trick. Plenty'a time."

Tony heard the front door slam. Three o'clock, the kid home from school.

"Hey, Dad, you home?"

"In here! All right, you guys know what to do. Take off. What's goin' on?" Tony said to his son from behind the storm door, watching Trick and the boys pull away. "Every day this week it's three, three-fifteen. Didn't know better I'd think you had a girl in the neighborhood."

"I don't have time for girls."

"You don't have time for homework either. When's the last time you opened a book?"

"I read," Jimmy said.

"Yeah," Tony said. "The tout sheet. Who the hell takes your bets, anyway? I catch 'im I'll break his legs."

"C'mon, Dad, you know I can't bet. I'm too young."

"You're too young for a lotta things. Don't stop you from tryin'."

"Like you always say, Dad, 'you can't pick it up if you don't lay it down.'"

Tony eyed him up. "And you can't wear a hat if you got no head. Come inside a minute. I wanna talk."

"You ain't gonna talk about college again?" Jimmy said, trailing his father to the living room.

Tony plopped in his fat-armed easy chair, across from the twenty-two-inch Zenith color console, pictures of Jimmy's real mother on top, staring back at them. Jimmy missed Rita and wondered how much Tony missed her. The way his father had picked up with Louise right away didn't seem right. And now this other bimbo, Eva Barone. Where the hell's he find these chicks? Jimmy wondered.

His old man was playing it slow, waiting for Jimmy to find a spot, settle in. He looked around for a place to sit, the couch covered with that plastic shit, hot in the summer, cold in the winter, freeze your ass to sit on, move and it sounds like farts. But Louise, that pain in the ass, had to change the house around, make it look like a frigging museum.

"Siddown," his father said. "I don't like lookin' up."

He sat on the floor, the couch against his back, legs outstretched under the big glass table. "Gonna tell me 'bout the birds and bees, Dad?"

"That's good," Tony said. "Make it easier, what I have to say." He lit a cigar, rolled it around. "It's no good bein' alone, you know? Now that Louise is gone—God rest her soul—"

"We're not alone. I got you and you got me."

"Sure, kid, and that's great and all." He waved his arm, blue smoke hung in the air. "But this house, needs . . . you know, like the woman's touch."

Jimmy knew where this was going. He'd heard the same crap eight years ago, when Louise walked in and took over.

"It ain't the house, Dad. It's you needs the touch. It's Eva, ain't it? Jesus."

Tony leaned forward, arms on his knees. "Now you listen. I know you didn't care much for Louise."

"I hated her."

"All right. I can buy that. Your mother dyin' and all, you bein' a ten-year-old kid. But you ain't a kid anymore."

"Since when?" Jimmy said. "I was a kid this morning."

"Don't get smart. You know what I mean."

"Yeah, I know. It fits the plan."

"Look," Tony said, "right now we got a maid who cleans and cooks for us."

Jimmy said, "That's enough. S'all I want."

"Well, I don't," Tony said. "Not for me and especially not for you. Kid like you needs a mother. All kids need a mother. It's healthy—mom and pop, that kind'a shit. You hear what I'm sayin'?"

"It *ain't* healthy. It's weird. How many mothers you gonna get me?"

"Whadaya want me to do?" Tony said. "I can't help it they get sick and die. Think I like the idea? I loved those women."

"That why you cheated?"

"Watch your mouth!"

"It's true. When mom was alive you cheated with Louise. When Louise was here you cheated with Eva Barone. Think I don't know? I can see good enough."

"What you're gonna see is the back'a my hand. I don't want no arguin' here. The way it's been, it ain't right."

"I know it ain't. Why can't we stay alone, the two of us?"

"Because I can't. Look at you. Torn pants, cruddy sneakers, hair all over the place. What is it? Don't you give a shit how you look? You're my son, for Chrissake!"

"Ah, man."

"C'mon, Jimmy, you know how it is. I wanna be here for you, but I can't. That's why I need Eva. What's the face for? She's all right, believe me. You get to know her, you'll see what I mean. I want you guys to get along."

"You're gonna marry her, ain'tcha?"

"Yeah. We're goin' to Vegas."

Jimmy sat up. "Vegas?"

"End'a June. Figured I'd take you along."

"You shittin' me?"

42

Tony smiled, puffed his cigar. "I need a best man."

"Oh, wow," Jimmy said. "Vegas. Awright!"

"Thought you'd like the idea. So how about it? You'll be my gumba. Pretty good, eh?"

"Shit, yeah, it's good."

"Only one thing."

Jimmy slouched. Here it comes.

"Hey. Can't pick it up if you don't lay it down. I'm not askin' much. All you gotta do is be friends with Eva."

"Whadaya mean 'friends'? Like do what she tells me, run the errands, vacuum the rugs? Go downstairs when you guys are upstairs? Like Louise, right?"

"No, no," Tony said. "Eva's different. We keep the maid. You do what you want, no hassles. Just treat her right, that's all."

There was nothing Jimmy could do or say would change his father's mind. Eva Barone was on the way in. Eva, what the hell did he know about Eva? Nothing, except what he'd seen. Eva in the short skirts and the red hair, a face load of makeup, bracelets jangling, you could hear them a block away. Those times at Patty's, Eva cruising up to their table like she was just passing through: "Oh, this must be Jimmy. Good looking kid, image of his daddy. Better keep your eye on this boy, Mr. Montello. He looks like a lady killer to me."

Phony bitch! Who was she kidding? But all right. Play the game a while.

"Okay, Dad," he said. "I'll give it a shot."

"Good, good," Tony said, head in the smoke and a dopey grin on his face. He stuck out his hand. Jimmy shook it. "She'll be here in a few minutes. Give her the glad hand. You know, make with the smiles. She thinks you're great, Jimmy. Really."

Jimmy said, "You won't take it back, will you? About Vegas?"

"Hell no. Already made the plans. Desert Inn. Got the rooms and everything. Coupla suites, one just for you. Figure we'll fly out right after the ceremony."

"What ceremony? You said Vegas."

"Not the weddin'."

"I don't get it."

Tony shook his head. "See what I mean? Where's your brain? In two months it's June, kid, remember? Graduation!"

Joey Cara had a thing for boats so he'd bought a house on the water in Mill Basin, a peaceful peninsula near Floyd Bennett Field, dropped a forty-foot Chriscraft off the private dock in his backyard and used it for both business and pleasure, even in winter. Joey loved the boat.

As usual, he was down below, in the galley which was more like a floating living room: wet bar, teak wood tables, full-length carpets, benches padded with leather. Sonny figured the cost at a cool quarter of a million; figured, too, that if Joey could afford a boat, he'd get himself a plane one day.

Sonny had called the meeting but chose not to rush to his purpose. They had a few drinks, smoked cigars and passed the time. It didn't seem to bother Joey that his main rival was running around Brooklyn like he owned it. Casually, Sonny reminded him of that fact.

Joey's round face went dark and he damn near chomped the end off his cigar. "I'd love to whack that bastard," he said, "about as much as he'd like to whack me. That's why it ain't gonna happen. Neither one of us can line up enough votes. It's like us and the Russians. We both got the hardware but nobody can use it. It's a fuckin' stalemate."

"Yeah," Sonny said.

Joey belched, blew out smoke and said, "We'll just have to wait. He'll make another mistake. Guaranteed."

Sonny said, "You know he's gettin' married again."

Joey laughed.

"What's so funny?" Sonny said. "I figured sure you'd be pissed. Your sister ain't hardly dead."

Joey said, "I would be if it was anybody else. Eva Barone? Shit, I know the broad. A real barracuda."

"I don't know," Sonny said. "I hear he's real happy about it."

Joey shrugged. "Let 'im. I know Eva. She'll have his nuts in a vise by the time they get back from their honeymoon. Serves him right, the rat bastard."

Sonny said, "Why don't we line up a few cowboys, let 'em do the job for us. Then I'll take care of the cowboys. Who's gonna know?"

"*Who's* gonna know?" Joey said. "Every hood in the country, that's who. Wouldn't matter if we hit Tony Montello on the moon. It's gonna come back to me."

"I guess you're right." Sonny looked disappointed.

"Of course, you can't ever be sure," Joey said. "Could be some other guys on the Council want Montello as bad as me. So far I ain't heard. But who's gonna say, with Montello sittin' there? Tell you what, Sonny. Lemme poke around. I hear anything positive, I'll send you out." He chuckled and thought about what he did know, and they didn't—that Montello was a marked man.

From outside came the sound and swell from an outboard motor. Cold waves slapped against the boat, made it rock like a baby's cradle. Joey eased back in his chair, drew deep on his cigar.

"Well?" Joey said. "Whadaya think?"

Beyond Joey's head, Sonny watched the dock going up and down. "I don't know."

Joey said, "I got a better idea. Get over to Greenpoint. Find Tricari or that jerk Diesel. Tell 'em I gotta see Montello. Tonight."

Joey's men looked surprised and troubled. "You sure, boss?" Sonny said.

"Go on," Joey said. "Get outta here!"

After his men were gone, Joey had second thoughts. He wondered if he ought to just let it happen. The thought of Montello iced brought a smile to Joey's face. But the vow he'd made was something he had to honor. Break it, and he'd carry the curse for the rest of his days. He spread the sports pages over his face and dozed for a while. An hour rocked by.

Joey felt the boat rock, knew someone had jumped aboard. He looked up and saw his driver coming down the galley stairs.

"It's all set," the driver said. "Twelve midnight at the Villa Maria."

"You sure?"

"Tricari set it up. He told Montello himself."

Joey checked his watch. Ten hours. The Villa Maria was out in Staten Island, on neutral turf. "Okay," he said, "let's go to the club."

There were two cars in the street, Joey's Lincoln and the driver's Chevy coupe. The driver headed for the coupe.

"Hold it," Joey said. He held out his keys. "We'll take the Lincoln. It's smoother."

The driver opened the back door but Joey shook his head. "I'll sit in front."

It was the last thing Joey ever said as the car launched itself straight up and onto the roof of the marina.

CHAPTER THREE

"So how's the arm?" Prize said as Dip slid into the passenger seat. Prize wanted to know about Dip's arm: Was it good enough to twist somebody else's?

"Comin' around," Dip said.

"You ain't gonna scare nobody with one arm, you know."

"Why? Where we goin'?"

"Forest Hills. Guy name DeSoto."

"How late is he?"

"Three weeks."

"He pay the vig?"

"He ain't paid shit, okay? That's why we're goin'."

"Who's he owe?"

"Who you think? Trick's hot on this guy. He's all over Paulie Jr."

"All right, let's go. I wanna get back by six. Gonna meet Robin at Patty's."

"Now there's a kick," Prize said, gunning the motor of his new Camaro, apple red exterior, white leather upholstery and one-way glass in the side and rear windows. He slammed a cassette in the deck: Mick Jagger and the Rolling Stones. Mick's funky voice cut through the speakers. Prize pounded out rhythms on the steering wheel.

"What's goin' with you and Tweets?" he said.

"I don't know. Look, just drive, all right?"

Prize shook his head. "Poor old Dipster," he said solemnly. "Stung in the ass by the love bug. Times are changed, beau. How many times I gotta tell ya? You don't have to love 'em anymore, okay? A shot in the bloomers twice a week, you got 'em for life."

Dip lit a cigarette and blew the smoke at Prize. He needed this shit right now like he needed DeSoto.

"You got a big mouth, Prize."

"What's the worse can happen?" Prize said. "Divorce?"

Dip said, "I don't tell her spit and you come in with your big mouth flappin' in the breeze."

"She knows the score," Prize said. "Come on."

"I just don't wanna remind her, that's all—cram it down her throat."

They eyed each other, Dip wondering what his friend had on his mind. He sensed the change in mood in Prize, a sudden downshift, as if Dip wasn't the only guy here had problems.

Dip reached out, punched him playfully on the arm. "It's all right, I still love ya."

Prize let out a sigh and said, "Gimme a smoke, will ya."

Dip gave him his pack, watched him light up. No doubt about it, the Prize was down all right. Except how do you reach him? Guy could be dying of cancer and never say a word about it. A real tight ass, Prize. Thirty years of friendship and Dip still hadn't broken the code.

If he led him on, maybe, got him going . . .

"I'm thinkin' about gettin' married," Dip said.

No reaction.

"Hey, Mr. Bustamente, I said I'm—"

"I heard ya. Whadaya want me to say—congratulations? Congratulations, okay?"

"That's it? Congratulations?"

"You love her, don'tcha? It's what happens when you love a chick. It's a good move, Dip . . . I guess."

"I'll need a best man," Dip said. "You interested?"

Prize, getting weirder by the minute, took a drag and grunted.

"Is that a yes or a no?"

"You gotta ask me? Who else you got besides me? Who gives a shit if you live or die except the Prize? Sure. Sure, I'll do it. Wanna be an asshole, that's up to you. Yeah, I'll do it . . . if I'm here."

"What's that supposed to mean? 'If I'm here.'"

"Nothin', forget it."

"Forget shit! 'If I'm here.' What's 'if I'm here'?"

Prize nodded a few times. "You of all guys," he said. "You're the one's always askin' about jobs. You're thinkin' about it, too."

"So I'm thinkin'," Dip said. "So what?"

"Thinkin' don't make it, Dip. You oughta be doin'. Robin, she wants you out. So get out, okay? Pack up and get the fuck out."

Dip cocked his head. Was he hearing right?

"Wait a minute," he said. "I had a few belts, could effect my hearing."

"You heard right," Prize said. "Look, you ain't a made guy any more than me. We're bustin' our hump for a buncha clowns don't know their asshole from an eight ball. Me and you, Dip, we're livin' on handouts—nickels and dimes, for Chrissake. And for what? I mean where's it gettin' us? I score two grand for Paulie and what'd we get? A hundred? Big fuckin' deal. We'll never get the big bucks and that's the fuckin' truth, okay?"

Dip said, "You gettin' out? That the story? Pack your bags and off you go. Like that?"

"I told you, I'm thinkin' about it. Guy can think, can't he?"

"Since when?" Dip said. "Only thing you ever think about is gettin' laid. Whadya do, read the want ads? Seen a job loadin' trucks? Union scale and two weeks off in the summer? I don't believe what I'm hearin'."

"Why?" Prize said. "I mean, they don't own me. Nobody owns me. I wanna split, I split."

Dip said, "You're a piece'a work. Nobody owns you, eh? You're gonna split, right? Try it, see how far you get. You love it here. Now, c'mon, cut the shit and tell me what's really buggin' you."

"I just told you, for Chrissake."

"Yeah, you told me. Bullshit you told me. What is it? Money? You into shys, that it? I got a few bucks. How much you need, just tell me what you need."

"What I need is to get outta here. I don't know—California maybe. L.A. Been thinkin' about it, coupla weeks now."

"L.A., huh? Like the Dodgers? Who you kiddin'? You'd be lost in L.A. Whadaya gonna do, cruise Hollywood and Vine? There's more whackos out there than we got over here. C'mon, you're messin' up my head."

Prize didn't say anything, just looked around, letting his gaze fall here and there. Dip had a strange feeling in the pit of his stomach. Like something was down there, something hard and getting harder. There was more to be said here, a lot more. Go after him, Dip thought, don't let it drop.

But Prize had already shut him out, leaving Dip without an opening. So they sat saying nothing, the knot in Dip's stomach growing larger, harder.

"You don't like women, do you, Prize?"

Prize covered his heart with an open palm. "Me? Don't like women? Come on, Dip, I get a cramp just thinkin' about them."

"Yeah," Dip said. "In your dick."

"Better there than my head. Look at you, for Chrissake. Tied up in knots, don't know where you're goin', what you're doin'. Least I know, okay? Or I did until . . ."

"Till what?"

"This music sucks," Prize said. He yanked Jagger out of his track and punched up the radio.

"Wait a minute."

"Ah, man, forget it, yeah?"

Dip studied his friend, the creases in his forehead. He'd seen this act before. Once, a year ago, when Prize caught a dose from some skank he met in Jersey. Time before that, when he knocked up some guy's wife, the broad wanting the baby, Prize flipping out.

They picked up speed over the Kosciusko Bridge. Then he said, "Hey, Prize."

"Yeah." Eyes straight out there, fixed on the road, the potholes.

"Remember little Rinaldi?"

"Orphan Annie? Shit, don't remind me."

Annie Rinaldi, castoff from a busted marriage. Fourteen years old, living with an aunt didn't give a damn what the kid did long as she wasn't around when the boyfriends popped in. Annie Rinaldi, taking notes from the aunt, working the neighborhood: twelve-, thirteen-year-old boys, boys like Dip and Prize. Little Annie, Greenpoint's town pump.

"A guy don't forget his first piece," Dip said.

"C'mon, Dip. Thirteen? Jesus."

"Know what I think? I think she's the one messed you up. Her and the aunt."

"She bit my dick, for Chrissake! Took a chunk out of it, okay?"

"Get outta here."

"Yeah? You saw the teeth marks. Anyways, it wasn't her."

"Then you admit it."

"Admit what?"

"You hate women."

"What is this? You in night school again? Psych One, Hard Ons for Women? There's only one broad in this world I can't stand. My old lady."

"Why? 'Cause she liked the sauce?"

"No. 'Cause she liked it better than me. Now drop it, yeah? You're pissin' me off."

"I'm tryin' to help you," Dip said. "Look, your old man got killed in the war. Times were tough and she folded, that's all. It happens. I mean she treated you good. Never hit you, right?"

"Never kissed me, either. Not that I wanted it. Stinkin' rye on her breath, knock'ya out, okay? Droppin' dead was the best thing

51

could happen. So get off it. You get me pissed I'll take it out on DeSoto."

"Wait," Dip said, raising a hand toward Prize. The radio was rattling off news bulletins, the announcement of Joey Cara's demise at the top of the local items.

Trick felt sweat running down the back of his shirt. His face was hot and his heart began to pound. He put his hand to his chest. *Thump-thump—thump—thump-thump.* What's going on here? Was it fear he felt? Or the first signs of a heart attack?

He heard someone cough, looked up, saw Diesel staring at him. "What the hell do you want?"

Diesel said, "Jeez, Trick, you look like shit."

"You come in to tell me that?"

Diesel shrugged. "It's the old man," he said. "He's out front raisin' hell. You want the truth, he looks worse'n you."

Trick nodded and went in.

Tony Montello was in no mood for bullshit or deadbeats. Which is what he found at the Good Fellows Sports & Social Club.

A dozen guys were sitting in folding chairs, pawing newspapers and flapping their gums over current events. In particular, the killing of Joey Cara whose picture was plastered over page one. They saw him coming and promptly turned away, as if by showing their backs they'd avoid the flack.

Squinting, Tony hacked his way through cigarette smoke, planted himself at mid-floor and roared at the back of their broad necks. "What the hell are you guys readin'? You oughta know what it says in the papers. We *make* the fuckin' news, don't we?" He leaned over, snatched the front page from the nearest hand. "Ain't this a coincidence," he said, slapping Joey's photo. "The very guy we were looking for. Right here on page one."

A low murmur rose from the chairs.

"I guess information's gonna walk in, eh? Say, 'Here I am'?" He

52

threw the paper on the floor, waved his hand in disgust. "You guys oughta stick to Lil' Abner. It's more your speed."

He looked around the room, spotted the back of Diesel's head. "Hey, numbnuts! Tell Trick I wanna see 'im. Right now!"

"I'm here," Trick said.

"Shit," Tony said and headed for Trick's office. He stormed in. Trick and Diesel followed.

"Tell me again, Trick," Tony sneered. "How much we payin' those guys? I want horseshit, I'd buy a farm."

"We're workin'," Diesel whined.

"At what?" Montello said. "Social studies? What's with you guys? You dense or what? I want to know *who!* This shit can ruin us."

"Sure, Tony," Diesel said. "I was just goin'."

"Where?" Montello yelled. "Where the fuck you goin'? Canada?"

Diesel glanced at Trick. Trick shook him off. Montello picked it up, said, "What's goin' on?"

Trick nodded to Diesel. "Go on, tell 'im."

"Boppy," Diesel said in a rush. "We're lookin' for 'im."

Montello hoisted his eyebrows. "I *know* that!"

Trick rose from behind his desk. "He was the shooter at the funeral home, Tony."

Montello thought it over, using the time to calm himself down. He rubbed his chin. "Boppy works for us. *Our* guy shot at *us?*"

"Looks that way," Diesel said, sweating. "A guy parkin' his car saw the whole thing, then dove under his dashboard. The description fit Boppy."

"He's a friend'a Prize's," Trick piped. "Maybe Prize knows where he is."

"Yeah," Diesel said. "Trick thought—"

"No," Montello said. "I wanna hear, Trick."

Trick said, "It's a long shot. Paulie seen 'em at Patty's a few times—Prize and Boppy. I wanna see 'im anyway so I figure what the hell, it's worth a look."

"Could be," Montello said.

"Yeah," Diesel said. "Boppy sure ain't around, can't find 'im nowhere."

Montello exploded. "What is it over here, a fuckin' plague? Guys are walkin' left and right and we don't know shit. This is *my* fuckin' town, for Chrissake."

"I'll get 'im," Diesel said.

Montello snorted. "Never mind. I'll get 'im myself. You couldn't get the clap in a Chinese whorehouse."

Trick said, "I betcha Dip knows where Prize is. They're always together."

"I know that," Montello snapped. "All right, Diesel. Get over to Dip's place. Tell 'im to be at my house tonight." He turned to Trick. "Okay. Now what's the latest on the Cara hit?"

"Musta been his own crew," said Diesel. "I mean, it wasn't us."

Trick said, "Lotsa guys hated Cara. Coulda been anybody."

"Yeah," Tony said almost to himself, his apprehension growing. No one had more to gain by Joey's death than he did. How long would it take for the Council to point a finger at him? Of course he could always swear innocence. But that was too degrading. He'd never copped a plea in his life and wasn't about to start. They wouldn't believe him anyway. He'd wind up having to fight the whole organization. Goddamn that Cara, Tony thought. He was as much trouble dead as alive.

Tony said, "We gotta find who's responsible. Top priority. Trick, I want you and Diesel out on the street. Learn what you can. I'll stay here with Paulie, make some calls. I gotta buy us time. They could be comin' after us so watch yourselves."

"How long you figure?" Trick said, "before Joey Cara's people try somethin'?"

"Depends."

"Okay," Trick said. "Stay close to Paulie."

"I will," Tony said, as Diesel and Trick left.

Tony's first call was to his lawyer. He knew the press would be hounding the guy and he wanted him to know where he could be reached. His lawyer told him not to worry, he'd keep the wolves at bay.

Tony said, "Case you're interested, I had nothin' to do with it."

"Whatever you say," the lawyer said.

He called a cop named Harris, a detective lieutenant on the NYPD. He'd had the man on his pad for years and he used him whenever the heat was on.

"Whadaya got on the Cara hit?" Tony asked.

"Nothing yet," Harris replied. "The guys in the lab are on time and a half."

"I want you to know," Tony said, "it ain't me they're lookin' for. I'm clear on this. I put some people on the street. They're gonna nose around so give 'em some room. Okay?"

"Right," Harris said.

Tony said, "Meanwhile you hear anything, give me a ring."

"You're covered," Harris said.

"My parents would like to meet you, Dip. They'd like us to come out for dinner."

Dip stopped midway over the table as he served her and Prize their dessert.

"Dinner? At their house? You kiddin'?"

"It's what families do, Dip."

Prize stuffed his mouth and said nothing.

"You'll like them, I know you will."

"Sure, sure," he said. "Just like that. C'mon, Robin, I can't go. How'm I gonna go? Can you see me? 'And what's your profession, Mr. Dippolito? Oh, a head breaker, huh? How nice.' Get real, will ya."

"I'm trying," she said. "I know the way it is."

"Then why this?"

"Because I want something to be normal."

"Whadaya want? Marriage? That what you want? If you're worried now, how's it gonna be after?"

"I haven't asked you to marry me," she said. "Have I ever said a single word about marriage?"

"No," he said. "But dinner with the folks—"

"It's only dinner, for God's sake. Don't you people ever eat with your parents?"

"*You* people?" he said, indignant. "*You* people? What am I, a freak or somethin'?"

"Of course not. But you're *acting* like one. Dinner!" she said. "One lousy dinner. It's . . . normal."

Prize waited to catch Dip's eye.

"Might as well answer her, Dip. She's not goin' away."

Dip said, "Jeez, Robin, I'm sorry about this, but I can't."

"Never mind," she said casually. "I need some air. It's also late." She got her coat from the closet and left. Dip and Prize listened to her descend the stairs. The front door opened and closed.

Prize checked the kitchen clock. "You got an hour before you gotta be at Montello's place," he said.

"Yeah," Dip replied and began clearing the table.

Dip had never been invited to Tony's house, didn't even know where Montello lived. So he felt good as he pictured himself at Tony's kitchen table, batting the breeze like an old friend of the family. The Family. Jesus, was this it? Had his time come? Nice raise in pay, an overdue shot of prestige, a little something to up his image.

Prize, bug-eyed, stared him down.

"So whadaya think?" Dip said. "The man wants me."

"What do *I* think? I think the weddin's off."

Dip said nothing and left.

Dip was on his way to Queens for what had to be a major turning point in his life, and all he could think about was *The Wizard of Oz*, those three sorry bastards: Scarecrow, Tin Man, and the Cowardly Lion. At least *they* knew what they wanted, what to ask for when they faced the Wizard. In a few minutes he'd be facing his.

He could see himself with Tony Montello, Tony saying: "I owe you, Dip. Anything at all. Power? Prestige? Money? You name it."

What would he tell him? Thanks, Mr. Wizard. What I really want are the brains, heart, and courage to say fuck you, I quit!

Right. You'll quit. You'll quit and fly to Kansas in a hot air balloon. You and Robin, dinner with her folks, and away you go. Meeting her parents, going straight.

Dip found the house, pulled over and parked. He had the address written down on the back of a matchbook. He checked it again. Tony may have been a wizard, but he sure as hell wasn't living like one. Sixteen Bridge Drive, a plain one-family brick that blended with the scenery. He'd heard about this kind of living: the big boys understating themselves, keeping a low profile for the benefit of nosy neighbors and nosier cops.

The house had a high brick stoop and a pitched driveway that led down to a one-car garage. He climbed the stoop and pressed the bell.

Tony answered. Tony, looking sharp in a charcoal gray suit, standing in the doorway for the whole frigging world to see. How easy it would be to hit this guy. Too easy. There had to be protection he couldn't see.

"Come in, Dip. Glad you could make it." Like Dip had a choice.

He waited for Tony to step aside but Tony turned around and walked away, leaving Dip to close the door. You'd never know the guy had enemies.

Meanwhile, where'd he go?

"In here, Dip. The kitchen."

The kitchen. All right!

Dip followed the voice through a short hallway, past the living room and a few doors on the opposite side. Tony was at the table, draped over a coffee cup.

"Grab a cup," he said. "In the cabinet. Pot's on the stove, help yourself."

If only Prize could see this, he thought. He couldn't wait to tell him.

Tony waited for Dip to settle in with his coffee. He said, "I been thinkin' about you, Dip, what you did at Charlie's."

Dip shrugged. "I saw the car, that's all."

Tony winked at him. "Ten guys out there but you're the one saw it. Know what that tells me?"

Dip couldn't imagine what it could tell him. So he sipped his coffee and pondered. "I got good eyes?"

Tony said, "More than that, Dip. You said it that night. Remember what you said? You said it was your job. That I pay you and you do it. Know what that tells me?"

Dip thought, What is this, a fucking quiz? He said, "No, I don't know."

Tony swallowed his coffee in two loud gulps. He smacked his lips and said, "Loyalty. Loyalty, Dip. I don't have to ask you what that tells me."

Just as well, Dip told himself, I'm running out of answers.

"What I'm sayin' here, Dip . . . well, what I'm gettin' at . . . want more coffee?"

Dip shook no.

"It's like this," Tony said, putting Dip on the edge of his seat. "I got a headache."

"With the Joey Cara thing?" Dip said.

Tony flapped his hands. "Forget Joey Cara, will ya? That ain't why you're here."

That ain't why you're here . . . Tony's words were a lullaby in Dip's ears. He could feel himself loosening up, growing confident. Let the hitters do the hitting. There were plenty of important jobs in this organization.

Tony said, "I need somebody here, Dip. In the house."

"In the house?" Dip said. He stiffened. "Like a bodyguard?"

"Sort of," Tony said. "I mean, yeah, in a way."

Dip was beginning to wonder just how these guys got anything done. Here's the big guy himself, in his own house, no bugs or wires to worry about, and what's he get? Pasta with horseshit.

"Whatever it is, Tony, just say it."

Tony said, "I know who the shooter is."

Tony let it sit for a while and Dip thought, Jesus, I'm on the street and I don't hear shit.

"It was Boppy," Tony said.

Dip gulped his coffee. "Boppy? He ain't a shooter. He's a shlunk."

Tony said, "Yeah. We got a rat, Dip. And he's close, too close to sniff without scarin' 'im off."

"Boppy?"

"Fuck no! The guy he's workin' for. The rat. He wants me outta the way, and if he can't ice me, he'll set me up. The whole fuckin' city thinks it was me did Joey. You hear what I'm sayin'?"

Dip nodded.

Tony said, "Look, I can take care of myself. That ain't the problem. It's Jimmy. He needs cover until I can straighten this out. I can't trust nobody right now so I'm turnin' to you. It woulda been Nickie if he was here."

"I don't know what to say," Dip said.

"Yeah," Tony said, then he jumped out of his chair. "Wait here a minute. There's more."

He watched Tony go down the hall, hook a right and disappear. A few seconds and he was back, holding an envelope which he dropped on the table.

"Go on, open it."

Dip's first thought was money, a bonus for signing on. He'd refuse it, of course, play it modest, make Tony force it on him. But the envelope was too skinny to be holding cash.

Cautiously, he opened it up and fished out a letter.

"Read it," Tony said.

He tried to read it, got as far as "Dear Mr. Montello," when Tony said, "It's from Jimmy's school. This shmuck, what's his name . . . Bell? Wants me to come up. Go on, read it."

"Dear Mr. Montello—"

"Imagine that scumbag? Tellin' me to come up. Like I ain't got enough headaches. 'Attitude problem!' What kinda shit is that? We all got attitude problems. Go on, read it."

" 'Dear Mr. Montello'—"

"Fuckin' asshole. Wants to leave 'im back if he don't pass geometry."

Dip ran his finger across the letter. "What about history and English? He's failin' that, too."

Tony said, "Geometry! What the fuck is that?"

Dip said, "Squares, I think. And circles'n stuff."

"Yeah, yeah," Tony said. "That stuff. You know about that shit, don't ya? Trick told me, said you went to night school. They teach you that stuff, right? Squares and circles?"

"Yeah, but—"

"Go on, read the letter."

Dip read the letter but skipped over *Dear Mr. Montello.* This guy, Henry Bell, wasn't too happy with little Jimmy. Words like "disruptive influence," "lack of initiative," "irresponsible." And right at the end, the big hit: no pass, no graduate, and "imperative we discuss."

He could see why Tony was pissed. Bell was calling his kid a bum. It was all true, but you don't tell a guy something like that. Especially a guy like Tony Montello.

Dip said, "This guy Bell needs a rap in the mouth. That what you want? Want me to—"

"You nuts or what? You don't slug a guy like that: fuckin' teacher. No, no. What I want you to do . . . I mean what I need for you to do is bullshit this guy, see? Like you're Jimmy's uncle come to straighten it out. I'd go myself, you know? But how's it gonna look? Face it, Dip, guy like me, coppin' a plea for his own kid. It don't work, you know what I'm sayin'?"

Dip blinked at him a few times. "You want me to talk to the man. About Jimmy'n all."

"Yeah, yeah. Talk to the man. Get 'im to . . ." Tony waved a hand in a circle ". . . to give you his word."

"About what?" Dip said.

"That he'll graduate 'im."

Dip said, "He won't graduate 'im 'less he passes."

"That's right," Tony said. "So what we do is this. You tell this meatball, you say, 'Hey, I'm gonna work with the kid. Study 'im up on circles and shit.' Then you get his word. Jimmy don't fail, he graduates 'im. Whadaya think?"

Dip couldn't tell him what he really thought. He said, "I don't know, Tony."

"Whadaya mean you don't know?" He was pissed. "I'm *tellin'* you."

"I know," Dip said. "But what I mean . . . I mean, what if the kid fails? He ain't gonna graduate."

"He ain't gonna fail, Dip. Know why?"

" 'Cause I'm gonna teach 'im," Dip said. "About circles and shit."

Tony banked his head to one side. "You're an asset, Dip."

"Asset?"

"A definite asset," Tony said. He winked. "Betcha never thought it'd pay off, eh? Night school? That's what I want Jimmy to see."

Dip said, "Look, I gotta tell ya. This thing about night school, what I got's a high school equivalency. Any dope can get it."

"Maybe so," Tony said. "But you're the one's got it. That's more than Trick's got. Or Diesel. Or anybody else for that matter. Besides, you know the kid, he's used to you."

"Already?" Dip said. "I only just met 'im."

"Wait a minute," Tony said, his forehead a bunch of lines and trenches, his eyes getting squinty. "You sayin' no? You won't do it?"

"Hell, no," Dip said quickly. "I'll do it, whatever you say, I told you that. But what I'm thinkin' . . . I mean, ain't it better you get a pro or somethin'? A regular teacher? You know, like a tutor?"

"You mean a civilian? In *my* house? C'mon, Dip, you're smarter than that." He paused. "You better be." Tony gathered himself up. "So what's the answer?"

Dip said, "When do I start?"

"I musta been nuts," Prize said.

He was talking to himself, alone in the car, on his way to a shack out in Rockaway Beach. "Friggin' Boppy. 'All you gotta do is drive, Prize. A quick five hundred and nobody gets hurt.'"

Right. Nobody gets hurt. Except Dip. Boppy with a gun all of a sudden, leaning over, pointing it out the window. *Hey, man, whadaya doin'?* Then the shot and down goes Dip.

Prize had never been that scared in his life. "A little job," Boppy had said. "Meet at Petrillo's. Pick up a few guys and head out." A dozen sluggers out front and Boppy pulls a gun. "Hit it!" he says.

They were lucky to get away, eighty miles an hour in a stolen car, Boppy running his mouth: "We fucked up! We fucked up!"

Jesus Christ.

And now the word's out: Find Boppy, bring him in. That maniac! Hiding out in the boonies like nobody's going to find him. A jerk like Diesel, he wouldn't find him. But then Diesel didn't know Boppy the way *he* did. You orgy with a guy, you get to learn more about him than the size of his pecker. Secrets. Boppy's hideaway. A beat-up bungalow off the beach on 105th Street. He'd been there a dozen times.

He drove up on the Crossbay Bridge, Playland straight ahead, shut down for the winter. He wasn't sure that Boppy would be there but it was worth a shot. He had to get to him before they did, find out for himself what the hell was going on, what he got himself into. Five hundred bucks.

"Musta been nuts," he said out loud.

Like all the bungalows on 105th Street, Boppy's had an old wooden porch in front. The place hadn't been painted in years and what was left was chipped and peeling, a losing battle against the salt air. It was early April and these were summer joints, no one around—except Boppy. He saw the car as he pulled up, Boppy's Grand Prix, sitting there like a big white elephant.

Prize parked, bounded up the porch and rang the bell. A few seconds, then, "Who is it?"

"Prize."

"You alone?"

"Me and my dick," he said. "Now c'mon, lemme in."

The door opened an inch or two. Prize had to peer into the crack to see Boppy's eyes. They were big and round, like two halves of a peach, yellow and red with brown pits in the middle. The guy hadn't slept in days.

"Whadaya want?" Boppy said.

"I'm sellin' magazines, okay? C'mon, open up."

"Go 'way, Prize. Go on, get outta here!"

"Can't do it, Bop. We gotta talk."

"Who sent you? Diesel? Trick?"

"Nobody sent me. I'm on my own, tryin' to save my ass, if you know what I mean."

A dry laugh. "Save your ass? What about mine? I'm the one they're lookin' for."

Prize leaned on the door, was ready to push it in if he had to. But the door opened up and Boppy stepped aside.

"Quick! Get in here!"

The house had a damp smell to it, damp and stale. Like his own house, years ago, his mother sucking up TV dinners and Seagram's 7. Here, there were three rooms, but it was mostly one, the big one in front. A living room with a fold-out couch, open now with wrinkled sheets and a torn pillow. There was junk all over the floor, yellow newspapers, cigarette butts, jelly-jar glasses, half a pizza in an open box, an electric heater blowing hot air.

He would have noticed more. But his eyes had locked on Boppy's hand. A shaky hand with a gun in it.

Prize smiled at him. Which wasn't easy with his jaws clamped shut, thinking, Jesus, this guy's got more guns than Billy the Kid.

Boppy said, "They sent you, didn't they? Sent you to find me."

"I already told you," Prize said. "Nobody sent me. Hell, nobody knows I'm here. So do me a favor, eh, Bop? Pull that sheeser outta my face."

Boppy stood rigid, studied him a while. Prize had no choice, he

63

studied back. He was tense but couldn't show it. Boppy, completely out of it, face twisted, mouth moving up and down with nothing coming out. A real flip job.

Prize said, "I need to know, Bop, what you got me into."

No answer. Just a nutty look. It gave Prize the willies.

"What's the matter with you, anyway? You nuts or somethin'? Hey! Whadaya doin'?"

Boppy had raised the gun to his own head, had it pressed against his temple.

Prize couldn't move. His knees were locked, feet nailed to the floor.

"Adios, Prize. See ya soon—"

"Wait!" Prize shouted.

Click went the gun. *Click. Click.* The chamber rolled but nothing happened. *Click.*

"What the fuck," Prize said. "It's empty, man. Killin' yourself with an empty gun?"

Boppy shook his head, the barrel of the gun stuck to his temple like hot ice on a cold sink. "There's one in there, Prize. One slug. Been doin' it all day." *Click!* "That's five."

Prize lunged, caught Boppy at the waist and threw him down. "Lunatic! Maniac! Gimme that fuckin' gun!"

He didn't have to work hard on Boppy. The guy was rigor mortis from the neck down, lying there, a friggin' zombie, head rolling from side to side like Little Stevie Wonder.

He got the gun out of his hand and threw it across the room. It hit the pizza box and fell on a slice.

"Lemme alone," Boppy said. "I'm dead anyways."

"You ain't dead," Prize said. "You only look it."

He helped him up then sat him down on the bed. "You got any booze in this dump? Take a shot, it'll help."

"That's what I'm tryin' to do," Boppy said. "Take a shot." He leaned forward, put his arms on his knees and stared down at his shoes. "I blew it, man. They're lookin' for me. Christ, Prize, what'd I do?"

Prize said, "I'll tell you what you did, Bop. You took a shot at Tony Montello. You tried to kill 'im, okay? And you brought me with you, you crazy bastard. Five hundred bucks. I oughta give you the gun, let you blow your face out. I won't say brains 'cause you ain't got none."

"I wasn't tryin' to kill anybody," Bop said. "Just take a shot. That's all, just take a shot."

"What the hell you talkin' about?"

Boppy sniffled. "Don't sweat it, Prize. I won't rat'cha out. I see 'em comin', I'll waste myself. I swear I will."

Prize said, "You always were a dumb fuck. Hey, Bop, remember those broads from Canarsie? Last summer, remember?"

Boppy tried a smile but it didn't work.

"Come on, man, get a grip, okay?"

"Easy for you to say," Boppy said. "They don't know about you."

"No," Prize said. "And I wanna keep it that way. But just in case . . . you . . ."

"Spill my guts?"

"Yeah. I need to know, Bop. What's goin' on? Who put you up to it?"

Boppy shook his head. "And you call *me* crazy. Whatchya don't know won't get ya killed. Go home, Prize. Go on."

"Who was it, Boppy? I gotta know."

"No way. Never."

"They're gonna find you, man. They'll *make* you talk."

Boppy said nothing. There was nothing to say. It was the simple truth. "Don't let 'em get me." Boppy was sobbing.

"Yeah," Prize said, sounding resigned. "Yeah." He helped Boppy to his feet. "Come on."

Prize led Boppy to the door, switched off the interior lights and guided him out.

He motioned toward the beach. "Walk," he said. "This way."

The moon was a toenail in a cloudless sky, the beach cold and deserted. The sliver of moon offered light but not much: thirty, forty yards maybe. Beyond that, black.

They crossed a ditch, Bop moving slowly.

"I can't see," Boppy said, looking over his shoulder. Prize was a yard behind him.

"You don't have to," Prize said. "Just follow the sound of the waves."

Boppy walked. Prize couldn't tell how far they'd gone, but they were out a ways, the sand squeaking underfoot, then turned hard as they neared the surf.

"That's far enough," Prize said.

"Lenny?"

"Yeah." Prize shivered in the chill air.

"I'm scared, man."

"I know," Prize said. "Now be a good guy. Look up at the sky. See the stars, Bop?"

Prize was so close to Boppy he could smell the fear on him. "Pretty ain't they? Count 'em, Boppy. Count the stars."

Boppy tried to talk but nothing came out. Prize raised the gun, cocked it.

"So long, Boppy."

CHAPTER FOUR

Eva Barone drove slowly down the exit ramp of the Clearview Expressway, her '71 Ford Fairlane belching smoke from a broken tailpipe. For the last mile or two she'd had her eye on the red Corvette, the young blonde dude at the wheel mouthing "I love you" as he pulled alongside. Just a kid, a rich man's son, high on grass no doubt, cruising the Clearview in his new sports car.

Go on, Junior, look all you want. Not bad for a broad pushing forty, eh? Yeah, not bad at all. Ten years over prime and still turning heads. Should have caught me in Freeport, kid. Queen of Lucaya, Number-One showgirl for thirteen years.

Talk about place and time. She'd been center stage, on the apron, footlights showing her stuff. From her spike heels to her feathered headpiece, nothing in between but a string of spangles up her ass. And Montello down below, table for twenty, whooping it up: "Yo, Red! What time you get off? I got D.P. on ice."

She'd met him after the show. Guy offers Dom Perignon you don't turn it down, not without a look-see.

"Where you from, Red?"

"Name's Eva. I'd ask where *you're* from but it shows all over. New York, right?"

"Brooklyn," he said. "Born and raised."

"Then you must know Scarsdale."

"Yeah. Scarsdale, the Bronx. Who you kiddin'?"

"Just testing." She smiled. "All right, I'm convinced. You're sharp. You want honest, I'll give you honest. I'm thirty-three years old," she said, cutting it down by a few years. "Never married. Never wanted to. But I look around now, see these kids alongside me—twenty, twenty-one—makes me think about the future, you know? You married?"

"For now."

She got up. "Have a nice time, Mr. Montello."

He snatched her wrist. "Whoa, slow down. It ain't what you think. My wife's a sick woman. Six months, maybe a year. What happens after?" He shrugged. "Who knows?"

She sat down. "So what are you doing, hedging your bet?"

He laughed. "You're pretty sharp yourself."

"Good for me," she said. "So now what? You bring me home, put me in the closet? I wait around for a funeral? I'll pass if you don't mind."

But she didn't pass. She spent the night with him. And the next day, and the next. She checked him out, asked around, made a few calls to New York. "Tony Montello? You kidding? . . . That big, huh? . . . Bigger!" She inquired about his wife's health. ("I was you, Eva, I'd hang in there".)

She played it easy, impassive. "I just can't pick up and leave," she told him, Tony naked, eyes rolling in his head, the culmination of Barone's famous tongue massage with cherry-flavored oil: takes a lickin' and keeps on tickin'.

She let him leave Freeport without a commitment. "You only want me because we're here, together. Go home, Tony. Back to New York, and your wife. A week or two, you'll forget all about me. I'll always remember, but it's okay, it's been worth it."

For three weeks he called every day. "I'm going nuts. All I think about is you, Eva. I can't stand you being down there, showin' yourself."

She said, "I miss you, too. But I'm down here thinking, his poor wife. It's no good, Tony. I couldn't do that to her."

A month later he was back in Freeport. "You gotta come with me. I'll take care of you—money, car, whatever you want."

She agreed, on one condition: "I don't sell my love," she said. "You wanna talk, all right, I'll be there. But no money, no gifts. It's the only way I can handle this."

She'd almost choked on the words. Here was the catch she'd been waiting for, the golden goose from Fat City. With only twenty-five grand in the bank, her one worry was whether her savings would hold out longer than Louise Montello.

So here she was, two years later, chuggin' along in a broken down heap, in debt up to her nose, closing in on the ultimate pay off. Were there problems? Definitely not with Tony. If only he didn't have that kid. She wasn't sure how to play the kid, hard or soft. Either way, she'd win him over. Man or boy, didn't matter. She'd never known one she couldn't handle. Like Anthony Montello.

He had told her his place was out in Queens: Highshore Estates, near the Whitestone Bridge. She'd pictured it over and over. Highshore Estates, Tony's home, up on a hill, the bridge in the near distance, iron gates and a circular drive. She'd tried to check it out, cruised the neighborhood a few times but got lost on the one-way streets and dead ends. But she'd seen the big Tudor homes, cars in the driveways, Caddies and imports, every other plate showing *MD*. Bridge Drive. If that wasn't class her name wasn't Rosalie Scalese.

Let's see now, right turn on this corner, up the block, another right . . . pass the 7-11. Seven-eleven? What the hell's that doing here? Attached houses? It had to be the wrong block.

She lurched to a stop next to a street sign: Bridge Drive. She counted off the house numbers and stopped at the Montello residence. The curtains moved in the darkened house next door in a creepy way.

"What happened? Thought you got lost," Tony said from the front door.

"Lucky I made it at all. That car of mine . . ."

"Shoulda let me get you one. Nice little Coupe de Ville. First thing tomorrow, I'll take you down. Friend'a mine's a dealer, fix you right up."

"Well, if you think so."

"I know so. Can't have you runnin' around in somethin' like that. Give my friends the wrong idea." He escorted her inside. "So whadaya think? The house."

"It's quaint."

"C'mon on, I'll show you around. In here's the kitchen. New cabinets, fixtures. It's a little small but don't worry, you won't have to cook anyway. Nobody's home during the day and I got a woman makes supper."

"Don't be silly. I can cook."

"I'll bet you can . . . Eva, in here. Got'cha full dining room. This set's an antique."

"Yes, I can see that."

"Hey. You don't like it, change it. Whatever you want. It's your home now."

"Not yet, Tony."

"Yeah. I want you to know, Eva, I appreciate you're waitin' all this time. You been great about everything. I won't forget it, believe me."

"It's all right, Tony."

"C'mere, gimme a kiss." They embraced, then separated. "Now, over here's the parlor."

"What's that on the walls? Flock? I haven't seen that in years."

"Louise put it up. It's all right, Jimmy hates it, too."

"Where *is* Jimmy?"

"Upstairs."

"He's home? You didn't say he'd be home."

"Hey, don't worry, huh? He's gonna love you. We talked it out, he knows the whole story. Oh, by the way. I told 'im he was comin' with us."

"With us? On our honeymoon?"

"No, no. Just the wedding. He'll stand up for us, gimme the ring and all. After that it's me and you. I got us a place in Acapulco. Way up in the mountains somewhere. You know the joint, the space guys go there when they're back from the moon."

"Las Brisas?"

"That's it. What'sa matter? Don't like the place? We'll change it."

"No, it sounds wonderful. Just . . . well, you know, I wonder if it's smart, taking a boy to Vegas."

Jimmy had crept toward the staircase, up on the landing where he could hear better, Eva acing him out. He was tempted to jump in, tell her, "Hey, bitch, mind your own fuckin' business. He said I can go, I'm goin'." But he waited. See how Tony handles it.

"It's only a few days, Eva. I promised 'im."

"You should've told me first, Tony. I mean it's only right. After all, it *is* my wedding."

"Look, it ain't definite."

"You just said you promised. If you promised something to me I wouldn't expect you to break it, go back on your word."

"My word's good, Eva. Ask anybody."

"I don't have to. You're Tony Montello, aren't you?"

"Fuckin' right."

"Okay then. He comes with us. But you know Vegas. You'll have to watch him, keep him out of trouble. We won't see each other much, but it's all right. It's good for a father and son to be close."

"Mother, too. Don't forget that."

"Of course I won't forget. I'm just worried, that's all. I don't think he likes me."

"He will. He don't, I'll break his neck."

"See, now that's wrong."

"You're a good woman, Eva . . . C'mon, I'll show you the base-ment. It's all paneled, cedar wood. Smells great. I got a poker table down there, case you wanna play with the wives. Louise use to enjoy it, before she got sick. I'll show you the bedrooms later. C'mon, through this door . . . Watch your step."

The tour didn't take long.

"Well," Eva said, back in the kitchen, she and Tony at the table drinking reheated coffee and smoking cigarettes. "You said it wasn't much."

"But you like it, right? You haven't seen the upstairs yet, but whadaya think? So far, I mean."

She hated the place. That basement, this kitchen, that crap on the living room walls. She wanted space: picture windows, swimming pool, central air, a sunken tub and a bidet.

"It's lovely," she said.

"You don't like it. Look, you gotta understand. I'm a workin' man. Got a W-2 form from a dress factory says I make thirty grand a year. How's it look I live in a big house? Feds'd be all over me, grab me on a tax rap."

"I understand," she said. "It's just . . . well, damn it, Tony, what good's having money if you can't spend it? I don't want much, not asking for the world. Just a house in the country. Long Island, maybe. Westchester."

Tony's head bobbed up and down. A quick drag, then, "I hear what you're sayin'. And hey, you're right. Hundred, ten percent, absolutely. Tell ya what . . . I'll ask around. Lawyers, accountants, you know. Gotta be straight here." He reached over, held her hand. "I'll work it out, Eva."

Lawyers? Accountants? She hadn't figured on them. Come to think of it, there was a great deal she hadn't figured. Cash flow, for instance. Asset management. How much does he really take home? And where is it? Not in the bank, or this house, that's for sure. So where does he keep it? The bread he'd dropped in Freeport: fifty grand at the craps table, twenty more in blackjack. Who's kidding who here?

She heard something overhead, a heavy thump and a metallic clank. "What's that?"

"Weights," Tony said.

"Weights?"

"Yeah, you know, dumbbells. Kid likes to work out, got a thing about buildin' himself up."

"He does that in his room?"

"Every day," Tony said, face full of pride.

"You've got the basement," she said. "Can't he do it there? Least it won't sound like a bowling alley."

Tony laughed, thought it was funny.

Eva said, "I think it's time your son and I got to know each other."

Tony left her sitting there, an oak table scarred with cigarette burns, casement windows you'd need a crowbar to open. Paradise in Highshore Estates.

"Here he is," Tony said. "Charlie Atlas. Jimmy, you know Eva. Eva . . . Eva?"

"Huh? Oh, oh yeah. How do you do? I mean, how are you?"

"Peachy dandy," Jimmy said.

He looked much older, more developed. And those tight trunks and no shirt, muscles in his arms, sweat she could smell . . . Close your mouth, Rosalie, that's your stepson you're gaping at.

Tony was saying, "So whadaya think, kid? Your new mom, she a looker or what?"

"I seen her before. Hair was different then. Not so orangey."

Eva patted her curls. "It *is* a tad lighter."

"Tad? What's a tad?"

"Hey," Tony said, "you know what? Eva thinks it's great, you comin' with us to Vegas. We'll have a ball, kid, all of us. Trick's comin', too. Diesel, Paulie Jr. We'll party it up, huh? How's that sound? Hey, I'm talkin' to you."

Jimmy had his head in the fridge, leaning over, mumbling to the milk. "Sure, it's great. Everything's great."

"Maybe he's tired," Eva said. "Worn out from dumbbells."

Jimmy's face appeared over the fridge door, a quart of homogenized in his hand. He snickered. "Right on, momma. Dumbbells, yeah. I can dig it."

Tony sighed while Eva pondered: little prick's going to be trouble. Take it slow, bring him around. She said, "So how you doing in school, Jimmy? Your dad says you're graduating. That's exciting."

Jimmy shrugged, started to speak then changed his mind, chugalugged his milk instead.

"The lady's talkin' to you, Jimmy."

"I heard." White moustache, tongue licking the milk, Eva getting antsy.

"Don't get smart," Tony said.

"Come on, fellas," Eva said, "let's not argue. These are happy times, a new start for all of us." No response. She snapped her fingers. "I got an idea. A graduation party. What do you think, Jimmy? We get a hall, cater, some music. Invite your friends."

"That's a great idea," Tony said. "You'll get a boost from the boys that'll knock your eyes out."

"No way," Jimmy said.

"Why?" said Eva.

"Yeah," Tony said. "Whadaya mean, no way?"

Jimmy shrugged. "Can I go up now? Finish my reps?"

"No," Tony said, "you can't. You got that look. I can see it. What happened? What's wrong?"

"I fucked up another test," Jimmy said. "I ain't gonna graduate."

Tony jumped from his chair. Eva flinched, spilled her coffee, cup rolling away. She snatched at it but missed, her eyes on Tony as he lunged at his son. Jimmy stood his ground, or tried, Tony with his hands around the kid's neck, pushing him back till his head hit the wall. *Thunk*.

"I *told* you! Didn't I tell you? You wanna be *dumb* all your life? Like Diesel and Paulie? Like—"

"Like you?" Jimmy said in a tight voice, barely getting it out.

"Yeah. That's right, like me."

Now Eva jumped in. She wouldn't mind him strangling the kid, the brat deserved it, but here was a chance for points: show them she cares enough to make the peace.

"Let him go, Tony! For God's sake, let him go!"

With a final push Tony dropped his hands. "I know, I know. Little bastard makes me nuts. Told him a hundred times: 'You're going to college, get a diploma.'"

Jimmy said, "*You* didn't get one."

The kid had balls, she'd give him that.

Tony said, "I told you, it was different then. Growin' up in the streets, nobody went to school. That's why I moved you to Queens."

"I hate Queens. I hate school. I wanna live in Brooklyn, learn the way you did."

"Don't be a jerk. Tell him, Eva."

Tell him what? Eva thought. I hate Queens, too.

"Listen," Tony went on. "I can teach you the streets. But it's not enough. You don't see it now, but believe you me, there's more to this than breakin' heads. Guys comin' up, they got ideas about business you wouldn't believe. Stocks and bonds, unions, foreign markets. I'm tellin' you, Jimmy, it's a whole new thing. You gotta be smart these days. Educated. You hear what I'm sayin'? Like high school. Like college."

"*You* did all right," Jimmy said.

Tony looked at Eva. "Will you talk to this thickhead?"

"Well," Eva said, "we *could* do this . . ."

"Who's she?" Jimmy said. "She ain't even here yet. Who's she anyway?"

"Shut up and listen. Go on, Eva."

"It's simple," Eva said. "You wanna see Vegas or don't you?"

"Yeah, but—"

"Then you'll graduate."

Dip's mind wasn't on his work. The kid was doing his share but Dip was out of it.

"Did you hear what I said?" Jimmy asked.

Dip was lying on the kid's bed, arms folded over his eyes. "I heard," he said.

"So what's the answer? Is it a noun or ain't it?"

"Look it up."

"Fuck!" Jimmy said. "You gonna help me or ain'tcha?"

"I been helpin'. Just look it up, all right?"

Jimmy nudged him. "Hey, man, I need ya."

Dip said, "What you need is a travel agent. Don't sweat it, you'll get to Vegas. May take awhile, but you'll get there."

"You're ticked," Jimmy said. "Hey, look, what's the difference? Long as I graduate, who cares why."

"Forget about it," Dip said. "I don't give a shit if you learn or not."

"Since when?" Jimmy said. "Listen, if it's my old man, don't worry about it. I'll set him straight, you know?"

Dip lowered his arms, raised himself on an elbow. "About what?" he said, cautious.

Jimmy looked down at his feet. "Nothin'."

"Whadaya mean nothin'? What's goin' on? What'd he say?"

"Nothin'. Jeez, you're paranoid, man."

Dip said, "It comes with the job. Think your old man's any different? So what is it, what'd he say?"

Jimmy raised his face, studied Dip for a while, like he wasn't sure. Then he got up and went to the door. Eva was downstairs singing to herself, messing with curtain rods. He came back and sat on the bed. "It's Prize," he said. "They're lookin' for 'im. Him and a guy name Boppy."

Dip's heart sank a little more. "What else?"

"I'm not sure," Jimmy said. "Except they know he's your friend. I was you, I'd tell 'em where he is."

"Thanks," Dip said.

Jimmy gave him the eye like he wanted more. Dip shook his head.

Jimmy said, "You better tell 'em, Dip."

"I already told 'em. Diesel asked me. I don't know where he is. Ain't seen 'im."

"What's it about?" Jimmy said. "How come they want 'im?"

"How do I know? You're the one tellin' the story."

Jimmy pouted. Dip said, "You better stick to your books, kid."

"Come on," Jimmy said. "Lemme help."

"For what?"

Jimmy shrugged. "I dunno."

Dip checked him out. Was the kid for real? He said, "Thought you didn't like me."

"Ah, man. Don't make it hard, yeah? I'm payin' you back, that's all."

Dip smirked.

"I'm serious," Jimmy said. "You got my word, man. You can trust me."

"Yeah, sure. I won't come in your mouth, right kid? Who you think you're talkin' to?"

"I swear to God," Jimmy said.

Dip got up, looked out the window, Eva's new Coupe de Ville in the driveway. Why not? he told himself. What's the worse can happen? He tell his old man? Let him. Can't hurt. Who knows, the guy just might believe him.

"Okay," Dip said, "I'll tell you. But it stays in this room."

"Hey," Jimmy said, "you kiddin' or what?"

"It's mostly Boppy," Dip said. "Word's out he did some work for Joey Cara. Boppy and Prize, they bounce together. So they figure, either Prize knows, or he's with Cara, too. It's all bullshit, kid. They got nothin' with Cara. They're with your old man, and that's the truth."

"If it's true," Jimmy said, "how come they're in the wind?"

Dip thought, the kid learns fast. "Who's your old man gonna believe, Jimmy? Them or . . . look, Boppy and Prize, they're small potatoes. Guys at the club, they point a finger, that's it, it's all over. So they run. Understand?"

Jimmy nodded several times and Dip wondered if he'd caught the message.

"Whadaya want me to do?" Jimmy said.

Dip grinned at him. "Mind your own business. You wanted to know, I told you. Now . . . that word, I think it's a noun."

"Dip! Oh, Dip, you up there?" Eva calling from downstairs, like he'd be someplace else, on the roof maybe, doing major repairs.

"Christ," Dip said.

"Would you come down here a minute? I need your help."

Jimmy looked up from his book. "Let her wait. My old man'll be home any minute."

"Wish I could," Dip said. He got up.

Jimmy said, "Watch yourself, eh?"

"Whadaya mean?"

"Just stay loose," Jimmy said.

Arnie pulled in behind Eva's car. "What time tomorrow?" he said to Tony Montello.

"Eleven o'clock," Tony replied. "Meanwhile get a coupla guys from Paulie's crew out here. I want 'em outside the house, day and night. You got that?"

"Got it."

Arnie waited for him to get in the house, give the sign it was okay to leave. Until they nailed down the situation with Cara's crew, he couldn't be too careful. The curtains in the house next door fluttered back in place.

Tony gave a wave and went in. He looked around, heard Eva's voice in the living room: "Harder! Harder, Dip. That's it, you got it."

"What the fuck?" Tony muttered. He rushed inside.

Dip was straddled over the top of a ladder, arms stretched, back twisted, his face straining red. "It won't go," he was saying.

Down below, Eva said, "It's only a screw, for God's sake. Use your muscles."

Tony looked up at a partially suspended travis rod. Eva held one end while Dip struggled with the other. He said, "You heard the lady, Dip. Use your muscles."

Dip flinched. The tool fell from his hand and the rod went right along with it.

Eva yelped. "Now look what you did," she said. "I swear, Dip, you're hopeless."

"Huh," Tony grunted. "Ask me, he's worn out. He needs a break. How about it, Dip? You and me, we go downstairs, have a drink."

Eva groaned. "Honestly, Tony. *Now?* I need him."

"I'll bet," Tony said. He motioned to Dip and headed for the basement. Dip didn't answer, just followed him down the stairs, Eva griping.

Tony waved an arm toward the poker table. He went to the bar, filled two pony glasses with Black Label.

They sat down across from each other. "Here's luck," Tony said, raising his glass.

"*Salude,*" Dip said.

They drank. Tony smacked his lips. Dip made a face.

"You're not much of a drinker, are you, Dip?"

"Once in a while."

"How about women?" Tony said. "You much with women?"

"Not really."

"But you got a girl, right? Sure you do, I seen her at Patty's once. Short? Black hair, light eyes?"

"Name's Robin," Dip said.

"Pretty name for a pretty girl."

"Thanks," Dip said.

Tony waved him off. "I got an eye for good lookin' women. Take Eva. There's a looker, wouldn't you say?"

"Very pretty," Dip said.

"But not for me, eh?"

Dip frowned.

"Come on," Tony said, "they all know what she was. A knock-around chick. A showgirl. Think I don't know what they're saying? 'Old man's losin' it, got his dick where his brain should be.'"

"I never heard that," Dip said.

"You wouldn't say if you did. But it's okay, Dip. You can tell me whatchya think."

"I think it's great. You're what, fifty-eight? You ain't that old that you shouldn't get married again."

Tony squinted at him. "That's good to know, Dip: how you feel. I'll remember that. But what about you? Got any plans?"

"Plans?"

"We're talkin' marriage, ain't we? So how about it? You and Robin, settle down, have kids."

"I'm thinkin' about it," Dip said.

Tony said, "That's the trouble with you young guys, you think too much. Don't think, just do it!" He rubbed his chin. "Tell you what. Comes June, we go to Vegas. Me, you, Jimmy, the whole fuckin' crew. You bring your girl. We hit the chapel: me one night, you the next. Bing, bing, it's all over."

Dip sat there, a blank look on his face.

"Come on," Tony said. "She'll love it."

"I don't think so, Tony."

"What'sa matter? She don't like me?"

"It's not you," Dip said. "Robin's never met you. It's . . . you know. Everything."

Tony nodded. "I get it. This Robin, she Irish?"

"Jewish."

"Almost as bad," Tony said. "Look, just tell her how it is."

"That's just it," Dip said. "What can I tell her?"

"Same as I do," Tony said. "You got a job. She wants you, she'll live with it."

"Maybe," Dip said.

"No maybe. You lay it down. It's this or nothin'. Besides, what the hell you gonna do, quit? Forget about it. We all go through it. Fall in love and right away we get religion. Face it, Dip. What you got here, it's your way of life. I know it's tough. But, hey, work hard, have patience, who knows? One day you'll be right up there. A made guy, money rollin' in. What's better, eh?"

He reached over, gave Dip a gentle slap in the face. Nice kid, he thought, I'd sure hate to clip him. Pointing his chin at the empty glass, he said, "How about it? Another hit?"

Dip shook his head no.

Tony poured one out for himself. Dip waited like he knew it wasn't over.

Tony sighed heavily. "Well," he said, toying with his glass, "so much for the small talk. I'm hearin' some nasty shit about your pal, Dip. I figure we sit down, set it right."

Dip said, "I'll take that drink if you don't mind."

Tony poured. Dip drank.

Tony said, "Trick's been talkin' to me. He ain't happy about the other night at Petrillo's. Me, too, but I got my own reasons." He paused. "What's Prize to you?"

"Friend," Dip said. "A friend."

"Only takes one bad friend to fuck things up. You oughta know that. This friend . . . Lenny, right?"

"Yeah," Dip said. His voice choked a little.

"Take it easy," Tony said. "You're in my home, remember? It's like bein' in church. All right, what's done is done. You're doin' good with my kid so I'll give you the chance to make it up."

"How?" Dip said.

Tony grinned. "Just tell me where he is."

It wasn't like Dip to ignore stop signs. Now the corner light was red and Robin could see he had no intention of stopping.

"Red light!"

He jammed the brake. "Sorry."

"They're not going to bite you, Dip."

"Huh?"

"Mom and Dad."

"Oh," he said.

The light changed, he pulled out. "It's not a good night," he said.

"It's good as any," Robin said. "You're just nervous. Don't worry, they'll like you."

Dip said, "I had a talk with Montello today. He asked about Prize. Wanted me to tell 'im where he is."

"You told him you didn't know?"

"Ten times," Dip said. "I think he believed me, but I ain't sure. I had to promise, I hear from Prize I tell 'im right away." He looked over at her. "It's a promise I can't keep."

If Dip was trying to frighten her, he was doing a damn good job. "What will he do?" she said.

"I don't know. But you don't lie to Tony Montello."

Robin's fear turned to anger. Who was this Tony Montello, anyway? How dare he threaten them. She said, "Does he honestly think you'll turn on your best friend? What happened to loyalty? Isn't that part of the creed?"

"What creed?" he said. "I work for Montello, not Prize."

She bristled. "More reason to quit."

"For Chrissake, Robin, we've been through this a hundred times. Maybe I *can* quit. But not now. He'd never let me."

There was a lot more Robin wanted to say. But Dip was right, they'd been through it a hundred times. Yet, everything he'd told her, everything she'd read about the mob, hadn't prepared her for this. Was Dip really a slave to Montello? Would it be this way for the rest of his life? And hers?

Dip said, "You still wanna go?"

"I can't disappoint them," she said. She pointed straight out. "Besides, we're here now."

He found a spot and pulled in. She said, "I know it isn't easy, Dip. But can't you let it go? Just for tonight?"

Dip tried to shelve Montello, his fear for Prize, block it out for a few hours anyway, get through dinner without screwing things up. It wasn't easy.

The main course was served around conversation. It came mostly from Esther Gold and all of it was directed at him.

"I understand you own buildings," Mrs. Gold was saying.

He suddenly realized that what he had on his plate was roast beef. "I'm sorry," he said. "What was that?"

"Buildings," she repeated, throwing a look at Mr. Gold. "You own buildings?"

Robin bailed him out. "Building," she said. "One building."

"Well," said Esther, "it must be a big one."

"Six family," Robin said.

Her mother looked puzzled. "Is that enough to live on?"

Mr. Gold cleared his throat. "I'm sure it is, Esther."

Dip saw him shake his head at her, enough with the questions. The old man hadn't said spit through the whole meal.

Dip looked at him, a skinny little senior citizen with sharp eyes and a friendly smile; laid back like he was checking him out. Dip understood and went along with it. He decided to open up a little.

"Robin says you do numbers," he said.

The old guy chuckled. "That's one way to put it. But yes, I'm an accountant."

"Right," Dip said.

Mrs. Gold jumped in. "You know, John, my husband can help you with your investments."

John? Jesus, Dip hadn't been called that since P.S. 26.

Robin said, "Why don't we clear the dishes, Ma? Let the men get acquainted."

"I suppose so," Mrs. Gold said. "But I'd like to hear for myself. Such a quiet boy. Is he always like this?"

"Esther!" Nate said.

"All right," Esther said. "So I'll make coffee. You like peach pie, John?"

"It's his favorite," Robin said.

"I hope so. We didn't do very well with the roast beef."

"It was great," Dip said, though he'd barely touched his food. "My stomach's on the fritz lately. Could be a virus or somethin'."

"That's what Ida Levine said about her husband. Turned out a tumor. Thank God they got it all. Sit," she said, "I'll get you the Pepto Bismol."

"Some peach pie oughta fix me up," Dip said.

She made a face. Nate Gold said, "It's a joke, Esther. Come on, John, let's go in the living room. I've got some fine brandy should put you right."

"You shouldn't drink," Esther said.

"One brandy, Esther," Nate said.

"I didn't mean him," Esther said. "You! *You* need brandy? With *your* blood pressure?"

Nate shook his head. "Come on, John. Before she calls for an ambulance."

Dip followed him inside—an old-fashioned parlor with old-fashioned arm-chairs, chintz draperies and polished tables that had seen better days.

"Nice place you got here, Mr. Gold."

"Nate," he said. "Call me Nate."

"Call me Dip. It's short for Dippolito."

"Sit down, Dip. I'll do the honors."

Dip sank into a thick sofa. Nate splashed some brandy into a snifter, then poured one out for himself. He settled in a wing chair, raised his glass. "Health," he said.

"*Salude,*" Dip said. The brandy felt good going down. "Smooth," he said.

"Private stock," Nate said. "For special occasions. Of course, every time Robin comes it's special to us. I have two other children, Dip. But Robin . . ." His eyes seemed to light up. "What can I say? She's a beautiful person. Inside and out."

"I'll second that," Dip said.

Nate Gold took a minute to scope him out. Dip returned the favor. It was easy to see where Robin got her looks. The nose and mouth, those gray eyes.

"You knew her husband, didn't you?" her father said.

"We met." He didn't know how much the old guy knew, about the beatings and all.

"She told me what you did. How you threw him out. I'm only sorry I wasn't there to see it."

Dip shrugged.

"Esther doesn't know," Nate said.

Dip said, "Better she don't."

"Hope you didn't mind the questions. You know how mothers are."

Dip flashed to his own mother, how she felt when his brother Nickie died. As always it hurt too much to dwell on.

"Your family?" Nate asked.

"Dead," Dip said.

Nate puckered his lips. "My daughter loves you, Dip. She hasn't said it, but I know. Truth is, she hardly talks about you. Esther gives a third degree. But Robin,"—he shook his head—"she keeps it in. Always the important things she keeps in. I never ask but I see. I look and I see. What I see, lately, is a troubled young lady. If I had to guess, I'd say it was you."

Dip nodded. "You're right."

Nate leaned forward, elbows on his knees. He looked Dip right in the eye. "I can't have that, Dip."

Dip said, "She brought me here to let you check me out. Guess I don't, eh?"

"I'm sorry," Nate said. "One marital mistake is enough. I doubt she could take another."

"Whadaya see?" Dip said. "I mean you look at me, whadaya see?"

"My only concern is for Robin. I don't know what you do for a living, but it isn't real estate."

Dip said, "I didn't come here to fool anybody."

"But you came."

He shrugged. "You know Robin. I put her off as long as I could. Woulda been better to wait a few months. But she pushed it, so here I am."

"I don't understand," Nate said. "What difference would a few months make?"

"I can't tell you that. All I can say is, that the way it is now, I could never marry her. I wouldn't."

"Does she know this?"

"I think so. Don't worry, Nate, I won't allow myself to hurt her."

Nate gave him a thin smile. "Neither will I, Dip."

CHAPTER FIVE

Dip spent the day searching for Prize. Old haunts, old girlfriends. He even took a drive to Calvary Cemetery.

Prize liked to bitch about his mother. But that didn't stop him from visiting her grave. Mother's Day, Easter, Christmas. Times when he got depressed, he'd grab a shovel, pick up a rose bush and head for Calvary. Dip would go with him on occasion. Dip, waiting in the car, watching Prize plant his flowers, talking while he dug. He'd say a few words to the headstone, then kick it and walk away.

He'd come back feeling more pissed off than sad, cursing under his breath, wanting a drink. One drink, then two. A bottle if that's what it took. "I want her to see how fucked up I am," Prize would say, red-eyed from tears or drink, Dip wasn't sure. "I want her to know, that's all."

He'd stagger out and Dip wouldn't see him for days. Then, one morning, there he'd be, at the door with a big smile, and a bag of hot bagels under his arm.

There were no flowers on the Bustamente grave. Dip hung around a while, but his friend never showed. So he drove to Manhattan and waited for Robin to finish work.

He parked in a no-standing zone on the corner of Broad and

Wall. The narrow streets and tall buildings gave him a penned-in feeling, like he envisioned jail would be. At 5:30 Robin came out, saw the car and went the other way.

"Shit!" Dip said.

He jumped out and chased her down the block, caught her at a subway entrance. "Where you goin'?" he said, puffing. "C'mon, lemme drive you home."

"I'll take the subway," Robin said, "like everybody else."

"It's no trouble."

"What you mean is, you're not doing anything anyway."

"C'mon, eh? Don't be like this."

"Like what?"

Dip pouted silently.

"You don't see it, do you, Dip? I mean how does it look? Every night, me getting a ride. My boss saw me the other day, getting into the car. Know what he said? He said he wished he had a chauffeur like I did. Then he said, 'Your boyfriend, doesn't he work?'"

"Whadya tell him?"

"I said you're a proctologist, that you work with assholes."

"Come on."

"Well, what could I tell him, Dip?"

"That's what I mean," Dip said. "It's not what you do, it's how it looks."

"Not in your case," she said. She brushed past him and headed for the subway. He followed.

"I wanna talk," he said.

That stopped her. She spun around. "Go ahead."

He looked around. "Not here, in the street."

"Oh," she said sarcastically. "I forgot. You're on the lam?"

"Come on, get in the car. Let's talk about it."

"Not too loud," she said. "Someone might hear you. God forbid you break the sacred code of silence."

"All right, I deserved that. You're still angry from last night."

She'd pressed him on the way back from her parent's: What did he and Nate have to say? Dip, blowing her off, saying nothing until they got home. You wanna come in? he'd asked, holding the door open. For what? she'd said, and ran upstairs.

"All right," he said. "I was wrong, okay? Now c'mon. Please?"

Ten minutes in the car and they were driving over the Brooklyn Bridge, Dip pleading his case. Or trying to. It wasn't easy admitting that his life had been a waste, that he wanted out but didn't know if he could pull it off.

Robin said, "We'll go away. Sell the house and move. Virginia, maybe. The Carolinas. We'll make out. It's not like we're broke."

"I wanna go," Dip said. "But I can't. Not now."

"When?" Robin said. "A year, five years? When they kill each other off? What am I supposed to do in the meantime? I want a family, Dip. I want my children to have a father they can look up to."

"I promise," Dip said. "I never promised before, did I?"

"Spare me the promises, Dip. There's nothing you can do in a year that you can't do right now."

"Not true," Dip said.

"Oh? Why's that?"

He knew it had to come down to this. All these months, holding back, never saying what he did or why he did it, letting Robin fill in the blanks. How do you build on that? Where's the trust? If *she* had problems wouldn't he want to know, expect to be told? Except this was different. In his line of work men were killed for talking too much.

"Well?" she said.

"Three months," he said. "Give me three months."

She frowned at him. "Cut the crap. You're in some kind of trouble."

"It's not me," Dip said.

"Not you," she said.

"Not exactly."

"That's what I figured. I've thought it over, Dip. I'm moving in with my parents. I won't worry about you bothering me. I know how you feel about family involvements."

"Whadaya want me to say? Jesus."

"The truth," she said. "Just once, I want the truth."

He didn't have to see her face. Now or never, she was saying. It wouldn't do just to say I love you. He'd have to back it up. But he couldn't do it now, too many complications: Trick on the warpath, Prize on the run. And Montello. What about him?

He felt like a man at the crossroads.

They drove over the bridge. He took the first exit, pulled over and killed the motor. Robin backed herself against the door.

He drew her close to him. "All right," he said. "You want the truth, here it is."

He told her the whole story. From Louise Montello's wake, to drinks with Tony. She listened quietly. When he finished, all she said was, "My God."

Dip said, "Listen to me, Robin. I don't wanna lose you. But if you walk, I'll understand. You see . . . I can't quit now. Prize and me . . . well, what can I say? I can't let 'im down, that's all."

She gazed at him for a while. Then she licked her lips, leaned over, kissed him. He returned the kiss, not sure if it meant good-bye or what.

Finally, she broke away. "I understand," she said.

"What?"

"I understand. I don't hate Prize. He's a conceited clown, but on him it works. Truth is, I like the shlump. You can't help but like him, his sense of humor, the way he flirts and carries on. You know what I mean? I guess I've been jealous of him. Just between us, he's fucking lucky to have a friend like you."

"I don't believe this," Dip said.

"Doesn't mean I'm not scared," she said. "I'm terrified, if you want to know. But I can't see you walking out on him. I know it sounds crazy, but I'd probably love you less if you did. So what do we do?"

"We?" he said.

"I'm in this now. I was the moment you told me."

He nodded. "Yeah, I guess so."

"Well?" she said.

"First thing to do is find 'im. I've been lookin' for 'im all day. I have to let 'im know what's goin' on. They got 'im tied in with Boppy. Won't be long they'll pull 'em in."

"Maybe he knows," Robin said, "and took off."

"Could be," Dip said. "But he'd need money."

She put her hand on his arm. "Let's go home. He'll get in touch. He always does."

"Where the hell is he?" Diesel said. "I'm gettin' hemorrhoids sittin' here."

They were out in Westbury, Long Island, in a diner right across from Roosevelt Raceway: Trick with Diesel and Paulie Jr., guzzling coffee, staring out the window of a corner booth, lights from the grandstand like a barn fire in the night sky.

"He'll show," Trick said, casual.

"He better show soon," Paulie Jr. said. "I drink any more'a this coffee I'll have to piss my way home."

Trick said, "He's got a mount in the eighth race."

"That's the triple, ain't it? The one we want?"

"Yeah," Trick said. "The big triple." He glanced at Diesel. "So what's happenin', Deez? With Boppy. Anything new?"

"Bupkis," Diesel said. "Guy must'a fell in a hole."

"You want me to tell that to Tony, that he fell in a fuckin' hole?"

Paulie had a mouthful of coffee. He swallowed, winced, said, "There must be somethin' to it, Trick. I mean, after what happened at Charlie's, I figured war for sure. You ask me, I'd say there's somethin' to it."

"I ain't askin' you," Trick said. "Boppy's the guy I wanna ask."

"We'll find 'im," Diesel said.

"You better," Trick said. "Just remember, when you do, I want 'im first."

He motioned for the waitress, a chubby chick in a tight white uniform, skirt two inches below her ass, legs like upside down duckpins.

She grabbed the Silex and rumbled over. "That's ten cups. Congratulations, you just broke the house record."

Paulie Jr. looked at her, let his eyes run her down. He was gazing at her meaty thighs when he said, "Didn't you used to be with the Olympics? Shot put, right? Olga Popotski from Poland?"

Paulie hacked and Diesel cackled. Even Trick smiled.

She waited for them to finish. Then she overpoured their cups, splashing coffee on the table. "Get bent!" she said and clomped back to her station.

Back to waiting.

Trick had his eyes on the parking field. He could see it clearly across the street. "They're lettin' out," he said as cars began to exit, spilling out in every direction, tires screeching, horns blowing, drivers with their heads out the window cursing other drivers.

"Look at 'em," he said. "Crazy bastards! You can always tell the losers, guys can't wait to get outta there."

Paulie said, "I know. They're the same guys can't wait to get in."

Diesel pushed his coffee cup across the table. "S'enough a *this* shit." He looked at Trick. "This thing with Greenwall. Think he'll go for it?"

"He'll go for it," Trick said. "He can't afford not to. Hey, there he is."

The man they were waiting for was Ed "Buddy" Greenwall, top driver for this winter's meet. Buddy Greenwall, the Canadian Tiger, handled a sulky like a shopping cart at the A&P, standing now by the register, a rolled-up newspaper in his hand.

Trick could see his eyes darting from side to side under a billed cap. He looked more like a farmer than a harness driver, flannel jacket, loose jeans, hands like leather from pulling back on the reins. Crooked son of a bitch! Ain't run an honest race in twenty years.

Greenwall spotted them, hustled over and slid in beside Paulie Jr.

91

"Bad place," he said. "Too close."

Trick said, "You wanna leave? We'll go outside, talk in the car."

"No, no," Greenwall said. "No, no."

The man was scared. Which suited Trick just fine. He said, "We all set for tomorrow night?"

Greenwall looked around.

"Hey," Trick said, "I'm over here."

"I don't know about this," Greenwall said.

"Come off it," Trick said. "You pulled races before."

Greenwall looked down at his hands. "Yeah, yeah, I know."

"Now you listen to me." Buddy Greenwall's head jerked. "You're into us for a bundle. What's the count, Paulie?"

Paulie smirked in the driver's face. "Seventy-five large."

Trick held out his hand, palm up. "Give it over." No response. "C'mon, Buddy, give it over."

"You know I don't have it. Would I be here if I had it? Don't make me laugh."

"Hey, prickface! You think I'm funny?" (Buddy Greenwall, the Canadian Tiger. Looked more like a sick alley cat.) "When you wanted cash to feed those plugs'a yours, was I funny? Think it's funny: borrow money you can't pay?"

"I told you," Greenwall whined. "I'm overextended. The bank's calling me in."

"So am I," Trick said. "Only I'm first."

Greenwall sighed. "All right."

Trick smiled. "That's better. So . . . answer the question. We set for the big night?"

Greenwall said, "What you're asking, it's not easy."

"Not easy? Makin' a hundred grand, that's not easy. And plenty more if you do it right. Look, Buddy, I seen you pull this shit a thousand times. Up on a horse, even money, red-hot favorite, best time by two seconds. Comes in fifth. Don't gimme that shit, 'It's not easy.' You wanna pull a horse, you pull 'im. Case closed."

"Yes," Greenwall said. "But a triple, that's different. Bet all the combinations you want, you still need the first three. Only way to win is to hold the others back. There's eight drivers in a race, you know. We'll need four at least, four drivers to pull it off. And that's the one race. You wanna do this once, twice a week, means I need about ten drivers on the pad. That's big, Mr. Tricari. I mean real big. Lotta mouths to feed. Lotta mouths that can talk."

"Don't worry," Trick said. "We'll feed 'em so much they won't be able to talk. Just remember, one guy rats and you all go down. And you'll be the first, Buddy. You hear what I'm sayin'?"

Trick could hear him gulp from across the table. Piece of cake.

"Now," Trick said, "we got that settled. Let's see . . . you had two months to work on it. I want the names'a those drivers, guys we can count on."

Without a word, Greenwall reached inside the breast pocket of his flannel shirt, pulled a sheet of paper and gave it to Trick.

Trick read it. "You sneak," he said. "Had it all the time. Whadaya think'a this guy? Real sneak."

"Understand," Greenwall said, "there's no guarantee. We'll do the best we can, but if conditions aren't right . . . I mean, they watch us, you know? Video tapes, like that. It's gotta look real."

"I gotcha, 'real,'" said Paulie Jr. "Ever watch those tapes? Guy gets a fuckin' hernia pullin' 'em back. Real? Real shit you mean."

"Just do what you can," Trick said. "All we need's an edge. Coupla big scores and we're gone. You got my word on it."

Greenwall pulled the cap lower on his face. "Okay," he said, "here's the set . . ."

"I shoulda took my car," Jimmy said,

"Where's the school?" Dip said.

"Up a ways," Jimmy said.

Dip stared out the windshield at the back of a city bus, heavy traffic on the main drag. "Wanna tell me about this guy Bell?"

"What's to tell? He's a moron. Sends letters to my old man like he's gonna come runnin'." Jimmy shook his head one time. "Every day, bustin' my hump to get home, snatch any letters before my old man does. Man, what a drag."

"Wanna talk about it?"

"You read the letters. I gotta pass the Regents exams at the end of the year or I don't graduate." He glanced over. "Do me a favor, will ya? Cream the sonofabitch."

"Maybe I will," Dip said.

"You're shittin' me," Jimmy said. "You'd do that? Belt 'im around?"

"Maybe. If he mouth's off. Hey, I been there, too, you know? Guys think they got college, they own the world."

"That's right," Jimmy said. "Too smart for their own good."

Dip said, "But they don't know shit, do they? Well, don't sweat it, kid. I'll straighten 'im out. First his teeth, then his nose."

Jimmy laughed, then got serious. "You wouldn't do that, would you? I mean, really?"

"It's what you want, ain't it?"

"Yeah, but . . . shit! I'll never graduate. They'll kick me out."

"So what," Dip said. "You're gonna quit anyway. Ain't that what you said?"

"Yeah, yeah. But that was before."

"Before what?"

"Look, Dip . . . just talk to the guy. No rough stuff. All right?"

Dip smiled. "Anything you say, kid. I'm here to help."

Jimmy pulled a text from under the seat. "I was lookin' at this stuff for an hour: simple algebra. If it's so simple, how come you can't even figure it out?"

It was true. Dip was as frustrated as Jimmy. Christ. How could he teach the kid when he couldn't understand it himself?

"All right," Dip said. "Let's forget algebra for a while. Do history." He grabbed the textbook sitting between them on the dashboard. "Did you read this shit?"

"Only the pictures," Jimmy said.

"You got a test tomorrow. How you gonna pass, you don't read the book?"

"I don't have to read the book," Jimmy said. "I got the test right here." Jimmy dug in his jeans, pulled out a wrinkled sheet of paper. He straightened it out, started reading. "Question one," he said. "Explain what is meant by the Monroe Doctrine. Answer: The Monroe Doctrine—"

"Gimme that!" Dip snatched the paper from Jimmy's hand.

"Hey! What the hell you doin'? Gimme that back!"

Dip glanced at the paper. "Where'd you get this?"

"Same place I'll get 'em all," Jimmy said. "I know the guy runs 'em off. I ask 'im nice, he gives 'em over."

"You mean you threaten 'im," Dip said.

"I gotta pass, don't I? Rate you're goin', I ain't gonna pass diddly."

"You ain't gonna learn diddly, either," Dip said.

"Who cares?" Jimmy said.

"You will," Dip said. "When you get to college and you don't know what the fuck's goin' on."

Jimmy laughed.

"Oh, that's right," Dip said. "I forgot. You're not goin' to college. You'd rather lift weights, be a jerk all your life."

"Like you," Jimmy said.

Dip glared at him. "You little bastard."

"Yeah," Jimmy said. "That's me."

They drove a while in silence.

"Drop me off here," Jimmy said.

Dip looked around for a school building, didn't see one. He pulled over. There were ten or twelve kids in front of a sandwich shop, a little dump called Rickie's.

Jimmy moved to get out. Dip said, "Hold it. It's eight-thirty, where you goin'?"

"I got business," Jimmy said.

"What kind'a business?"

"You writin' a book or what? Just do what you gotta do and leave me alone."

Smartass kid, taking back all he gave. "I thought you wanted to graduate."

"It's what I *always* wanted," Jimmy said, with sarcasm. "Don't sweat it, Dippolito. I can't miss with you on my team." He laughed and jumped out, didn't even tell him how to find the school.

Dip watched him swagger toward his friends: five-hundred-dollar Italian leather jacket, tight Levis, hands in his back pockets, throwing his head to the wind. Cocky little bastard.

Dip put it in gear and drove in the direction of the school. Three blocks later, there it was. Hawley High, four-story, brick, couldn't miss it from the main drag, big air raid siren up on the roof—a state-of-the-art educational facility. He parked and went in.

Some guard with acne pointed him toward Mr. Bell's office. He went in, saw an old lady with blue hair punching keys on a fossil of a typewriter. She looked lost behind the big desk.

He said, "Excuse me, Miss."

The keys kept clattering. "I'm not a Miss," she said without looking up.

"Excuse me, Madam."

"And I'm certainly not a Madam." She took one hand off the keyboard and pointed at a nameplate attached to the near corner of the desk.

Dip read it: Miss Condon. He could almost hear the kids snickering, calling her Miss Condom. He said, "Excuse me, Miss."

She scowled at him.

He blinked back at her. "Sorry."

"What do you want, young man?"

"I'm here to see Bell . . . about Jimmy Montello."

"Are you his father? You certainly don't look like his father. The communications specifically said—"

"I'm his uncle. His father couldn't make it."

"Hmmm," she said through her nose. "Doesn't he think it's important enough? A conference with Mr. Bell?"

Dip shrugged.

"Hmmm," she said again. "Might've known." She got up. "Very well. I'll see if Mr. Bell is in."

Dip could see Mr. Bell was in, caught his shadow in the next office, through the pebble glass, name on the door frame: Mr. Henry Bell.

He could hear their voices behind the glass. Shadows moving closer. She poked her head out the door. "This way," she said, as if he couldn't figure it out from himself.

Henry Bell was sitting at his desk, head down, pulling papers out of a folder. He wore a starched white shirt with a red bow tie and he had a bald spot on the top of his head, right in the middle like a bull's-eye.

Dip waited for him to look up, check him out. But the guy was in no rush, kept looking down at the folder. Dip figured, what the hell, grab a chair, take a load off.

"Have a seat, Mr. Montello." Henry Bell was talking with his face in the folder. He had a loud voice, like he was used to giving orders.

"Name's Dippolito."

That got him. Down went the folder, up came the face. Late thirties, dark eyes, rough olive skin. A flat nose and a three-inch scar on his left cheek, smaller one on the right. If the guy wasn't a fighter, he used to be.

He said, "I thought you were Jimmy's uncle."

"I am," Dip said, "on his mother's side."

Bell said, "Right," then reached out a hand.

Dip took it, a hard paw with big, bony knuckles. Dip squeezed and Bell squeezed back. A standoff.

Dip said, "Tony asked me to see you. That's Jimmy's father."

Bell kept smiling. "You mean your brother-in-law."

"What?"

"Right," Bell said. He gazed up at the ceiling like there was something wrong with the lights. "Why do guys like you always think guys like me are imbeciles?"

Dip said, "Huh?"

Bell lowered his chin. "You heard me."

Dip said, "I don't think you're an imbecile. Job like yours, you gotta be smart, right?"

"And what about you?" Bell said. "Your job. You have to be smart for a job like yours?"

Dip said, "Wait a minute, back up. Let's start over."

"Let me tell you something. I know all about your boss. I know what he is and I know what he does. And the same goes for you."

"How do you know me?" Dip said. "I just walked in."

"My name wasn't always Bell. It was Bellino. I grew up on Mott Street and what I know about guys like you can fill a book. Montello sent you here to strong-arm me. Well, it's not going to work. He can't throw his weight around. Not here he can't. So go on back and tell him. His boy's no different from anyone else. We don't pass students because their parents have . . . clout."

Dip said, "You finished?"

"Yes," Bell said. "Unless you want to make something of it. In which case I'll meet you any time, any place. Just say the word."

Dip liked the way the guy cut through the bullshit: Here's what I think, take it or leave it. He wondered how a guy who'd been raised in Little Italy could become the Dean of Boys at Hawley High, Queens. Jesus, he thought, that could be me sitting there in a starched shirt, talking high principles.

Dip said, "You're right. About Montello . . . and about me. But it don't really matter. I mean, the problem ain't us. It's Jimmy. He's a smart kid, but he's got his head in wrong places. I would, too, if I was him. Too much goin' on he shouldn't know. But I had a talk with 'im this morning and you know what? He wants to graduate. He really does. If it's too late, then all right. Just tell me and I'm outta here. But if there's any chance at all—well, it don't matter what his father does—he oughta have it."

Bell said, "How well do you know Jimmy Montello?"

"Not as well as you," Dip said, "but I'm workin' on it."

"You really his uncle?"

"I'm just a mug."

"I've seen worse. So? Where do we go from here?"

"Just tell me this," Dip said. "Does the kid have a shot or don't he?"

Bell said, "What do they call you?"

"Dip."

"You like the ponies, Dip?"

"Once in awhile."

"Then you know about long shots. How does fifty-to-one sound?"

"Depends. On who rides 'em."

"And who trains them."

"That's right."

"You think you can train Jimmy Montello?"

"I don't know," Dip said. "But I'm his only chance—besides you."

"The boy needs a swift kick in the butt. You know that, don't you?"

"I wear size twelve."

Bell smiled. "And Montello? He'll let you do it?"

"He wants what he wants. If it takes a kick, Jimmy'll get it."

Bell had a thing with the lights, kept looking up. He looked up and said, "Okay. Let's lower the odds."

"Just tell me how," Dip said.

Bell looked at him. "It's more than grades. He's failing now, but he's got the brains to pass. He does well on impromptu quizzes. It's when he has to prepare that he fails. He doesn't study at all and he never turns in homework."

"He will," Dip said. "I'll work with 'im. Just tell me how."

"You're serious about this, aren't you?"

Dip nodded.

"Why?" Bell said. "Why's it so important? I mean are you doing this for Jimmy or his father?"

Dip wanted to say, neither. I'm doing this for me. He said, "I just wanna do it. I don't know why."

"That's honest," Bell said. "All right, come in this afternoon and every day after this. I'll get you his assignments, explain what's needed. It won't be busy work, so don't worry about that."

"Busy work?"

"Some of our teachers like to assign work just to keep the kids busy. They've got thirty-four students to a class. That's a lot of people to monitor, much less motivate. Half those will get F's." Bell swiveled back and forth. "There's more to James Montello's problem, too. I really think you can help."

"Like what?" Dip said.

"There's been complaints. From parents."

"What kind'a complaints?"

"I think Jimmy's trying to emulate his father."

"Emulate?"

Bell nodded. "He's taking book, right here in school. Baseball, football. Even hockey. And if that isn't bad enough, he's forcing the kids to bet money they don't have. Lends it out at one hundred percent interest. He's got himself a goon squad to help him collect. We've got four thousand students here. That's quite a population base for that kind of thing." Bell leaned back. "Sound familiar?"

"Yeah."

"We've lost two kids in two years. Shot dead. Dealers. Not on school property, but nearly. There are more guns in here than in Canarsie. We should have metal detectors at the doors, but the principal is too chickenshit to declare the school dangerous. At least your kid isn't into that."

"Sonofabitch," Dip said. "There's a sandwich shop a few blocks over. That Jimmy's hangout?"

"That's it. His base of operation. It has to end. If it doesn't, it won't matter what he scores on his tests."

"I hear you," Dip said. He got up, stuck out his hand. Bell took it.

Ten minutes later Dip was outside Rickie's Sandwich Shop. He wasn't there to look for Jimmy; it was well after nine o'clock and the kid was bound to be in class. What Dip wanted to do was check out the place, get a fix on the kid's action.

He figured Dean Bell was making more out of this than there really was. After all, what's the harm in taking a few bets? Hadn't Dip done the same thing at Jimmy's age? Dip and Prize, with their own sports book, clipping school kids for twenty-five-**cent bets:** baseball games, football. Same as Jimmy.

But this was different. He knew it the instant he walked through Rickie's front door. These weren't high school kids he was looking at. No fucking way.

Dip checked them out. There were about fifteen of them, and not one student in the lot. Big guys with shaved heads or short ponytails: dressed in heavy leather, spiked bracelets, and pointed steel-tipped boots. They were all over the place, swarming the half dozen video games, smoking grass, and getting off on mock gunfire and the clang and boom of mid-air explosions.

Along the far wall was a long glass case filled with cold cuts and salads, a waist-high counter to one side, behind which he saw no one.

He ambled over, ignoring the wisecracks coming at him from all sides: "Check it out, man. It's Ken Wahl." "Hey, slick, where's your Tommy gun?"

Dip reached the counter, looked around. "Anybody here?"

There was another room on the left side. Dip hadn't noticed it until now. But it was there, cut off from the rest of the place by a lopsided drape that hung loosely from a warped cafe rod.

"Hey!" he called. "Anybody back there?"

"Whadaya want here, man?" Someone behind him.

Dip turned for a look. There were three of them. Three shaved heads. Three black bomber jackets graced with silver studs and thick shoulder chains.

"Whadya say?" Dip said.

The one in the middle, the tall one, with rows of tiny diamonds in his earlobes, did the talking. "You heard me. Whadaya want here?"

Dip eyed them up. Lightweights. "I like your outfits," he said. "Who dressed you this morning? Darth Vadar?"

No reaction.

"Where's the owner?"

The tall one smirked. "He took a shit and the hogs ate 'im." He pulled his jacket aside, giving Dip a look at a large caliber automatic tucked deep under his belt. It looked like a .44. "You wanna join 'im?"

Dip blinked, wasn't sure he was seeing right. Here he was with a .32 on his ankle, and this punk had a piece big enough to knock out walls. What happened to zip guns? Saturday night specials?

"Very impressive," Dip said, bowing his head toward the automatic. He wanted to grab the damn thing and cram it down the punk's throat.

"It ain't meant to impress," the guy said, placing his hand on the gunbutt. "It's meant to kill."

"Yeah," said the guy on the right, and the three of them moved closer.

"We don't like aliens," the tall one said. "You an alien? From Mars maybe? The Bronx?"

The place was quiet now, the games on hold, all eyes on Dip while he figured his options.

"Tell you what," he said. "Why don't the four of us go outside. Leave the hardware, and I'll show you where I'm from."

"I don't think so," the leader said. He called over his shoulder. "How about it? Should we go outside with this turkey?"

"No way!"

"You hear that? They don't think so either." He nudged his friend. "Lock the door!"

Dip backed up, felt the counter against his legs. He heard a noise behind him: a swishing sound, the back room drapes sliding open.

"What the fuck's goin' on?"

Dip didn't turn. He knew the voice.

The tall one grinned. "Just in time," he said. "Check it out, Jimmy. We got us a real live wiseguy. Down from the Bronx." He sneered at Dip.

"Leave 'im alone, Roof," Jimmy said, stepping in, pushing the tall one aside. "I know the guy."

"So what?" Roof said. "I know my old man, too. Don't mean I wouldn't cream the fuck."

Jimmy glared at Roof. "What about me, Roof? You know me, too. You wanna cream me? Wanna try?"

A nervous laugh from Roof. "C'mon, man, you know better'n that. You're the man, right?"

"Right!" Jimmy said. "Go on, all'a ya. Do your doobs and play the games. I'll handle this." He looked at Dip. "Outside!"

Dip went out first, Jimmy close behind, watching his back.

"What the fuck was that?" Jimmy said the moment they hit the street.

"That's *my* question," Dip said. "You're supposed to be in school, for Chrissake."

"And you're supposed to be in Brooklyn."

Dip said, "I'm where your father wants me to be. Which is right up your ass until you graduate. The way I see it, it ain't gonna happen. I talked to Dean Bell. He knows what's goin' down over here. He says it don't matter what you do on the Regents. It won't mean shit, unless you blow this joint. So what's it gonna be?"

"Get off my back, will ya? I know what I gotta do."

"Then you better start doin' it," Dip said.

"I am."

"Yeah," Dip said, "I can see that." He gestured toward the sandwich shop, a half dozen punks staring at him through the window. "That's quite a gang you got there."

"That's right," Jimmy said. "I told you. When my time comes, I'm gonna be ready."

"Sure you will," Dip said. "You're gonna make your bones in a fuckin' sandwich shop." He shook his head. "You're outta line, kid. Way outta line."

"Dip! Dip, wake up!"

"Huh?"

"There's someone at the door," Robin said.

"What time's it?"

"Two fifteen."

Dip heard the doorbell ringing, but he rolled over anyway. "Go back to sleep," he said.

"Aren't you going to answer it?"

"Why? It's kids from the club again raisin' a little hell in the streets. Who else'd ring doorbells at two o'clock?"

The ringing grew louder. Robin threw off the covers and got out of bed.

Dip groaned. "Where you goin'?"

"To yell at them. They'll wake up the whole house."

"So what," Dip said.

"Oh, for heaven's sake. Where's your robe?"

He opened one eye, watched her rummage through the closet, fish out the robe he hadn't worn in years. She put it on and went out to silence the racket.

He heard the door open, then Robin saying, "My God! You look awful!"

Dip jumped out of bed. It was not unlike Prize to pop in after a rough night on the town, face flushed from booze, clothes a mess, cracking wise and looking to sober up with a pot of black coffee. Dip found his briefs and put them on. Then padded inside to calm Robin down. Dip stood in the bedroom doorway, taking it in, watching Prize. He was a mess, all right. But it wasn't from booze. He could tell Prize hadn't touched a drop. No jokes, no grab-ass. Prize had always been a happy drunk, no worries, no hassles, a carry-over from his free and easy life style. Dip liked to tease him about it, call him a clear-headed bastard.

There was nothing clear-headed about Prize tonight but that look on his face.

Dip said, "Hey, ski ball, you want coffee or what?"

Robin carried on for a while, but Dip wasn't listening. He was watching Prize who was motioning behind her back, waving at the door, the message clear: Get her out of here!

Dip said, "Leave us alone, let me talk to 'im."

Robin's head was swiveling from side to side. First Dip, then

Prize. Then back again. The way they were staring each other down, two close friends in a mind lock.

"What is it?"

"Go on," Dip said gently. "Go upstairs to your place. I'll call you tomorrow." He took her arm and walked her out.

"Is he all right?" she whispered. "I've never seen him like this."

"Neither have I," Dip said, and kissed her on the nose.

He went back inside to find Prize splashing Cutty in a glass, spilling most of it on the floor.

Prize checked him out. "Put your pants on, Dip. You make me nervous in those tight bloomers."

"Cut the crap," Dip said.

Prize took a healthy hit, swallowed and said, "I'm in deep shit, my man. Heavy-duty."

"I know."

"How? Whadya hear?"

"I'm on the street, too, Prize. It was Boppy took the shot at Montello. They want 'im, Lenny. You, too. But you know that, or you wouldn't be here lookin' like shit."

"Swear to God, Dip. I didn't know what he was gonna do."

"Hold it. You were with 'im?"

"Yeah."

"That's great, Prize. Fuckin' great."

"No lectures, okay? Just help me out."

"Help you out? What I oughta do is smack you around. Boppy's an imbecile. How'd he talk you into a bone-headed move like that?"

"I just told ya, I didn't know. He offers me five hundred for a job. I figure, how bad could it be, right? Next thing I know we're outside Petrillo's, I'm behind the wheel, okay? Like, where are those guys, when do we leave? I turn around and the fuck's got a gun—bang—you're goin' down and I'm haulin' ass. Boppy never said a word, just did it—like that. Swear to God."

"Beautiful," Dip said. "Are you fuckin' nuts?"

"I know," Prize said. "I screwed up. But afterward, I figured, what the hell? Only guy that knows is Bop and he can't say shit anyway. And it's not like we killed anybody."

"No," Dip said. "But you came damn close. Lemme tell you."

"Hey, look man, I'm real sorry about that. I didn't see it comin'. The way it went down—so fast—I didn't think."

Dip said, "Imagine if you *did* think. Do me a favor, Prize. Don't think. Rest that friggin' mind of yours."

They went silent, Prize sipping scotch and smoking his cigarette, Dip with his coffee and cigarette.

Dip said, "We gotta find out what it was. It don't make sense."

"No shit," Prize said.

"What about Boppy?"

"He was scared, is all I know. He'd give up his grandmother to get out of this. Jesus, ya think they'll get 'im?"

Dip rubbed his face. "Whadaya think?" Dip ran it through his mind, tried to put it in order: what they knew, what they didn't know. He said, "Let's talk about this."

"We been talkin'," Prize said. "Trouble is, we ain't said nothin'. Maybe it ain't so bad. I mean, Tony don't even know me."

"Yeah," Dip said. "Think again."

"Shit," Prize said, looking pale.

"Hang loose. It might take 'em months to track Boppy down. Meanwhile, who knows? Boppy had his reasons for pullin' that stunt. We find out, it's gotta help. Hey, maybe the hit was for real."

Prize screwed up his face. "Boppy? Come on, the guy's no button. You shoulda seen 'im with that gun. It was strictly an ad lib."

"So what's the answer?" Dip said.

"If I knew, would I be here shittin' bricks? Only reason I'm still here is 'cause I ain't got money to run. What I need is a heavy score. A one-way ticket to Portugal."

"You mean Petrillo's funeral home," Dip said. He shook his head. "Don't worry, it ain't gonna come to that. We gotta find Boppy, open 'im up."

"*We?*" Prize said. "What the fuck can *I* do? They grab me, I'll be suckin' hind tit."

"Bop's got a place in Bushwick, don't he?"

"Yeah. Dumb fuck still lives with his mother. But forget about it, okay? You won't find 'im there."

"So whada I do?" Dip said. "Put an ad in the papers? What about chicks? There's gotta be *one* he sees regular."

Prize snorted. "You kiddin'?"

Dip thought it over. "Hangouts," he said, snapping his fingers. "Where does he bounce?"

"All over."

"Hey, Lenny, eh? Gimme a break over here."

Prize looked at him. "Whadaya want me to say? All right, look. Try the Polka Dot Lounge."

"That joint in Canarsie?"

"Yeah. He's been goin' there lately. Got a friend works the bar. Name's Hack."

Dip said, "You gotta find a place and mole out for a while. I got about five hundred bucks here—oughta help. You need a piece?"

Prize smirked. "What the fuck am I gonna do with a piece? Comes to guns, I'm worse than Boppy."

"Yeah," Dip said. "You never did like the noise. Wait here a minute." He went inside, came back with the money and gave it to Prize. "Keep in touch, all right?"

They shook hands. Prize said, "Thanks, Dip. I mean it."

"I know," Dip said. "Look, you're my best friend. I'd stop a bullet for you."

"You already did," Prize said.

CHAPTER SIX

"What's so funny?" Tony Montello said from the rear seat of his Sedan de Ville. Arnie Randazzo up front, chuckling under his breath, eased the big car up to the curb.

"I was just thinkin'," Arnie said. "This place . . ." He laughed.

"I'm glad you're amused," Tony said. He looked out at the old granite church, it's ivy-covered walls and heavy carved wood doors, a buttressed steeple with a stone cross on top, sunshine glinting off the stained glass windows. *The Church of Our Lady of Perpetual Peace.* "You see any cars?" he said.

"Up the block," Arnie said. "Fresina's town car." He turned back to Tony. "His brother, he runs the joint, don't he?"

"He's the monsignor," Tony said. "And it ain't a joint. It's a church."

"Well," Arnie said, "you gotta admit. It's a funny place for a sit-down."

Montello grunted and Arnie clammed up.

Sure, Montello thought, it's a funny place to meet. That's why they used it. Not the church itself, but the building alongside, the new gymnasium built from monies pledged by the "friends" of Dominick Fresina. "It's for the kids," Dominick had announced. "To keep them out of trouble." Then, with a sly wink, he'd added,

"And us, too, eh?" Even Tony had pledged two grand.

The parishioners loved the new gym almost as much as they loved their monsignor—and his brother. The old hypocrite, every Sunday receiving Holy Communion, tipping his hat to the ladies, walking the grounds like he was ready for sainthood. What did they care that the Fresinas were blood cousins to Lucky Luciano? So long as the money rolled in. Don Dominick and his weekly tithes were making The Church of Our Lady of Perpetual Peace the richest in the diocese.

Tony had planned the time of his arrival. He knew that Dominick always came early to talk with his brother, and Tony wanted to see the old man before the others got there. Word was out that Tony Montello was scheduled for a call-down about the Cara hit, and he had to see the don first, feel him out.

He got out of the car, straightened his jacket. "Drive around the corner and wait," he told Arnie, and headed for the gym.

The door was closed but unlocked. He let himself into an anteroom, beyond which was the basketball court. He could see the big round table at the far end, and the five chairs, one of them upside down on the table. It was a message from Don Dominick that Joey Cara would not be joining them for their regular meeting.

Tony scanned the hall. There was no sign of Dominick or the monsignor. He walked the length of the floor, took his usual place, and stared at the inverted chair.

It was going to seem strange without Joey, Tony thought. Joey with his guinea cigars, blowing smoke across the table, shouting invectives at his archenemy: him. And Fresina, sitting there, calming them down: "You're on hallowed ground!" As if cursing was their worst transgression.

Tony remembered vividly his first meeting with the Council, and the way Dominick had greased it for him. A unanimous vote was required and Tony had been worried about Ray Vitale. Vitale was Joey Cara's boss and there was no way he'd go for Tony. But Dominick knew how to get his way without using force or promoting a grudge. He had found out that Ray Vitale was sick—a bad heart—and that he'd already named Joey Cara to succeed him. Dominick said he would get Vitale to vote "yes" if Tony promised to reciprocate when it came time for Joey Cara to take his seat. Tony agreed. Three months later he and Joey Cara were both members of the Council.

Tony wondered now about Joey Cara's replacement. Whoever he was, he would hate Tony as much as Joey had. What Tony had to do was convince the Council that he hadn't ordered the hit, that he would never pull a stunt like that even though he had cause. Of course they wouldn't believe him. Only Dominick Fresina could make them listen.

Footsteps. Tony looked up, saw an old man with thinning white hair coming toward him, his dark blue suit hanging limply off narrow shoulders, white shirt with its stiff collar, the skin under his chin flapping around like a turkey's. Dominick Fresina, eighty-year-old relic, with as much juice now as he'd had anytime in the past half century.

He shuffled over, took his chair and gazed at Tony. "You're early," he said.

"A few minutes. I wanted to say hello to the monsignor."

"He's busy. But that's not why you're early."

"I thought we'd talk before the others got here."

Dominick Fresina shook his head, his neck shook with it. "Can't do it, Tony. Not this time."

The front door opened. Voices flooded the hall. Tony tracked the sound. Louis Gola from Manhattan, John Conessa from the Bronx, and Vinnie Musto from Queens, were all coming in.

They went directly to Fresina, gave him the usual hug and a kiss on the cheek. Tony got a limp handshake. They took their places at the table. Fresina opened the proceedings.

He thanked them for coming and each of them took a moment to stare at Joey Cara's chair. "As you can see," Dominick Fresina said, "we're only five today."

"Terrible thing," Gola said.

"Yeah," said Musto. "A real kick in the ass."

Dominick Fresina said, "It's worse than that. It's a breach'a trust. We agreed, didn't we? Right here at this table, we each swore an oath to the Holy Mother: No violence between us!"

All eyes fell on Tony Montello. He said nothing. Tony waited. He wanted to know how bad it was and who stood where before he made his pitch.

"What happened to Joey," Vinnie Musto said, "could happen to any one of us. I say we find who done it and do *him*."

"Me, too," said Conessa.

Gola nodded. Tony glanced at Dominick Fresina. The old man pursed his lips. "You see how it is, Tony?"

Tony Montello said, "You sound like you've made up your mind. C'mon, Dominick, you think I'm crazy? I know when I'm well off. I respect this Council, and that means more than my dislike for Joey Cara. Besides, the guy was my wife's brother."

Musto snorted. "I know guys who'd whack their own son if they had to. Ask me, I think you *had* to whack Joey. Save face for what happened at Petrillo's."

Tony scowled at Musto. "I ain't askin' you, Vinnie."

Musto leaped to his feet. Tony got up with him and for a moment they just glared at each other.

Don Fresina raised his hands, palms open. "We're here to talk."

Musto, red in the face, took his seat. Dominick Fresina turned to Tony, who nodded and sat down.

"That's good," Fresina said. He rubbed his chin, then said to Tony, "I saw Joey the day after you and him had that scuffle. Couldn't believe it. His sister's wake and you guys throwin' punches like two crazy kids. But all right, Joey was hot and you had'a do what you had'a do. But he told me, it wasn't him took the shot that night. I believed 'im. Still do."

"So what are you sayin'?" Tony said.

Fresina scratched his head. "We have to explore the possibilities. After all, you been after Joey for years."

"That's right," Musto said.

"Yeah," Tony said, "and he was after *me*."

"That's right, too," added Conessa.

"Not any more," Musto said.

Fresina eyed Montello. "How do we know that thing at Petrillo's wasn't a setup?"

"Whadaya mean?"

"Well," Fresina said, "let's look at it. You and Joey have words. An hour later he's shootin' at you. You want a war, what better way to start it. See?"

Tony said, "You're tellin' me it wasn't Joey. You're sayin' it was me, a bogus hit to make it look like Joey."

"It's possible," Fresina said. "You bring it to us, ask for help." He shrugged. "Who knows, eh? So now we got headaches. Joey's got a hundred men on the street who want revenge."

Tony gestured toward Cara's chair. "Who's takin' over? We oughta get 'im here, talk it out."

Fresina shook his head. "It's too late for that. We don't know who's in charge. Could be Sonny DeMarco. Anyway, that's why the chair's empty." He waved a frail arm around the table. "I speak for all of us. We don't want a war over this. So whatever happens, Tony, no reprisals. That's our final word."

Tony sat there, stunned. From now on, Fresina was saying, it would be open season on anyone who worked for Tony Montello. Worse than that, he couldn't retaliate. If he did, he'd be fighting them all.

Fresina cleared his throat. "Don't look so unhappy. They'll take out one or two of your guys and that'll be that. After that we'll put a lid on them."

Tony said, "Thanks, Dominick. That's real considerate."

"It's the best we can do," Fresina said. He looked around the table. They all nodded.

"I'm supposed to sit by?" Tony said. "Watch my guys get taken out?"

Fresina shrugged. "It's a small price."

"Sure," Tony said. "But what happens if I'm one'a the guys gets hit?"

112

Vinnie Musto laughed under his breath.

Fresina said, "Lucky survived the Castellammerese War. You can survive this. Just watch yourself, that's all. You'll get through it."

Tony figured he had little choice: blow his top and he'd get killed for it. Play for time and maybe, with luck, he'd cope with this. "Okay," he said. "If that's your final word."

"It is," Fresina said.

They started to get up.

"Fair enough," Tony said, and got up, too.

On the way out, Dominick Fresina pulled Tony aside. "I like the way you handled this. You coulda played it hard. But you didn't. That shows you have strength. You'll need it. Joey Cara's people ain't gonna be soft-hearted."

Tony nodded and they stood there for a moment, Fresina looking at him like he had more to say. He did. "I been thinkin'."

"Yeah?"

"Yeah," Fresina said. "Lucky used to say, 'You got trouble, first place to look is your own home.' I was you, Tony, I'd do that. You hear what I'm tellin' you?"

Tony said, "I hear you, Dominick."

Dip didn't know the origin of the territories, how Brooklyn had come to be cut into sections, and why the various outfits got what they did. All he had to know was that Canarsie—from Flatlands Avenue to Beach Park—belonged to Joey Cara. A guy from Patty's once stopped at a gin mill on Flatlands Avenue. He'd gone in for a quick beer and had come out with two broken arms.

The more Dip thought about it, the more he thought that Charley Bop wasn't playing with a full deck. That stunt at Petrillo's was crazy enough. But this—. A thousand joints in Brooklyn and Boppy picks one in Canarsie. The Polka Dot Lounge, right on Flatlands Avenue.

Dip parked across the street, away from the bar lights, where he could watch the place without being seen. It wasn't much. A mid-block tavern with a souped-up facade and a neon sign flashing: LIVE MUSIC NIGHTLY. The band was playing tonight. He could hear it whenever the front door opened. Which was often. Even now, at 2:30 in the morning, there were men and women going in and out.

He decided to go in now rather than wait till it emptied out. He'd belly up to the bar like any other guy on the make. But first came the man at the door, screening the clientele: taking money with one hand and maintaining order with the other.

Dip took a deep breath, secured the revolver to his ankle and got out.

"Fi' dollar cover," the guy said, looking Dip over, raising his chin like he was smelling him out.

"Sure," Dip said. He gave him the money and waited for him to stand aside. The guy hesitated just long enough to roll his shoulders, flex his muscles to impress the new face.

"Okay," he said finally. Dip went in.

It was pretty much what he'd expected: dark, loud, and hot as the subway on a summer night. The air was stale and smelled of spilled beer and perspiration.

He looked around, ready to go at the first sign of trouble. The crowd was thin. Some on the dance floor, some near the bandstand, gazing up from tables at the four rockers making noise disguised as music. The crowd appeared to be straight. But he still had the bar to check. And that was mobbed.

It was shaped like a horseshoe. He ambled toward it, using his size to elbow his way in. A few guys grumbled, but no one challenged. He stood there, scoping the faces.

"Hack! Yo, Hack!" This from the guy right next to him, a skinny kid with thin lips and a hawk nose. "Give us a brew over here, will ya, Hack? My fuckin' throat's closin' up."

The guy mixing drinks was a tall dude with a high forehead, big round shoulders, and an incipient swag belly.

"Hold your nuts!" Hack called. Then he sauntered over like he was used to this kind of thing. They all wanted drinks, and he'd keep them waiting until he was damn good and ready.

He noticed Dip right away but ignored him, placed a bottle of Miller's in front of the kid, and walked away.

Dip called after him. "Yo, Hack!"

Hack stopped, gave him the eye, then came back. "I know you?" he said, loud, over the thumping guitars.

"A friend'a mine," Dip said.

Hack leaned across the mahogany bar. "Who's that?"

Dip leaned over, too, putting his face close to Hack's. "Charley Bop," he said.

Hack closed one eye. He stepped back and looked around. Dip wasn't sure what to make of it. Was Hack looking for help? Or checking for snitches? Dip waited.

Again Hack leaned over. "You got somethin' for me? He send you to give it?"

Dip nodded, going along with it.

"Lay it on the bar," Hack said.

Dip went for his wallet, took out fifty bucks and put it down in front of Hack.

"C'mon, Hack," someone called from the other side. "You on a break, or what?" Hack snatched the money and went to serve the loudmouth.

A moment later Hack returned. "Where's the rest?" he said to Dip.

"You'll get it," Dip said. Hack peered at him, like, Where is it? Hand it over. Dip said, "He's supposed to meet me here. You seen 'im?"

Hack was quick on the uptake. He knew bullshit when he heard it. "That bread ain't from Charley," he said. "It's from you. You're lookin' for 'im, aint'cha? Tell ya what. I'm gonna keep the fifty on general principles. You want 'im, try lost and found." He started to walk.

"Fifty more," Dip said. He didn't like uping the ante when what he wanted to do was reach over and belt the guy.

Hack turned on his heel, smiling now. Dip slid him the money. Hack looked at it.

"Tell you the truth," he said. "I ain't seen 'im."

Dip grabbed his forearm, squeezed it hard. "Don't fuck with me, Hack."

Hack grimaced. "Take it easy." Dip let him go. Hack said, "Tell you what. There's a chick in here, name's Arlene. Real tight with your friend. Check her out, you'll see I'm right."

"Where?" Dip said.

Hack shrugged. "Ask around. The whole joint knows Arlene." He rubbed his arm and swaggered off.

Dip cursed under his breath. The kid next to him started to laugh. Dip glared at him. "Something funny?"

"Could be," the kid said. He raised the beer, tucked it under his nose, and took a swig. "Arlene," he said, smacking his lips. "You really want her?"

"That a problem?" Dip said.

"Not for *me* it ain't." The kid chuckled and threw a thumb over his shoulder. "She's back there, holding court. You dig what I'm sayin'?"

"Yeah," Dip said. But he didn't like the sound of it.

The kid laughed. "Take a leak," he said. "You'll see what I mean." Then he took his beer and blended in with the crowd.

Dip thought about it. Arlene, Canarsie's version of Annie Rinaldi, pulling tricks in the men's room, for Chrissake. And Boppy, that asshole. The guy would screw anything if the price was right.

The last thing Dip wanted to do was confront some whore in the pisshouse at the Polka Dot Lounge. For all he knew, Hack was pulling his chain. More likely, Arlene wouldn't know Boppy from any other john.

The men's room was in the back, by the service bar. He went in expecting the worst: guys lined up for Arlene, standing on a piss-covered floor, the stink so bad it would make him woozy. But the room was surprisingly clean and there were only two guys inside, one of

116

them in front of the mirror combing his hair. The second, zipping his fly, shaking his head, was saying, "Out-fucking-rageous!"

"Told ya," the comb said. "Didn't I tell ya? Twenty bucks, man. Is she worth it or what?"

"Yeah," said his friend. "But let's get outta here. I don't wanna see her in the light."

They left Dip alone. With Arlene. He couldn't see her but she was in here, behind the stall. He bent down and saw a pair of pink vinyl boots. That was all he had to see. He left the club and went straight to his car.

Dip had paid for sex only once in his life. That was ten years ago. He remembered the girl, a kid about nineteen. He had tried to talk to her, ask her what was so bad in her life she had to give herself for money. He could still picture her, looking at him like he couldn't be serious. "There ain't *nothin'* bad in my life," she'd said. "I fuck 'cause I like it. Simple as that."

Sure, Dip thought now as he lit a cigarette, keeping his eyes on the front door. Simple as that. Until some joker says: *I don't wanna see her in the light.*

He was on his fourth cigarette when Arlene came out, a chubby blonde in a pink mini-dress, the taps on her vinyl boots clicking away as she crossed the street in front of him. He started the engine, poked his head out the window. "Arlene!"

She stopped, peered over, securing her shoulder bag.

"It's okay," he said.

She looked behind her and for a moment Dip thought she'd call out. But she didn't. Instead, she looked back at him. She seemed tentative, taking a few steps, then stopping.

He said, "C'mon, get in the car."

"Jesus Christ," she said and came around and got in beside him.

Without saying a word, he pulled away, glad to be putting distance between them and the lounge. He chose a dark street, turned off and parked under a budding maple tree.

She stared at him. "What is it with you guys?" she said. "Don't you get enough at home?"

"That's not what I want," he said.

"Yeah, sure."

"Arlene," he said. "I wanna talk, that's all."

She groaned. "Just what I need. Another Jesus freak. I had twenty bucks for every sermon laid on me, I'd retire. Save your breath. Just drive me back, all right?"

Dip said, "I wanna hear about Charley Bop."

"What about 'im?" she said flatly.

"Whatever you know," he said. "Who he sees, who he hangs with, when you seen 'im last."

She said, "I tell you what you want, will you let me go? Stop hasslin' me?"

"I'm listenin'."

She sighed. Her breath was sour. "All right. I seen 'im."

"When?"

"I don't know. A month, maybe two."

"Where?"

"He's got a dump out in Rockaway Beach. I don't know the street. He took me there for a session. You know what I mean?"

"Alone?"

"No."

"Name," Dip said.

"Hey, look—"

"Name!"

"Whadaya tryin' to do to me?" she said. "These are made guys I'm talkin' about."

"Boppy's a punk," Dip said. "An odd-jobber. Who was the other guy?"

Arlene took out a tissue, blew her nose. "I don't know," she said. "We weren't introduced."

"What'd he look like?"

"Oh, wow!" she said. "You know how many guys I see in a month? To me they're all alike."

"Was he tall? Short? What?"

"Tall . . . I think."

118

Tall, Dip thought. He knew a hundred guys who fit that. Starting with Prize.

Arlene was getting antsy. She said, "Look, that's all I know. Whadaya say, eh? Take me back?"

"Not yet. This guy, was he good lookin'? Nice white teeth?"

"No."

Dip relaxed a little. It wasn't Prize. He said, "Did he and Boppy talk to each other? Say anything?"

She squinted at him. "Are you for real? Guys gettin' laid."

"Well, they must've said *somethin'*, for Chrissake!"

She took a moment to think it over, twisting the tissue while she gazed out the window. "Come to think of it," she said, "they did say somethin'. Some club in Greenpoint. The other guy belonged to it. Kept sayin' he was in a hurry, had to get back and see the man."

"What man?"

She shook her head. "That's it."

"All right," he said. "But if you see Boppy, tell 'im to call me. The name's Dippolito. Jack Dippolito."

"Sure, Honey. Anything you say."

CHAPTER SEVEN

Jimmy slumped in his desk chair. "Almost forgot," he said to Dip. "I got a ninety-two on that history test."

Dip said, "Big deal. You had the questions, should'a got a hundred."

"Yeah?" Jimmy said. "That's how much *you* know. He didn't give us that test. Changed it the last minute. Gave us ten questions, multiple choice."

"And you got a ninety-two?"

"I read the fuckin' book," Jimmy said.

"You're fulla shit," Dip said. "Only way you'd get a ninety-two is to cheat."

"Fuck you, Dippolito! I don't have to cheat. I got a brain."

"Guess so," Dip said. "Your name's Montello, ain't it?"

Jimmy pointed a finger in Dip's face. "And don't you forget it," he said.

"Right, right. I'm goin' downstairs for a beer. Read the book some more. I'll be back to ask questions."

"I can hardly wait," Jimmy said. He turned on the cable TV and threw himself across the bed to catch the late scores.

Dip went quietly down the stairs. Tony and Trick were in the kitchen. ". . . even better'n we thought." Trick's voice. Dip stopped and listened.

"I'm worried about Greenwall," Tony said. "The guy's a real *strunze.*"

"Sure he is," Trick said. "But he's comin' through for us."

"For how long?" Tony said. "I seen a few'a them races. They look like shit. Won't be long before they pick it up."

"So what? We got a guy on the pad."

"There's more than one commissioner," Tony said. "Things get hot and he's gotta back off."

Dip shifted his weight and the floorboards creaked.

"What's that?" Trick said.

Dip lowered his head and started for the kitchen. He looked up suddenly. "Oh, hi. Didn't know you were here. How's it goin', Trick?"

Trick glared, said, "Make some noise next time. I don't like bein' sneaked up on."

"He's all right," Tony said. He looked at Dip. "How's my scholar doin'?"

"Comin' along," Dip said. "Mind if I grab a beer?"

"Help yourself."

Dip opened the fridge, took out a can of Bud. He snapped it, took a swallow and said, "I'm gonna quiz him in a few minutes. Okay if I hang here a while?"

"Get lost," Trick said. "Can't you see we're talkin'?"

"Let 'im stay," Tony said. "He's on the team, ain't he? Siddown, Dip."

Dip took a chair.

"Okay," Tony said to Trick, "tell me how you work it."

Trick squinted at Dip. "What I say you keep in your sock. There's too many guys already know about this."

"He's good," Tony said.

"Yeah," Trick said, but he didn't sound convinced. "All right, what happens is this. It's the eighth race, right? The big triple. Now we don't know if it's set until the post parade. They'll come by the

121

stands on the first warm-up. You seen 'em, Tony: nice, nice, in a straight line? They come around and head back toward the paddock. We keep our eyes on Greenwall. If it's go, he'll pull up and make his turn first. You can't miss it 'cause the rest'a 'em keep goin'."

"Why so complicated?" Tony said. "Why not tip his cap or somethin'?"

"We tried that," Trick said. "The second night three'a them jokers tipped their caps and we didn't know what the fuck was goin' on. No, this'll work for a while."

This wasn't what Dip wanted to hear. But it sounded big so he worked on his beer and paid close attention.

"Who else we got besides Greenwall?" Tony said.

Again Tricari looked over at Dip. Dip turned away, studied the paint job on the kitchen wall. Trick said, "We got twelve altogether. I'll give you the names later."

"How much we hit 'em for last week?" Tony said.

"About two hundred grand," Trick said, casual. "But we're startin' slow, twelve, thirteen hundred a race."

Dip glanced at the newspaper on the table and took a sip of beer, holding it in his mouth.

"How many we hit?" Tony said.

"Four outta seven," Trick said. "So far the biggest price was fifteen hundred. We made sixty grand on that one. But you wait, one'a these nights we're gonna hit for telephone numbers, see a price like ten, twenty grand. That's a half million to us, Tony."

Dip barely managed to swallow. Half a million on one race! Jesus.

Tony said, "Who collects? A score that big means IRS, social security numbers, shit like that. We need somebody clean."

"No problem," Trick said. "We get the old farts from down the club. Guys on pension. We guarantee their income tax and throw 'em an extra grand. They're happy just to hold that much money."

"Sounds good," Tony said. "We'll do it a few more weeks then pull out. I don't want any heat. Which reminds me. What's the word on the Joey Cara thing?"

Trick flicked his head in Dip's direction. Dip knew what that meant. So did Tony Montello.

"Better get upstairs, Dip. The kid'll be waiting for ya."

Dip wasn't at all keen on crashing Montello's racetrack party, but Tony surprised him. He put a sappy grin on his face Wednesday night and Dip knew: the man was really glad to include him. Not so with Trick.

Trick's eyes went icy and his face turned beet red when Montello said, "Move over, Trick. I want 'im next to me," as they arranged themselves in the grandstand one row behind Eva and Diesel.

Everyone slid down one seat and Dip found himself sandwiched between the two bosses, so close he could feel heat from their shoulders.

Tony said, "Jimmy tell you he passed the big test?"

"Yeah," Dip said.

Tony laughed. "Little bum's gettin' ready to make his fortune over here." He shrugged. "What the hell, all work and no play . . . he deserves a night out." Then he leaned over and whispered. "You, too, eh, Dip?"

Tony had barely finished when Trick leaned over and whispered in Dip's other ear. "You don't hear too good, do ya, numbhead?"

Dip kept his eyes straight ahead, Tony in one ear, Trick in the other.

Tony Montello whispered, "Keep your eyes on the board."

Trick said, "I wanna talk to you later."

Montello squeezed Dip's knee. "You're doin' good with the kid. Keep it up."

Two seats over, Eva Barone, looking back at him, giggled.

"The Marshal calls the pacers!"

"Here we go," said Paulie Jr.

They got up on their feet. All but Dip. He sat there worrying. A fun night at the track.

"They're off!"

Just then, Jimmy showed up. He saw Dip, gave him a high five then turned his face toward the track. "Here," he said, slipping Dip a fistful of tickets. "My old man said to bet this for you."

"That's Happy Hanover in the lead. Two lengths back it's—"

"What's he doin'?" Jimmy yelled.

"Shut up!" Tony said.

Dip got up. What he saw was the five horse, Happy Hanover, three lengths in front, drawing away. The final odds flashed on the board. Happy had dropped from even money to three-to-five.

"They go to the half in fifty-eight seconds flat!"

A wave of boos began rising out of the bleachers. Driver Buddy Greenwall was burning up his horse.

"Fuckin' moron!" Trick muttered.

"Boooo," the crowd droned.

"They'll put 'im down if he loses," Tony said.

Trick said, *"I'll* put 'im down if he don't."

They hit the top of the stretch and Buddy Greenwall's horse began to fade.

The crowd was shouting insults: "Fix! Throw 'im out!" The race ended. Happy Hanover, dead last.

The boos rained down on Greenwall. Buddy G. was a bum, a fuckin' crook. Somebody down by the finish line grabbed a wire mesh wastebasket and heaved it over the fence onto the track. Security arrived. They tussled. The fans jeered, threw programs and containers of beer.

Trick had his eyes fixed on the tote board. "Who you make it?" Trick said to Paulie Jr.

"Two-three-eight," Paulie said. "Definitely two-three-eight. Don't worry, we got it." Dip had it, too.

Jimmy and Eva were dancing in the aisle, waving their tickets in each other's face, a brief truce. One of those horses, the eight, had gone off at ninety-to-one.

Through all of this, Tony Montello remained silent, his face a stone. Dip knew the reason, but he kept his yap shut. Whatever

Tony had won wouldn't matter, what with the heat he'd have to face if Buddy Greenwall was called in.

The place went nuts. A two-dollar bet on numbers eight, two, and three had returned $31,580.50.

"You see that?" Tony Montello barked. "You see it?" He rolled up a program and slammed it against his thigh. "It stinks!"

Trick said, "Jesus, Tony! We just hit 'em for four hundred grand."

"You saw the race," Montello said. "He stunk out the joint."

They were downstairs under the grandstands, huddled in a corner, Dip nearby, trying to listen over a squealing Eva Barone. She and Jimmy were still celebrating, thirty grand to the good and dancing a tarantella to show it off. Dip's ticket was worth fifteen G's.

Tony waved him over. Dip approached. Montello was saying, "I told you, Trick, no heat. Ain't that what I said?"

Dip stuck his nose in. "You want me to hang around, Tony?"

"Just a minute," Tony said. He wasn't finished with Trick. "I don't want nobody touched till I see how it goes. You got that?"

"Yeah, yeah," Trick said.

To Dip, Tony said, "I want you to take Eva home. Jimmy, too. Take my car, I'll get it tomorrow." He went over to Eva. Dip stood there, alone with Trick.

Trick said, "I ain't got time for you now, asshole. But we're gonna talk, that I promise."

He walked away, picked up Diesel and Paulie Jr. They moved aside and waited for Tony Montello.

Dip scanned the place. The whole joint was in an uproar. What could he tell them: Prize hadn't left town yet but already he could feel the hole in his life where his friend used to be?

They left in Tony's Caddie. Eva didn't need a car, she could have flown home on the high she was riding. Jimmy, too, though the kid was starting to come down, giving Eva the eye like, Wait a minute, we're enemies.

Leaning forward, Jimmy spoke around Eva's compact. Eva with the lipstick and eye shadow, checking it out.

"What's goin' on, Dip?" Jimmy said.

"How do *I* know?" Dip snapped.

"What's *your* problem?" Jimmy said. "You on Trick's shit list?"

"I don't know," Dip said.

Eva chirped, "God, that was beautiful! I feel like celebrating. Whadaya say? I know a place near here. We stop, have a drink?"

"Forget it," Dip said. "The man said to take you home."

"Party pooper!" Eva said. "You better cheer up by June."

Jimmy frowned, changed the subject. "There's gonna be trouble, ain't there? About tonight. That's why he's mad, right?"

Eva sat up. "Trouble? What trouble?"

"No trouble," Dip said. "Everything's fine."

"You're lying," she said.

"Back off," Jimmy said.

"Listen, you."

"No, *you* listen!"

"Knock it off!" Dip said.

They clammed up and the mood went sour. From the corner of his eye Dip could see Eva's wrinkled brow, dark thoughts behind those bright blue eyes.

He pushed the big car to seventy.

She said, "If Tony's in trouble I've got a right to know."

"It's none of your business," Jimmy said.

"I'm going to be his wife, Jimmy."

"Don't remind me."

Eva flushed. "You're acting very mean. Tell him, Dip. Tell him he shouldn't treat me this way."

"That's his father's job," Dip said.

"You know what your trouble is?" she said. "You don't know when you're well off. If I wanted, I could make it very difficult . . . for both of you."

Jimmy said, "Hey! Go see who you gotta see, yeah?"

Eva said, "Just wait, you little brat. Comes June, we'll see who sees who."

"Right."

Eva said, "Drop me off last."

Jimmy said, "Drop *me* off last."

Sure, Dip thought. If he had his way, he'd stop the car right there, get himself a cab and let these jokers battle it out.

He'd stick with Jimmy. At least the kid wouldn't try anything cute to get answers.

Eva yapped when they passed Queens, headed for Brooklyn. But she had no choice. When they pulled up, she got out and slammed the door.

Jimmy said, "I hate that bitch. She's the worst yet."

"Maybe so. But you better learn to live with it." Dip waited for Eva to get inside her building, then pulled away.

"This fuckin' wedding," Jimmy said. "If only I could talk him out of it. Whadaya think, Dip. Any chance?"

Dip shrugged. "You know 'im better than me."

"Yeah," Jimmy said, "guess so." He slid down in the seat, stared at the windshield.

Dip headed back to Queens on a roundabout route.

Jimmy said, "Did you talk to my father at all?"

"Not really. Why?"

"I don't know. He was pretty hot."

Dip looked over at him but Jimmy didn't look back. Dip said, "Hey, don't worry about it. He'll work it out."

"Sure," Jimmy said like he was all alone. "He'll work it out."

Now and then Dip checked the rearview. On the second look he spotted a canary yellow Toyota closing ground. What shooter would ever drive a Toyota? Or was it juiced up?

A left turn would have taken them back to Brooklyn. As a precaution, he went right. The Toyota followed.

He began to worry. They drove for about a mile, slowing down, then speeding up. The yellow car stayed with them. He tried to make the driver through the windshield, but the street lights reflected off the hood like a welding torch.

Jimmy sat there, deep in his thoughts, paying no attention.

"Hold on!" Dip said.

He hit the gas and made a skidding turn down a one-way street. Jimmy's head hit the side window.

"What the fuck!" he squealed.

"Shut up and get down!" Dip said. He checked the mirror. The car followed. "Goddamn it!"

By now Jimmy had caught on. Turning to see, he said, "That guy's flashin' his lights."

Dip looked. Sure enough. "It's a fake out," he said.

"I don't think so," Jimmy said.

"How many you see?"

"One. Check it out. He's wavin' at us."

Dip looked. "He's wavin', all right. I'm slowin' down. Try and get a look."

Dip slowed to a crawl. The guy actually tapped his bumper.

Jimmy said, "Look at that maniac. He's givin' us the finger."

"It don't matter," Dip said. He swerved and threw the stick into park. "I'm gonna tear it off for 'im."

Dip twisted around for a look. The face he saw was grinning at him through the windshield. "I don't believe it," he said. He opened the door and jumped out.

Prize, showing a new mustache and bleached hair, rushed to meet him. "I saw you pullin' out," he said, throwing his arms around Dip. They hugged, slapped each other on the back.

With a broad grin, Dip said, "How the hell did you find me?"

"You kiddin'?" said Prize. "I been all over Greenpoint lookin' for you." He lifted his chin toward Dip's car. "Who's that with you?"

Dip looked back, saw Jimmy scoping them out. "Oh, shit," he said. "You better get outta here, Lenny. It's Montello's kid."

"Christ," Prize said. But it was too late: Jimmy was out of the car, coming toward them.

"How much does he know?" Prize said.

"*Now* you worry about it," Dip said. "Look, lemme handle it." He intercepted Jimmy and pulled him aside. "I guess you know who that is, right?"

Jimmy didn't answer.

"Look," Dip said, "this ain't what you think."

"I don't think nothin'," Jimmy said. "He followed *us,* didn't he?"

"That's right," Dip said. "Listen, I gotta talk to 'im. You want in, okay. But you gotta keep it to yourself."

"I ain't no fink," Jimmy said.

Dip winked at him. "C'mere, I'll introduce you." Together, they went over to Prize. "Lenny, this is Jimmy Montello. Don't worry, he's okay."

Prize stuck out his hand. "How they hangin', kid?" They shook hands and Prize said, "We can't talk here, Dip. I got a place not too far. It's my girl's. She shleps booze at the Stardust over in Hoboken. That's her car. C'mon, we'll sit, drop a few beers." He turned to Jimmy. "You don't mind, do you, kid? We got some catchin' up to do."

Leading the way, Prize took them on a trek down to the Brooklyn waterfront, and pulled up alongside a weather-beaten camper perched on crumbling cinder blocks. The only redeeming feature was the view of the river.

Jimmy said, "Man, what a dump."

"Whadya expect?" Dip said. "He's on the run. Check it close, kid. And hope it never happens to you."

"Forget it," Jimmy said, shaking his head.

"Just remember," Dip said. "We're trustin' you."

Jimmy nodded.

"Keep your mouth shut and your ears open. You say anything about this and I'm dead meat. You understand?"

Jimmy nodded again. "Yeah."

Prize waved them in, pointing to a booth under a small window partially blocked by a rusted air conditioner. "Grab a seat," he said. "I'll get the beer."

They sat on a padded bench that flanked a formica table. The table was chipped and badly scarred with cigarette burns.

While Prize fished a six-pack from a miniature icebox, Dip took the moment to look around.

Inside, the camper was cramped and messy, the bed unmade, dishes in the sink, towels and clothes on the floor. Prize was a fanatic about neatness in his own apartment. He wouldn't serve a drink without putting a coaster underneath. The guy had to be desperate to live in a hole like this.

Prize joined them, placed three cans of beer on the table. He saw Dip looking around. "I know," he said. "It's a fuckin' mess. Lani's a great lay, but she ain't worth shit at keepin' house."

"Whadya do to your hair?" Dip said.

"Bleached it. It's supposed to be blonde but it came out orange. I grew the stash, too. It's all part of my cognito look. Cute, eh?"

"Yeah," Dip said. "How long you been livin' here?"

Prize shrugged. "Too long. I met Lani a couple of days after I saw you. Good thing, too. I was runnin' out of bread."

"Here." Dip opened a drawer, tossed a bundle in and shut it. "I got lucky tonight." He glanced at Jimmy.

"Fifteen grand?" Jimmy said, incredulous.

"Hey," Dip said. "So tell me, what's goin' on?"

Prize jabbed a thumb at Jimmy. "How about the kid?"

Dip said, "I trust 'im."

"What?" Jimmy said.

"All right," Dip said. Dip took it slow, explaining carefully how it was that Boppy took the shot at his old man, how Prize had come to be driving, and how he never knew what Boppy had in mind. "Somebody set it up, Jimmy, to put the heat on your old man."

Prize said, "Somebody wants 'im to go down, kid. Me and Dip, we been workin' on it. So far, nothin'." He beamed at Jimmy. "So, whadaya say?"

"Hey," Jimmy said. "I'm here with him. I don't know from spit."

"We're partners," Prize said. "All the way."

"I don't know," Jimmy said.

Prize saw it all getting away.

"All right," Jimmy said. "I was never here."

"Okay," Dip said, then to Prize: "Lenny. You gotta go away. This is no good. Jimmy and I will take care of business."

"How?" Prize said.

"Don't worry about it." He checked his watch. "It's late. I gotta get Jimmy back." He slapped Prize on the shoulder and hustled the youngster out and back into the car.

Prize came out to watch. He lit a cigarette and leaned back on the trailer. Dip saw him. "Wait here," he told Jimmy and went back to Prize.

Prize smiled at him. "What's the matter? Miss me already?"

"Where you gonna go?" Dip said.

Prize shrugged. "One thing about trailers. They move."

Dip said, "I seen Hack."

Prize jerked himself off the trailer. A breeze kicked up off the water, rustled his hair. "What'd he say?"

Dip stood silent.

"Come on, Dip, don't fuck around."

Dip said, "He put me onto some hooker. Name's Arlene. You know her? Works the lounge?"

"How the fuck would *I* know her?" Prize said. "Think I'm nutty enough to cruise the Polka Dot?"

Dip shrugged, playing it cool while inside his guts were churning. If Lenny wasn't lying, then he didn't know him as well as he thought. "You didn't tell me about Rockaway, Lenny."

Prize squinted at him. "Whadaya mean?"

"*Now* who's fuckin' around," Dip said. "We're lookin' for Boppy, ain't we? Why didn't you tell me he's got a place in Rockaway?"

"Nothing to tell," Prize said. "I checked it out, okay? He wasn't there."

"You and Boppy ever do a scene out there with Arlene?"

"You kiddin' or what?" Prize said. "I don't do whores. Especially fat ones."

"How'd you know she's fat?" Dip said. "You never seen her."

Prize flushed. "What is this shit? You with me or not? Call me a fuckin' liar." He shook his head. "I dunno, man. It's pretty fuckin' discouragin'."

Dip said, "I'm tryin' to help you, you dumb bastard."

"Then help, for Chrissake. Forget about Boppy. Find the guy he was workin' for."

Dip frowned.

Prize said, "I'm worried about that kid. Will he stand up, or what?"

"You heard 'im," Dip said. "He was never here."

"Yeah. You're gettin' pretty tight with 'im, ain'tcha?"

Dip shrugged. "I'm trying to straighten 'im out."

Prize grinned. "Get serious, will ya? You ain't gonna straighten that kid out. His old man'll do it. And a lot better, too."

"That's what I'm worried about," Dip said.

"Ah, man," Prize said. "You're really losin' it. Ain't you heard that sayin' about acorns? They don't fall far from the tree, you know?" He flicked his head toward Dip's car where Jimmy was watching them intently. "That kid belongs to Tony Montello. And he's the biggest fuckin' oak in Brooklyn."

Dip said, "The kid's tryin' to make his bones in a sandwich shop, for Chrissake. You oughta see his setup. He's got a dozen dropouts packin' hardware."

"Then he's a jerk," Prize said. "Why fuck around when he can make his bones right in his own house?"

"Yeah, sure."

"Why not?" said Prize. "Look at us, we're out on the street. Listen't'a me. You ain't gonna change that kid any more than you can change yourself. So get real, man. It's how it is."

"We'll see," Dip said.

"See what, Dip? I'm lookin' at you and what I see is an asshole the size'a the Lincoln Tunnel. One day that little shit's gonna run the whole outfit. He's gonna look back, say, 'Dip? Yeah, I remember him. Broke my balls when I was a kid.' You fill in the rest, Dip. If you ain't too blind to see it."

Dip said nothing, just shook his head.

"Go on," Prize said. "Take off before the little punk gets cataracts checkin' us out."

Dip nodded. He stuck out his hand. Prize looked at it, hesitated, then took it.

"I need you, Dippolito."

Dip pumped his hand. "Hey," he said. "We're friends, ain't we?"

Dip had Jimmy home before he realized the kid hadn't said a word. He pulled into the Montello driveway. Jimmy sat there, a cloudy look in his eyes.

Dip said, "Hey, meatball! Don't worry about it."

"Sure," Jimmy said, but he didn't get out.

"What's the matter?" Dip said. "You won a bundle tonight. I was you, I'd be doin' back flips. Thirty grand? Christ."

Jimmy said, "Who cares?"

"Who cares? You kiddin' me or what?"

Jimmy looked at him. "Get real, yeah? That ain't my money. He lets me bet, but I don't keep it. What am I gonna do with that much bread? A few hundred, yeah. But thirty grand? Forget about it."

Dip figured maybe Tony knew what he was doing. Let Jimmy have his fun. But keep him on a leash, pull it in when he has to. Still, it surprised Dip.

The kid was still giving him the eye. "It ain't the money," he said. "I get all I need."

Dip said, "I don't get it. The way you hustle them kids in school. If it ain't for money, then what?"

Jimmy smirked at him. "Who's teachin' who?" he said. "Christ, you're dumb." He opened the door.

Dip pulled him back. "Get over here!"

Jimmy closed the door, slouched.

Dip said, "Who you callin' dumb?"

"All right," Jimmy said. "You ain't dumb. You're blind."

"You're pissin' me off," Dip said.

Jimmy said, "He tells me he's gonna teach me. But nobody taught *him*. He learned on the street. I ain't doing nothin' he didn't do."

Dip said, "That's all you care about? Bein' a wiseguy? You're only—how old, for Chrissake?

"Nineteen. I got left back in the fourth grade."

"You oughta be thinkin' about girls . . . baseball."

"And school," Jimmy said.

"That's right. 'Less you wanna be a punk all your life."

"You're only a punk when you're not the boss," Jimmy said. "You're a pain in the ass, Dip, but you ain't a bad guy. Thing is . . . like, you and me, we're miles apart, you know?"

Dip thought for a second. "I wasn't born with the silver spoon," he said. "But the rate you're goin', you won't be any different than me."

"What's that supposed to mean?"

"Look," Dip said. "There's more than one way to make it in this business. All they care about is money. The more you bring in, the easier it is to move up. With the pull your old man's got, you can do it easy. You won't have to break heads. That's why he wants you to go to college."

"Get the fuck outta here," Jimmy said.

"It happens," Dip said. "Shit, I know guys who been made that never touched a gun in their fuckin' lives. Think about it. I mean what's better? Whackin' guys in a dark alley, or sittin' in an air-conditioned office, dreamin' up deals? You don't have to be like your old man, Jimmy."

Jimmy sneered. "Except for one thing. I wanna be."

CHAPTER EIGHT

Dip thought he heard rain. What he heard was the shower, Robin getting ready for work. Used to be two, three nights a week she'd stay over. Now it was five, six nights, his closet filling up with skirts and dresses, getting closer to a permanent stay. He didn't mind. But there were times, like last night, when it would have been better to be alone.

She wanted to talk about them. He wanted to talk about Prize: Where would he go, would he see him?

He waited for the shower to stop, then he rolled out of bed. His head was swimming. Robin was in her underwear, drying her hair. He tried to squeeze past her. She grabbed his arm and turned him around. "All right, Dip. What is it?"

"Nothin'."

He turned on the water and was stepping in. She said, "I see. You always take a shower in your shorts. You're either in trouble, or the washing machine's broken."

He pulled off his shorts, threw them angrily in the hamper. "You're gonna be late," he said and got into the tub.

"What happened last night?"

"What? Can't hear with the water runnin'!"

"Last night," she bellowed. "You were out with Montello."

"Just go to work," he hollered back.

"Oh, sure. Go to work and worry all day. Thanks a lot, Dippolito."

"I'm tellin' you, nothin's wrong."

"And I'm Orphan Annie," she said. "I *hate* this."

He heard the bathroom door slam shut, felt the walls tremble. No good, he thought. It's never going to work. If not this, something else. You don't tell her, she's pissed. You tell her, she's scared. It ain't right. Ain't fair, either.

"Shit!" he said.

He closed the tap and called out to her. "Robin! Hey, look, I'm sorry, all right? C'mere, will you?" No answer. He snatched a towel, went out to get her.

He looked around, saw the open closet, her coat missing. She had gone upstairs to her place.

He thought about going after her. Then he heard a pounding on the front door.

"Hey! Numbnuts! It's me, Diesel."

Dip could feel the blood rushing out of his face, tried to remember, had Diesel ever been here before?

Diesel banged on the door. "Let's go!"

"Whadaya want?" Dip said, stalling, wishing he had a back door instead of a window ten feet above a concrete slab.

"I want the car," Diesel said.

Tony's car. He'd forgotten. He hurried into a pair of trousers, then opened the door. Diesel came in. "S'about time," he said. "You got a broad in here or what?"

"You didn't have to come," Dip said. "I woulda drove it back."

"No books today, Dip. You got the day off."

"What's goin' on?"

"Read the paper," Diesel said. "Greenwall, that asshole. Never made it home last night. Tony's climbin' the fuckin' walls. Like me and Paulie got nothin' else to do. Trick says, 'find this guy,' Tony says, 'find that guy.' What the fuck are we, Missing Persons? You're lucky, sit home on your ass, watch TV."

"Yeah," Dip said. "Lucky."

"You better believe it," Diesel said. "You got the world by the short hair. You and your asshole buddy. Where is he, anyway?"

"Who?"

"Who you think? Prize." Diesel chuckled. "Trick ain't happy with that one. Which reminds me. He wants to see you chop-chop. He's at the club."

Dip turned away, tried to cover the look on his face. He gave it a second and turned back. "What's the big deal?" he said.

Diesel paced, his long legs covering the room in four strides. He lit a cigarette. "Lemme ask you somethin'. You know Boppy, don'tcha?"

Dip swallowed. "Like that. I see 'im around."

"Not lately, you ain't. But him and Prize are real tight. That true?"

"Nah," Dip said. "You know Prize. He knows a hundred guys like Boppy."

Diesel took a hit on his cigarette, exhaled. "Yeah. A real social butterfly. Well . . . you see Prize any time soon, tell 'im I wanna talk. Now gimme the keys, I gotta go."

Dip waited until Diesel drove away. He finished dressing, but wasn't anxious to start his day.

It's piling up, he thought. Enough bullshit to get me buried. He'd already lied to Montello and Diesel. Now it was Trick's turn.

Dip could have walked to Trick's club. But like everybody else in Greenpoint, he always drove no matter how far he was going. It wasn't until he reached the corner that he realized the street up ahead was cordoned off by construction. Backhoes were tearing up the asphalt and a team of hard hats were drilling the sidewalks with jackhammers. The mess forced him to detour and he wound up walking two blocks anyway.

There were a number of clubs like Trick's in the neighborhood and Dip didn't care for any of them. He might have though, if the members treated him better: got someone else to fetch the coffee and newspapers. It's why he preferred hanging out at Patty's, where most of the inhabitants were like him and Prize, knock-around guys who did odd jobs for Montello. The neighborhood called them "half'a wiseguy."

Tricari's club had a metal door painted black. A sign said: NO SOLICITORS! There was no bell. Dip knocked and was let in. There were three guys in the room playing cassino on an old card table. The fourth, the one who'd let him in, hurried back to the game. Dip knew the four but only casually.

"Trick around?" he said.

"In his office," the pale one said without looking up. "Your play," he told his partner.

Dip crossed the room to Trick's office and went in. It was small and dismal-looking, empty except for an old dispatcher's desk with nothing on it but a telephone and a goose-neck lamp pointed right in his eyes. He was about to call out when the door to the bathroom opened and Trick appeared, head down, securing his belt while the toilet sputtered. He raised his head and jumped when he saw Dip.

"That's a lousy habit you got," Trick said. "Sneakin' in on people." He went behind the desk and sat down, leaving Dip to stand.

"All right," Trick said. "I wanna know what's goin' on."

"About what?" Dip said.

"Yeah, that's right. There's a coupla things you oughta be tellin' me about. But what I wanna know right now is this: What's goin' on with you and Tony?"

Dip was puzzled. "Whadaya mean?"

Trick slammed the desk. "You! With your fuckin' diploma. What I'm askin' ain't in Greek. It's American! You got somethin' goin' with Montello. I wanna know what."

Dip shrugged. Either Trick was jealous or he was nosing around where he shouldn't be.

"Well?"

"Nothin'," Dip said. "His kid's got a problem in school. I'm helpin' out."

"I know that part," Trick snapped. "What else?"

"That's it," Dip said. "Comes June, it's all over."

"Is that right? Comes June . . .? You think you're pretty smart, don'tcha? Well, you ain't. I know what you're doin', even if Tony don't."

"What am I doin'?" Dip wanted to know. He wasn't trying to rile Trick, but everything he said was coming out that way.

"Don't act dumb," Trick said. "We got a scam all worked out, no loopholes, everything set. Then you sneak in, grab a beer, and everything turns to shit. You know what happens if Greenwall spills his guts?"

"Sure," Dip said. "What's that got to do with me?"

The more Dip talked, the redder Trick got. "You want me to spell it out for ya?"

"You got it wrong, Trick."

"No," Trick said. "*You* got it wrong. I ain't got a son, like Montello. You don't come in here and feed me a line. I know guys like you. You want in so bad you forget where you come from, tie up with the wrong people. Lemme tell you, it ain't gonna happen. Not while *I'm* here, it ain't."

In all the years Dip worked for the outfit, he'd never once lost his temper with the wrong guy. But Trick was pushing him.

"You can call me what you want, Trick. Think what you want. It don't mean shit to me. Not anymore."

"Huh!" Trick grunted.

Dip said, "You don't know nothin', Tricari. Least of all, about me. I know what I am and I know what I mean to this organization. Nothin'! Zero!"

"You got *that* right," Trick said smugly.

"Okay," Dip said. "We agree. That's why I'm tellin' you now: soon as I'm done with Jimmy, I'm outta here. I quit and you can keep your fuckin' pension!"

Trick laughed. "You'll quit, Dippolito. When we fuckin' tell you."

"Stuff it!" Dip said, then he turned and walked out.

What Tony Montello really wanted was to put a hammer to Buddy Greenwall, close him out before he could rat to the State Racing Commission.

He'd spent the whole night in Greenpoint, him and the boys sucking down coffee in the back room of a one-time fruit and vegetable store that had become a members-only club where bets were taken, cards dealt, and plans made. They had it all worked out. Trick would pay a visit to Buddy's home, see his wife and kids. Except for one thing: they had to find the bastard's family. They had disappeared and so had Buddy Greenwall.

Tony paced the kitchen floor.

Trick said, "Take it easy, Tony. If I know Buddy, he's up in Canada by now."

Tony's head throbbed, his tongue felt parched and ragged. "Canada, huh?" He ran it through his mind, his contacts in Toronto. "Call Toronto," he said. "Give 'em the word: Buddy's disappeared. They make sure it's for good."

"It's gonna cost," Trick said. "Could be all we made on the race."

"Whadaya want me to do?" Tony said. "Wait'll he comes back, cuts a deal with the D.A.?"

"Don't worry about Buddy," Trick said. Trick got up but didn't seem to be in much of a hurry. "You ain't gonna tell me, are you?" he said.

"Tell you what?"

"The Council. What'd they say?"

Tony smirked. "The usual bullshit. You know Fresina. He thinks he's a fuckin' diplomat."

"Like his cousin," Trick said. "I don't like it, Tony. This thing with Buddy Greenwall, it's bad timin'."

"Then clean it up," Tony said. "Make the call."

The man got lucky. He was in a neighborhood gin mill when he looked up from his drink and saw Whizzy, one of his moles, a cokehead with a four-hundred-buck habit. Tall and lanky and, from the look on his face, definitely corded out.

"I found you," Whizzy said. He took a deep breath and blew it in the man's face.

"So you found me. Quit breathin' on me."

"Been lookin' all over," Whizzy said. "Fuckin' feet are killin' me."

"It's your breath killin' you."

Whizzy's eyeballs looked like two radishes in a Mix Master. They kept rolling around.

"I gotta score, man. You help me out?"

"I don't deal that shit."

"Yeah, sure. I know that. But just in case."

"In case what?"

Whizzy kept looking around. Nobody in the joint but he kept looking around like there were cops in the woodwork.

"Park it," the man said.

Whizzy took the stool next to him. "Check it out," he blurted. "The Canadian guy. I got 'im for ya."

"You better know what you're tellin' me."

"This kid I know," Whizzy said. "Works out at the track. He seen 'im this morning at the stables."

"Where is he now?"

"The kid?"

"Hey, snowbird! Who we talkin' about? Greenwall! Where's he at?"

"Some joint in Westbury. The Carriage Motel. The kid followed 'im, called me right up."

"He there now?"

"Far as I know."

He checked the time. Four o'clock. He told Whizzy to hang loose while he made some calls. When he came back Whizzy was humming a tune, strumming an invisible guitar and bouncing his legs with the rhythm.

"Come on," the guy said, "you're comin' with me."

Whizzy turned white. He stopped strumming and rolled his

eyes like there was something behind them he wanted to see: his future, maybe. What there was of it.

An hour later they pulled up outside the Carriage Motel. There were two men in a car waiting for him, free lance sluggers who worked by special arrangement. He had never seen them before and didn't plan to see them again.

Their car was a Buick Riviera. He blinked his lights and the Rivie blinked back.

"What's goin' on?" Whizzy said.

"Shut up!"

Whizzy groaned.

The two men approached the car; one guy in a suit, the other in a suede jacket. The guy lowered his window.

The suit came over, leaned in. "He's in there. Room 111."

"Okay. You know the setup."

"What about me?" Whizzy whined.

"Sit here! I'll take care of you later."

Tony Montello had passed the word he wanted Greenwall in one piece. Buddy's room was on the ground floor, facing the parking lot. They knocked on the door.

"Who's there?" came Buddy's voice.

"Police."

"Police?"

"That's right. Open up!"

They waited.

"Come on," he said. "Open it up!"

"Show me your badge," Buddy said. His voice sounded closer.

"Through the door?" he said. "Gimme an inch and I'll show it."

They slid to either side while Buddy fussed with the chain. The door opened a crack.

"Get 'im!"

Buddy tried to slam them out, but he wasn't quick enough. They hit him together, the suit and the suede jacket. Buddy went down in a heap.

He stayed on the floor, covering his face; a sorry sight in work boots and gray underwear. "I never said nothing," Buddy cried. "Swear to God!"

They picked him up, threw him on the dresser chair. "Gun," he said.

The suit took a .38 from inside his belt. He screwed a silencer into it and gave it over.

Buddy's eyes were like hubcaps. "Oh, Jesus," he said. "Oh, Christ."

"Stop yappin'. This ain't what you think."

"You're lying," Buddy wailed. "You're here to kill me. I'm gonna die!"

"Not if you do what I tell ya."

"You're lying."

The suit smacked him. "Keep sayin' that and you *will* die."

Buddy rubbed his cheek. "If you're not here to kill me, then why the gun? Whadaya want?"

"I wanna help you, Buddy. You're gonna write a letter. I'm gonna help you do it."

"Letter?"

"You know what they say. Confession's good for the soul."

"Wait a minute," Buddy said, shifting his glance from the man to the gun, back to the man. "Who sent you?"

"Mother Teresa." He turned to the suit. "Check around. . . Oughta be paper here somewhere. A pen, too."

"Here it is," said the suit.

The man pulled a note from his pocket: Greenwall's confession. Names, dates, Montello, the whole shmear. He had typed it carefully in advance, made sure there'd be no question who was involved.

"All right, Buddy. Start writin'."

Buddy read the note. "I don't get it."

"Go on, do it!"

With a shaky hand, Buddy started to write. "What happens after?" he said.

The man grinned, gave him a friendly pat on the back. "You go south with my friends here. Lay on the beach, get the sun. A paid vacation, you know?"

Buddy's eyes went glassy. He sniffled. "My stomach hurts," he said. "I gotta go to the bathroom."

"That gonna help you write? All right, go 'head. You got two minutes."

Buddy rose slowly. They moved aside to let him pass. He grabbed the chair and threw it. It struck the suit in the chest. He toppled backward and hit the floor. The gun went off. Then Buddy hit the floor.

"Sonofabitch! Stupid sonofabitch!"

The sluggers rushed over to Buddy. The suit took one look, shook his head.

Whizzy died five minutes after Buddy Greenwall. The suit and the suede jacket took the contract. "What the hell," the suit had muttered. "We're here anyway."

They buried Whizzy in Staten Island, then headed for JFK, leaving Buddy in the overnight parking before they left town.

CHAPTER NINE

At 11:05 A.M., Tony Montello, wearing a dark suit, white shirt and striped tie, paced his living room floor, waiting impatiently for Arnie Randazzo. He'd been ranting and raving for the last five minutes. "I'll crucify that lazy bastard!" he shouted. It was the first time Arnie had ever been late picking him up. But it made no difference to Tony.

He'd arranged a rendezvous with Detective Lieutenant Fred Harris. They'd planned to meet in the parking field behind Alexander's Department Store on Queens Boulevard. Harris had phoned earlier that morning. He had the report Tony wanted.

Tony hadn't even bothered to brush his teeth. He had a man out front, but he was there to watch the house, not drive. So he'd phoned Arnie. "Be here at eleven sharp."

"You got it," Arnie had answered. And now here it was, a quarter past, and no Arnie.

Driving alone would be unwise, but he figured Harris had a lead on who it was that hit Joey Cara. He also figured that if Harris knew, then so did a lot of other people. Like Joey's crew, for instance. But he could easily imagine Sonny DeMarco saying: I don't care who it was. Tony Montello gave the order. Case the house. He comes out alone, nail 'im.

Tony went downstairs to the basement, opened the inside door to the garage, and peered in. It was a small one-car garage and the Eldorado was wedged in tight. He wasn't worried about the car being wired; he'd put it away himself the night before. Still, he held his breath when he got in and turned the key; he didn't exhale until it started. With the remote control, he opened the outer door and pulled out, giving his man a wave before heading for Alexander's. As he turned the corner, he lowered the armrest to cover the gun on the seat next to him.

When he drove into the parking field, Harris's unmarked sedan was parked in its usual spot in the last row, as far from the store as he could possibly get. Tony eased the Caddie alongside. Harris, sitting in a cloud of cigarette smoke, saw him pull in. They nodded to each other. Harris got out, checked the field, and hurried over.

Tony watched him. Freddie Harris, a twenty-year veteran with visions of peaceful retirement, playing shuffleboard under a southern sky. It was Tony's cash that had bought Harris that sweet little condo waiting in Boca Raton.

Lt. Harris got in. "Where's your driver?" he said.

"He didn't show."

Harris shook his head. "I was you, Mr. Montello, I'd get a new driver. It's a bad time to be tooling the boroughs on your own."

"Whadya hear?"

"DeMarco," Harris said. "He's making waves. Spent a ton'a money importing help. Shooters from Phillie and Buffalo. They're coming in by the carload. We already busted a few on possession."

"Thanks," Tony said.

Harris shook him off. "It won't stop him. Word's out. It was one of *your* guys who waxed Cara."

"Yeah," Tony said.

"Yeah?" Harris said. He looked shocked. "You told me different. You said it wasn't you. What's going on?"

"I'm workin' on it," Tony said.

Harris gave him a doubtful eye. "You wouldn't kid me, would you, Mr. Montello?"

"I said I'm workin' on it."

"Yeah," Harris said. He stared out the window, then turned himself around toward Montello. "What are we gonna do? I can't just sit on my hands while you guys blow the fucking town apart."

"It ain't gonna happen. I'm gonna find the cocksucker and turn him over."

"Sure. But what happens in the meantime? What's the body count gonna be?"

"Take it easy," Tony said.

Harris made a face. "Yeah, sure."

Tony said, "I'm gonna need your help, Harris."

"I figured as much," Harris said.

"You got a snitch near Sonny, don't you?"

"Yeah, but—"

"Who is it?"

"Jeez, Mr. Montello. I can't tell you that. Only guys that know are me and my captain. I let him out and they'll make me for sure."

Tony pointed a finger at him. "Listen to me, Freddie. You're too close to the end to fuck it up now."

"I know."

"Then give me the guy. He'll be all right, I guarantee it."

Harris took out his cigarettes, offered one to Tony. They fired up. Harris said, "Okay, Mr. Montello. But you play it wrong and it's my ass on the rack."

"Don't worry about it," Tony said.

Harris said, "You really don't know who it is? *Your* guy, I mean?"

"I told you, I'm workin' on it."

"I'll tell you this," Harris said. "I'm not so sure this snitch knows either."

Tony took a drag, held it. "So let's find out, eh?"

"Okay. But this ain't a made guy we're talking about. Fact is, he's a nobody. We busted him a while back for selling crack to some jig in East New York. That's how we turned him. Now he works the

147

bar in one of Sonny's joints: the Polka Dot Lounge. His name's Rudy Farmer. They call him Hack."

"Good," Tony said.

They shook hands and Harris got out.

Tony wasted no time getting to a telephone. He called Trick and set a meeting at Trick's club. "Get as many as you can," he told him. "Whoever has a crew, get 'em down there in half an hour."

"That ain't much time," Trick griped.

"Do it!" Tony said.

As he drove to Greenpoint, Tony pictured his boys sitting around the club, trading dumb looks and wild rumors. The boys loved to spread rumors. Trouble was, they were always negative: gloom and doom and no way out.

He drove slowly, but he still got there five minutes early. The City was tearing up the street and the adjoining sidewalk was being redone with fresh concrete. He found a spot nearby and hustled toward the club.

Someone had placed wooden planks over the wet cement, two-by-eights running perpendicular to the street and the metal door. He picked his way across the planks and let himself in.

There were seven men in the front room and they were all talking at once. One look at Tony and the room went dead silent. Tony stood there, eying the group, performing a silent head count.

"Where's Paulie?" he asked Trick, who'd been standing just inside the door when he came in.

"Couldn't reach 'im. Where's Arnie?"

"He didn't show."

The words had barely left Tony's mouth when the bullshit began to fly: "You hear that?" "They grabbed Arnie." "Paulie, too." "Nah, he's out in Jersey. He's comin', give 'im time." "No way. They grabbed 'im, I tell ya."

"Shut the fuck up!" Tony roared.

They stopped in mid-sentence, mouths hanging open, gaping at their boss.

"If you guys are that scared, I'll call the cops, get you protection.

Now shut up and listen. I'm gonna say this once. Somebody's gotta pay for what happened to Joey Cara. And that's us!"

"Wait a minute," someone said.

"Pipe it!" Trick said. "Listen to the man."

Tony said, "I know what you're thinkin'. Fuck the Council. Well, we can't fuck the Council. Sure, we can hold our own against DeMarco. Same goes for Vinnie Musto. But it ain't just them. What I'm sayin' comes right from Dominick's lips. We're gonna eat shit for a while. How long I don't know. But we're gonna take it until *I* say different."

"What the fuck!" Diesel said. He'd been off in a corner by himself, taking it in. Now he stepped forward, an arrogant look on his bony face. "I don't know about *these* guys," he said. "But *I* ain't rollin' over. Fuck 'em in the ass. That's what *I* say."

"Yeah," someone said.

"Right," said another.

Tony glared at Diesel. "What *you* say is what *I* tell you to say. We wouldn't be in this mess in the first place if you'd done your job, Diesel. I tell you to find one lousy punk and you can't do it."

Diesel flushed and lowered his face.

Tony stared at the rest of them. One by one they lowered their eyes.

"You guys make me laugh," he said. "One minute you're shakin' in your boots, the next you're all heroes. Like Audie Murphy, eh? Storm the bunker, blast DeMarco? Make up your fuckin' minds!" He stood there, head swiveling, waiting for flack.

"What is it here?" he said. "Think I don't know what I'm doin'? How many years we been on top . . . ? Ten? Fifteen? Who got us here, eh? Me! And I'm gonna keep it that way. *Capeesh?*"

Tony loved this. Seven men, killers, each and every one. Look at them! Squirming around in their chairs like little kids who gotta take a leak. He let his eyes scan the room until they fell on Diesel.

Diesel shrugged, then grinned. He reminded Tony of Stan Laurel and that sappy grin he'd lay on his fat partner whenever he fucked up.

Trick broke the silence. "So what's the plan?" he said.

"DeMarco's buyin' help," Tony said. "Keep your eyes open for new faces. Don't go for walks with guys you don't know. Travel in pairs. Carry a piece. Anybody fucks with you, fuck 'im back. But don't start it, don't go lookin' for trouble. We're not supposed to dish it out. Any questions?"

The room was silent.

"That's better," Tony said. "Now . . . what's the story on Buddy Greenwall?"

They kicked it around for a while, but no one had any leads. Then Paulie Jr. burst in, his face brick red, eyes popping out like he'd just swallowed his cigar.

"Did you see it?" he said. "Out front, ya see it?"

"See what?" Tony said, annoyed.

"Out front," Paulie said. He gestured toward the door. "In the cement."

Tony went out and the rest of them followed. They stopped short when they saw it.

"What the fuck is that?" Diesel said.

"What's it look like?" Tony asked.

Moving slowly, Tony inched his way over the planks. Near the curb, planted in the wet cement, stood a marble gravestone. *R.I.P.* it said. Underneath was Arnie Randazzo's name in red spray paint.

Dip rang Montello's doorbell.

Jimmy answered. "Come in quick," he said. He looked rattled. Dip went in. "What's up?"

"Downstairs," Jimmy said. "He wants to see you."

Dip went down to the basement. Jimmy followed. Tony was sitting at the poker table, a tall drink in front of him, a cigarette burning in the ashtray.

Tony looked up. His face was pasty and he had dark circles under his eyes. "Siddown," he said. "Both of you."

Jimmy hurried, took a chair and leaned forward. Dip hesitated.

"It's all right," Tony said. "I want 'im to hear this."

Dip sat. Tony poured him a drink. "Sonny DeMarco made his move," he said.

"I just heard," Dip said. "Too bad about Arnie."

"Yeah."

Dip didn't know how to respond. All he could think of was what he said: "It's a bitch."

Tony sipped his drink, studied Dip over the top of the glass before putting it down.

"I told you I had a rat."

"Yeah," Dip said. He was nervous, thought for sure Tony was going to press him about Prize.

"I wasn't sure then," Tony said. "But I am now. Two hundred guys. Another two workin' for us and, the way it stands, the only ones I can trust now are the men in this room." Tony moved close, leaned in. "I need someone out there, doin' my leg work. A guy nobody's gonna worry about if he starts pokin' around."

He squashed the cigarette, stared at Dip. "Find 'im, Dip. Find my rat."

Dip said, "That's a big order."

"I know," Tony said. "Find 'im and you can name your price."

"My price?" Dip said.

"You deaf or what?" Tony smiled, his face softened. "And I'm givin' you the best guy I got," he said, and slapped his son on the shoulder.

"No," Dip said. "I do this alone."

"What kinda shit is that?" Jimmy said, an angry look on his face. "I don't believe what I'm hearin'.."

"Can it!" Tony said. He took another sip of his drink, pondered a moment. "Jimmy goes with you."

"Way to go!" Jimmy said.

Dip sighed. "Tony, somethin' happens to 'im I'm dead meat."

Tony said, "The kid's gotta learn some time. He goes." He winked at his son.

"All right."

Tony went on. "Now, here's a lead for ya. There's a guy works one of Sonny's joints, the Polka Dot Lounge. I want you to squeeze 'im, open 'im up."

"Who is this guy?" Jimmy said.

Tony filled them in, but Dip wasn't listening. He already knew him.

"Maybe we oughta call the place," Jimmy said.

"And do what, leave a message?"

"Suppose he ain't there?"

Dip didn't answer, kept his eyes on the road. He dropped the blinker and took the next exit off the Belt Parkway.

"So what's gonna happen?" Jimmy said. "Whada we do?"

"*We?*" Dip said. "*We* don't do shit. I do it. You stay in the car and watch."

"That's cool," Jimmy said.

Dip glanced over at him. "That's it? No argument?"

"Hey," Jimmy said, grinning. "You're runnin' the show. I'm here to learn."

Dip said, "Listen to me. This ain't the senior prom. We ain't out for laughs so you better get serious."

Jimmy shook his head. "Take it easy, will ya? I know it's serious."

"Then act it, for Chrissake."

Dip made the turn onto Flatlands Avenue. He drove slowly for several blocks until he sighted the Polka Dot Lounge up ahead. He drove by, took a look, then gunned the motor.

"What are you doin'?" Jimmy said. "You passed the place."

"No shit."

"I don't get it."

"Whada you blind? Didn't you see?"

"See what?" Jimmy said. "A coupla guys out front. Big deal."

"Jesus Christ," Dip snapped. "Whadaya think they're doin'? Waitin' for Take Out? They work for Sonny."

Jimmy looked at him, his eyes getting wider. "How do you know?"

"I know," Dip said. "Now be quiet and lemme think."

He drove for another block then made a U-turn and doubled back. "I'm gonna make another pass," he said. "Lemme know if they look."

"They're talkin' to a chick," Jimmy said as they drove by.

"Did they look?"

"I just told ya—"

"Answer me!"

"No, for Chrissake!"

He kept going until he was sure they couldn't see his tail lights. Then he turned the car around and headed back again.

"This is great," Jimmy said sarcastically. "I shoulda brought a pad and pencil, take notes on how to shake a guy. Step one: Drive back and forth until you run outta gas."

Dip found a spot a block before the lounge and pulled in. He killed the lights and peered down the street at three burly goons and a tall blonde. They were laughing, joking around.

"Now what?" Jimmy said.

"We wait. He's gotta go home sometime."

"Yeah," Jimmy said. "If he's *in* there. But how do we know? I got better things to do than sit on my ass all night."

"Like what?" Dip said.

Five minutes went by. Jimmy said, "How long we gonna wait?"

"They close at three," Dip said.

Jimmy looked at his watch. "Christ, that's an hour and a half."

Dip gave him a smirk. "You oughta come out with me and Prize sometime. Once we waited ten fuckin' hours for this guy to come home, the two of us pissin' in coffee cups, freezin' our asses. We finally get the bum and he's got fourteen bucks in his pocket. I thought Prize would kill the guy."

Jimmy sighed. "This sucks. At least put the radio on, gimme a cigarette—somethin'."

"Tell you what," Dip said. "Next time we do this we'll invite a few chicks. Have a party while we wait."

"There you go," Jimmy said.

"Shut up!" Dip said.

The minutes passed slowly and Jimmy grew more restless. "Listen, Dip. They don't know me. I can walk right in."

"Forget it."

"At least we'll know if he's in there. C'mon, whadaya say?"

"You move and I'll break your legs."

"All right," Jimmy said. "But I still think it's a good idea."

Dip turned away. That was all Jimmy needed. He threw open the door and jumped out.

"Hey!" Dip said. But the kid was on his way and it was too late to chase him down. "Shit!" Dip said.

Jimmy was doing a fast-walk toward Sonny's boys. *If they make him, we're both dead. Sure, I have my gun. But what good's it gonna do if they snatch the kid?*

Jimmy wasn't even there yet and already Dip could feel the knots in his stomach. They grew tighter when Jimmy was stopped.

Dip hunched over the steering wheel, watched them talk, saw Jimmy take out his wallet. Dip was frantic, torn by the risk of going out after him, and the anxiety of doing nothing. He was ready to get out when suddenly a path was cleared and Jimmy walked right in.

He took the gun off his ankle and held it on his lap. Time dragged. Ten minutes, twenty. Twenty-five. Then the front door opened and Jimmy popped out. All smiles, he waved "so-long" to the bad guys and headed back to the car.

Dip blew a long, heavy sigh as Jimmy walked casually away from the lounge.

Jimmy got in, propped himself straight up and looked over at Dip like he wanted praise. Dip glared at him. "You ever pull that shit again, Jimmy, I swear to God I'll—"

"Yeah, yeah," Jimmy said, the smell of beer wafting across the seat. "Now come on, we're wastin' time."

"Whada you talkin' about?"

"Hack," Jimmy said. "He's got the night off. I asked around. There's a joint out by Kennedy Airport: the Travel Inn. It's where he goes when he ain't workin'."

Dip smirked. "It took you that long to find out?"

Jimmy smiled at him. "Whadaya want?" he said. "It's my first time out."

Dip said, "The Travel Inn, eh?"

"That's it. You know the place?"

"I know it. It's a motel for husbands and wives who don't wanna be. Rooms by the hour, piano bar, that kinda shit."

"Then let's go," Jimmy said. "Before it closes."

Dip wanted to chew him out, but he was too busy thinking about the Travel Inn, what he'd do when they got there. He knew the place well. He and Prize had been there several times to collect vig money from a middle-aged sleaze named Stevie Rodman. It was one of those joints that featured dim lights and dark corners; cozy booths along the wall where the cheaters groped each other while they waited for rooms.

It was nearly closing time when they got there. A light mist was drifting in off the bay. Dip pulled off the service road into the parking lot that surrounded the building. He circled the place, well-lit in the front, dark in the back. The headlights picked up a guy changing a flat tire in the rain. It was Hack. Dip eased into a spot. He killed the engine and lights and looked over at Jimmy.

Dip flicked his head. "Outside." He and Jimmy got out. They walked up slowly and stood over the man.

Hack's eyes were sliding back and forth, looking for help he couldn't call on. Dip grabbed him by the elbow.

"What is this?" Hack said.

Dip pulled out his gun. "Shut up and get down on the ground."

"Yeah, sure," Hack said. "Whatever you say. Just take it slow with that thing." He hit the ground on his stomach. "Look, man, if it's about that chick, forget it. I got nothin' with her. I mean, I don't want no trouble, you know?"

"Face up," Dip said. Hack rolled over. "Under the tire."

Hack didn't move. But his eyes were getting wider by the second. Dip hunkered down, pressed the gun to Hack's cheek. "You got a choice," he said. "Take it now, or get under there."

Hack raised his head, saw the gap between the ground and the elevated tire: about a foot high—just enough to squeeze under.

"Okay, okay," he said, trying to sound calm. "But what's this about?" He squirmed under the car until the only part of him Dip could see was his head.

"We're gonna talk," Dip said. He didn't know where Jimmy had hid himself, but when he got to his feet the kid was standing beside him. "Get on the jack," he told him.

Jimmy looked down at the man under the tire. "Hey, man, that's excellent," he said. He moved to the front of the car where the jackhandle protruded from beneath the bumper. He gripped the handle and waited for orders.

"All right, Hack," Dip said. "Let's talk."

Hack's head was swiveling from side to side. His face was wet from the mist and he had to squint to see. "Who's with you?" he said. "He's too close to the jack. Get 'im outta there!"

Dip looked at Jimmy. "When I say the word, drop in a notch. Go on, do it."

Jimmy pumped the handle. The jack made a clicking sound and the car rocked gently, dropping an inch.

"Oh, Christ," Hack said. "Jesus. Jesus."

"Relax," Dip said. "We ain't even started."

"Who the fuck *are* you?" Hack cried. "Whadaya want?"

"Information," Dip said.

"Sure. Anything you want, only get me outta here."

"You know what happened to Joey Cara?"

"Yeah, sure. They blew 'im up."

"Who's 'they'?"

"How the fuck do *I* know? I'm a bartender."

Dip raised his chin at Jimmy. *Click.*

"Oh, shit!" Hack wailed. "I don't know, man. I swear."

Jimmy lowered the jack another notch. Dip said, "Lemme help you, Hack—get you started. Word's out it was Tony Montello. That true?"

"Yeah," Hack said quickly. "That's right."

"How do you know?"

"I heard talk."

"Who?"

"Sonny DeMarco and some other guys."

"How do they know it's Montello?"

"I don't know. I mean, *they* don't. Not for sure, anyways. Sonny says, 'Who else *could* it be?' He's plenty sore, that's all I know."

Dip said. "Listen good. You're in the Polka Dot every night—"

"Now I know you!" Hack half-shouted. "You're the guy was lookin' for Charley Bop."

"That's right. And you owe me a hundred bucks, 'cause I ain't found 'im yet."

Hack's face lit up. "Is that what this is? A hundred bucks? I'll give it back, man. No problem."

Dip pointed at Jimmy. The car dropped an inch.

"Fuck!" Hack yelped. "What's your story, man?"

Dip said, "It wasn't Montello did Joey Cara. You oughta know that before you go spreadin' rumors."

"I heard that, too," Hack said.

"Heard what? Whadya hear?"

"That it wasn't Montello."

"Hit it!" he told Jimmy.

The tire was an inch above Hack's neck. He groaned, his eyes wet with rain. "Please," he cried, "gimme a chance."

"Why'd you say it was Montello?" Dip banged the front panel with his fist. The car swayed a tiny bit.

"Okay," Hack said. "One of his guys, one of his guys did it. I mean, what difference does it make?"

Dip leaned closer. "Did you get a name—the Montello guy?"

"I already told you. It don't matter to them. To them it's the same thing."

Dip was right in Hack's face. "Let's talk about Boppy. You know he works for Montello. How come he comes to your joint and hangs out? How can he do that?"

"I don't know. The guy comes in, I serve 'im. If he wasn't okay, he'd never come back."

"Who else comes in from Montello's crew?"

"Nobody."

"Say again," Dip said. "You got two more clicks before you say goodbye to your Adam's apple."

"I swear to God," Hack pleaded. "Only one ever came in was Charley Bop."

"But you talked to 'im, right? You loaned 'im money so you must've been friends."

"I gave 'im a few bucks. Don't mean we're asshole buddies."

"He ever say who he works for? Besides Montello, I mean."

Hack twisted and squirmed, tried to stretch his neck from under the tire. "I never got a name," he said. "Some heavy hitter. Boppy was scared shit of the guy."

Dip got up, his leg bones cracking. He thought for a moment, then crouched again. "I want you to find out who he is. You hear me, Hack?"

"Yeah," Hack said. "Now get me outta here, will ya?"

Dip motioned to Jimmy. The car was still going up when Hack scrambled out.

"Yeah. Yeah, I hear you. But how? Only guy that knows is Boppy and if *you* can't find 'im, how the hell can I?"

"That's *your* problem," Dip said. "But if I was you, I'd start at the Polka Dot."

"What am I supposed to do?" Hack whined. "Ask Sonny De-Marco? Jesus, man, gimme a break!"

Dip said, "If Boppy can drink there, then somebody's sayin' he's okay. Forget about DeMarco. Ask around. Get me a name. I'll do the rest."

Hack gave it some thought. "All right," he said. "I'll do what I can. How do I reach you?"

"I'll reach *you*," Dip said. "But make it fast, Hack. You hear what I'm sayin'? All right. Beat it!"

CHAPTER TEN

Dip got out of his car and was immediately hit with the smell of dead fish. He'd expected the smell but it didn't make it any easier to take. Across the street, on the opposite corner, was what he was looking for: a long flat building with a large wooden sign on the upper facade—PARISI'S WHOLESALE. He waited for traffic to clear, then jogged toward it.

He went around the side. A small procession of ten-wheelers were waiting their turn in front of several loading bays, backed against the platforms while crates of iced fish rolled out on conveyor belts. On one of the platforms was a fat guy in bib overalls smeared with blood. He had a clipboard in one hand and a pencil in the other. He was counting the crates and trying to look important.

Dip climbed the platform stairs. "I'm lookin' for the Fish Lady," he said.

The guy didn't say anything, kept writing little checkmarks on his clipboard.

Dip said, "She here, or what?"

"She's always here," the guy said. "Inside. Up the stairs."

Dip went in, stepping lightly over a concrete floor, awash with slimy water and fish entrails. There were six rows of work benches, each about forty feet long, covered with chipped ice and freshly cut fish. Each bench had two men assigned to it. They were dressed in the same type of overalls he'd seen on the fat guy; the only extras were rubber boots and blood-covered carving knives.

Along the near wall, about ten feet up and running parallel to the benches below, a catwalk led straight to a corner office. The outer wall of the office was sheer glass. Behind it, a middle-aged woman peered down at him. She was Angie Parisi, the Fish Lady.

Angie had inherited the business from her late husband, Gino. Gino, and their eldest son, Gene, had both been associates of Tony Montello, and the business had been merely a front. Nowadays, Parisi's Wholesale was strictly legitimate.

Dip was crossing the catwalk when Angie opened the office door. "He ain't here," she said, gruffly, stopping him in his tracks.

She was small and slim, wore straight-legged jeans, a flannel shirt, and a black sweatband that held a thick head of white hair off her forehead. She had a square jaw, a wide mouth, and dark, sunken eyes. About sixty years old, but she might have passed for forty-five.

"Who ain't here?" Dip said.

"My son. I ain't seen him in months." She backed inside the office.

"I'm his friend," Dip said, getting it out before she could close the door in his face.

She squinted at him. "I know all'a Charley's friends. You ain't one'a them. Now make an about-face before one'a my guys gets nervous."

Dip looked down at the cutting benches, saw three of the workers glaring at him. "I'm Jackie Dip," he said.

"Dip," she said, and her eyes brightened. "You're friends with Lenny?"

"That's me."

"Why'n ya say so right away?" She stepped forward, leaned

over the handrail. "It's okay," she called down. "Back to work!" She tossed her head toward the door. "Come on in."

The office was small and uncluttered: a simple desk, two chairs, and file cabinets along the far wall, beneath a nicely done mural of saltwater fish. The desk abutted the glass. It gave Angie a clear view of the work area below. On the mantel behind her desk were two urns.

"You want some coffee?" she asked.

Dip looked around. "If you have it."

She smiled. "How do you take it?"

"Hot."

She went behind the desk, opened the side drawer, and pulled out a handsized microphone. She barked into it and her voice crackled from speakers Dip couldn't see. "Nelson!" She looked down at one of the workers who raised his head and gazed questioningly at the Fish Lady.

"Two mugs!" she squawked. "Right away!" The worker nodded and scurried off.

She looked at Dip. "I got sixteen men on my payroll," she said. "I talk and they jump. Not bad for a sawed-off old widow, huh?"

"You ain't old," Dip said.

She chuckled. "You sound like Lenny. Where is that good lookin' sonofabitch, anyway? I ain't seen 'im lately."

"He's been busy," Dip said. "Got himself a lady."

"A lady! What the hell am I, a pickled herring?"

Dip pictured Prize flirting with her and Angie eating it up. He could see them liking each other. Hell, he just met her himself, and he liked her, too.

She said, "Hey, he's not serious, is he? I mean, Lenny's a doll. But God help the girl he marries."

"Nah," Dip said. "It's just a fling."

She sighed. "A fling. Been thirty years since I had a fling." She winked at him. "Except for Lenny, that is."

The door opened. The worker came in, placed two steaming

mugs of coffee on the desk, and walked out. The stink of fish stayed behind.

"Are *you* married?"

"No."

"No," she said, "you wouldn't be. So many nice young men in this neighborhood." She shook her head once. "I tell Charley all the time: Find a young lady, quit the street. But he doesn't listen. He says yes, but he doesn't listen. Your mother, she tell you to find a nice lady?"

"She used to," Dip said, "when she was alive."

Angie shook her head. "You should have listened to her. Coffee all right? Want sugar?"

"This'll be fine," Dip said. He was starting to feel uncomfortable, the way she kept staring at him, searching him out, her eyes asking what she wasn't ready to ask: Can I trust you?

He waited, sipping coffee.

She said, "Who you with?"

"Nobody."

"I can see that. No, I'm talkin' about the mental giant that sent you. You know how many guys been around here askin' for Charley? I tell 'em, 'Hey, you lost him, you find 'im.'"

"You got it wrong," Dip said. "I'm not lookin' for Charley for the same reason. I wanna help 'im."

"Help? Charley? What is it, you walk on water or what? My nephew, Louis, he comes here, tells me the same thing. Louis and Charley are close, like brothers. If anyone can help Charley, Louis can. But he comes back all pissed off and I know there's nothing can be done."

Dip didn't answer. He couldn't.

"What'd he do this time?" she said. "You're Lenny's friend, I'll believe you."

She sat there a while, her eyes drifting. Dip could only imagine she was thinking if she would see her son again.

"I'm not sure," he said. "But I can't do anything for 'im unless I know where he is."

She took a cigarette from her shirt pocket, lit it, and exhaled smoke across the desk. "You couldn't help Charley," she said, "if he was sittin' in my lap blowin' you kisses. Charley's my kid, but I know him for what he is. A fuck up! Maybe it's not his fault. He was too young when he lost his father and his brother. All he had to go on were the stories he heard about 'em. They had guts, those two. Never took shit. Ask Montello, he'll tell you. The Parisis were stand-up guys." She inhaled. "Charley's a wimp. Always has been. I want 'im back, but if he *has* fucked up then that's it. He'll have to pay." She turned her face toward the mantel. "See that?" She nodded toward the two urns.

"I was wondering about those," Dip said.

"The one on the left, that's Gino. The other one's Gene. They found 'em in the river. Ironic, ain't it? Two guys in the fish business? I got room there for Charley. But to tell you truth, he don't really belong with them."

"You sound like you gave up on 'im," Dip said.

"What can I say?"

"I gotta find 'im," Dip said. "It's not just for him. It's Lenny, too."

"Oh, for Chrissake." She squeezed the bridge of her nose. "I thought Lenny was smarter than that."

I thought so, too, Dip wanted to say. "Does Charley have an address book?"

She blinked. "Who would he put in it? It's only Lenny and Louis that he sees."

"Does Lenny know Louis?"

"I suppose so. I never saw them together, but I guess so."

"What about your son's place in Rockaway Beach?"

"It was our summer getaway," she said, "when my husband was alive. Louis said he wasn't there."

"Where is it?"

She gave him the address.

"Charley's cousin," Dip said. "Louis."

"Parisi," she said. "My brother-in-law's son."

"What's he do?"

"What does he do?" she said. "What does my Charley do? And you."

Dip colored.

She waved him off. She said, "Louis owns a carwash on the side."

"Listen to me, Mrs. Parisi. It's important. I wanna talk to Louis. If he's really on your side, then ask 'im to talk to me. Tell 'im that I can help Charley. Would you do that?"

"If that's all you want? Yeah, I can talk to him."

Dip wasn't sure if he'd be sticking his neck out with Louis Parisi. Chances were good that the guy was connected with Sonny De-Marco's crew and that he wouldn't open up no matter what the Fish Lady asked. But maybe Louis and Boppy were as close as she claimed.

He got up, said goodbye and wished her well. "We'll work it out," he told her. "Don't worry."

She looked up at him from behind the desk. "It ain't Charley I'm thinking about," she said. Then she turned back toward the mantel, the little shrine for her late husband and number-one son. "It's just that they ain't gonna want Charley up there."

Hack lived in a frame house off Remsen Street, not far from the Polka Dot Lounge. Dip parked and trotted up to the front door. There were three doorbells. The first two didn't answer. The third got a side door to open.

"Over here!" came a man's voice from the driveway.

Dip went around the side, saw Hack leaning out. He was dressed in his underwear and he looked as if he just woke up.

"Oh, man," Hack groaned. "Not you!"

Dip pushed him aside and went in. A short staircase led down to a basement apartment. "Come on in," Dip said.

"Thanks," Hack grumbled.

Downstairs Dip found himself in a small, dark living room.

There were rumpled sheets on the couch and the portable TV was showing an old black-and-white movie.

"I know you're in a rush," Hack said, following him down. "But this is ridiculous. I just got up, for Chrissake."

Dip said, "Tell me what you know about Louie Parisi."

"Jesus," Hack said.

"How heavy is he?"

Hack went to the couch, pulled a cigarette off an end table. "He ain't a made guy," he said. He struck a match, held it out while he thought it over. "But he will be. He's in pretty good with Sonny D. You want my advice, you'll go light with Louie Parisi."

"Do you know he's Boppy's cousin?"

"I don't get it," Hack said. "You know all this shit, whadaya talkin' to me for?"

"Is Louie the reason Boppy's allowed to hang around the Polka Dot?"

"Could be," Hack said. "They're real tight."

"How far would Louie go to protect his cousin?"

"I don't know. Blood's thicker than water. But Louie Parisi . . . he's a hungry dude. My opinion? He'd give 'im up if he had to."

"Him and Boppy," Dip said, "what are they into?"

Hack shook his head. "I got no idea."

"Lemme ask you somethin'," Dip said.

Hack smirked. "You kiddin'? That's all you been doin'."

"I need somebody close to Cousin Louie."

"Only one I know is Charley Bop," Hack said, grinning.

"Hey," Dip said. "You wanna get under a car?"

Hack blanched.

"Okay then. Gimme somebody."

"I already did," Hack said. "Arlene Consolo. She and Louie have one of those love-hate things. Last I heard, it was more hate than love. Catch her right, she'll tell you his life's story. Won't even cost you."

"Where does she live?"

"You talked to her, don't you know?"

"I didn't get her address."

"Then you got problems, 'cause I ain't seen her since that night. You must'a scared her pretty good."

"Find out where she lives," Dip said.

"Christ!" He took a drag on his cigarette. "All right. It's an apartment house. Sea Cliff Arms on Coney Island Avenue. But what happens if she ain't there? For all I know she's pullin' tricks in Houston, Texas."

"Who else?"

Hack shook his head. "All this for Charley Bop? You must want 'im pretty bad. Tell you what," he said. "You get me some coke and I'll help you out."

"Coke?" Dip said. "What is this, bargain day? Forget about it."

"It ain't for me," Hack said. "It's for Ralphie Scimone."

"Who the hell's he?"

"He works at Louie's carwash on Bushwick Avenue. Louie's in and out, on the phone all the time. If anybody knows what Louie's doin', it's Ralphie. Give 'im some blow and he'll talk your fuckin' ears off."

"I'll think about it," Dip said.

Tony Montello had received another letter from Mr. Henry Bell at the high school. Tony read the letter and immediately called for a sit-down. In attendance were Eva, Jimmy, and Dip.

They were waiting impatiently at the kitchen table when Tony announced, "We're goin' to Vegas. All of us!"

Jimmy slapped the table. "Awright!"

Tony waved Dean Bell's letter like a checkered flag. "It says here that what Jimmy did only proves that anybody who applies himself can make the grade." He beamed at his son. "I'm proud'a you, kid."

"I *knew* I aced them tests," Jimmy said. He looked at Dip. "Didn't I say it, Dip? Didn't I tell you? Oh, *man,* I can't wait to hit them casinos. They ain't gonna know what happened. I'll rake the joint."

Tony laughed heartily, thought it was cute: his only son, a chip off the old block. "We're gonna celebrate tonight," he declared. "The four of us. No, make it five. Dip's girl will go with us. Go on, Dip, call her right now. Tell her dinner at eight, wear the best she's got. Eva, you pick the place."

"Lutece," Eva said.

Jimmy had no idea what he was eating. Some kind of meat drowning in wine sauce; broccoli in creamy shit made it look like green oatmeal. He couldn't wait for the night to end. Here he was, in one of the swankiest restaurants in New York City, wearing his best suit, a new white shirt with initialed cuffs, a silk tie he'd allowed Eva to pick out for him; his first real shot at the big time, and all he could do was brood.

He wished Tony would shut up for a while. They'd been here less than an hour and even the cooks knew what they were celebrating. "The most important night of my son's life," he was telling everyone. As if they cared. Hell, Jimmy didn't care himself. At a nearby table sat two watchdogs Tony had brought along for security. Jimmy poked at his food, shoved it around his plate, then lowered his fork.

Tony snorted. "That's a hundred bucks you're pushin' around. C'mon, kid, *mangia*."

Eva chuckled. All night she'd been chuckling—everything funny, everything cute. "*You* should talk, Tony," she said. "You didn't do much better yourself."

Tony made a face. "You'd think a joint like this could make pasta with lentils. If I'd a known, we'd a went to Patty's."

"Honestly," Eva said. She leaned across the table, toward Robin. "You ever been here before, honey?"

"First time," Robin said.

"It's Tony's fault," Eva said. "If he paid his people more, they could afford a place like this."

Tony said, "God Almighty couldn't afford a place like this."

"It's not every day your son graduates," Eva said.

Jimmy glared. "Knock it off, will ya."

"You believe this kid?" Tony said. "Passed every test and he acts like it's nothin'. Don't get modest on me, Jimmy. I wouldn't know you."

Dip said, "He'll lighten up when he gets to Vegas."

"Yeah." Tony nodded. "But you'll have to stay with 'im, Dip. See he don't blow his whole wad the first night. Those joints ain't like candy stores, you know."

"I'll watch out for 'im," Dip said.

Jimmy threw his father a look. Tony winked back.

Eva reached over, took Robin's hand. "Why don't you come with us?" she said. "With so many men around, I'm afraid I'll get lost in the shuffle."

"I doubt it," Tony said.

Eva ignored him, stayed with Robin. "We'll have fun." She smiled. "It's a great town. We'll shop, sun by the pool. Massage."

"Hey," Tony said. "No massage."

Eva giggled. "It's a woman, silly." She clucked at Robin. "He's so jealous. Honestly, if another man just looks at me, he goes crazy."

Tony said, "It's not hard to look. Ain't that right, Dip?"

Before Dip could answer, some guy in a tuxedo came over. Behind him was a cart loaded with sweets: gooey stuff he called dessert. He waved it closer and gave them a rundown.

Jimmy didn't look at the cart, but he was still hungry so he listened, heard "chocolate mousse" and said, "Yeah, gimme that." He figured he'd get a hollow piece of chocolate shaped like a reindeer. What he got puzzled him: a cup with brown mush in it. Disgusted, he let it sit there.

Dip's girl noticed he wasn't eating. "Would you like to switch, Jimmy?" she said. She held up her plate. "I don't remember what he called this, but it tastes like apple pie."

They made the switch.

Suddenly, Tony dropped his fork. "Now what!" he said, looking past Jimmy.

Jimmy tracked his father's glance, saw the two bodyguards talking to Paulie Jr. Jimmy hadn't seen Paulie come in, but it had to be important for him to show up like this.

Paulie looked over, gave Tony the eye.

Tony said, "Eva, go dust your nose. Take Robin with you."

"For heaven's sake," Eva griped. "Doesn't he know it's a private party?"

"Just do it, Eva. All right?"

Eva sighed. "I guess so. Come on, honey," she said to Robin. "I know it's hard to look better than we do, but let's give it a try."

The women left and Paulie lumbered over. He seemed out of breath, like he'd run here all the way from Brooklyn. He took Robin's chair.

"I got news," he said.

"Now there's a shock," Tony said. "Is it good or bad? Don't make it bad 'cause I ain't in the mood."

"It's good *and* bad," Paulie said.

Tony wrinkled his forehead. "I ain't in the mood for riddles, either."

Paulie flicked his head toward Dip and Jimmy.

"Talk," Tony said. "You just wrecked a hundred-dollar meal."

Paulie lowered his voice. "Greenwall's dead."

Tony smiled. "Good! Who got 'im?"

"That's the bad part," Paulie said. "We don't know."

Tony went red in the face. Jimmy pulled back, waited for the explosion.

"Whadaya mean, 'We don't know'? It's us, you dumb jerk. It had'a be."

"I know it had'a be," Paulie said, "but it ain't. Least we don't think so. I just left Trick. He got a call. They found the guy in a car at the airport. Been there for days."

"That don't mean shit," Tony said. "It was *our* contract. Who else would want the guy?"

"That's what Trick said. Except whoever done it ain't comin' forward. Not to us, anyway."

Tony rubbed his chin. "I see what you mean. Maybe he's layin' low. Don't worry, he'll come around. Them guys don't do work for charity."

"Sure," Paulie said. "But what if he don't come around?"

"What of it?" Tony snapped. "We wanted the guy, didn't we? Who gives a shit who it was. He did us a favor."

"Yeah, but—"

"Never mind. Now go on, beat it. Tell Trick I'll catch 'im later tonight."

Paulie was still shaking his head when he walked out. Tony waited until he was out of sight. He looked at Dip.

"Whadaya think?"

Dip shrugged.

Jimmy said, "Maybe he owed the shys."

"He did," Tony said. "Except that's us." He paused. "Somethin' stinks."

Robin had always thought that when it came to applying makeup, there was no woman in the world who was slower, more meticulous than she. She'd been wrong.

It had taken Eva ten minutes to apply mascara, another five for eye shadow. Now it was lipstick, which was no easy chore.

If only Eva would shut her mouth long enough to put the damn stuff on, Robin thought.

"Just like that," Eva was saying. "One look at Tony and I knew it was time to quit. Not that I had to, mind you. My legs are tight as ever, and my bust . . . well!" She threw her shoulders back. "See for yourself. Thirty-eight D and not one ounce of silicone. Would you believe I'm pushing forty?"

Forty-five, Robin wanted to say. "Is that a fact?" she said instead.

"Well." Eva giggled to herself in the mirror. "Give or take a few months. What about you, hon?"

"Thirty," Robin said. "Give or take a few months."

Eva grinned at her. "What they don't know, right, sweetie?" She brought the lipstick to her mouth, tried again but gave it up. She tsked. "I just can't seem to get this right."

"Try humming," Robin said. "It works for me."

"Hmmmm. No," said Eva, "it doesn't work. Tony tells me you're taking the plunge." She tittered. "Or should I say, taking the dip?" She waited for Robin to catch on. "That's a joke, honey," Eva said.

"I gathered," Robin said.

"You going to have children? You should, being thirty and all. I used to love kids, always felt bad I never had any. Now I'll have Jimmy. Boy, there's a package, eh? Ever see that kid in a pair of shorts?"

"No," Robin said. "I never have."

"Outrageous," Eva said. "Say, wouldn't it be nice if after we're married we got close."

"Who?" Robin said. "You and Jimmy?"

"What!" Eva said. "No, no. I meant us, you and me." Then she spoke to her own image, gazing at it with admiration. "My God, imagine what Tony would do." She shook her head. "Oh, well. You know, Robin, you oughta be proud of Dip. The way he helped Jimmy with school. Tony's so grateful, he's ready to give him the world."

"That's nice," Robin said.

"Nice? God, but you're a cool one. Don't be surprised if Tony makes Dip his number-one guy. How would that be, huh? You and me—we'd be like those broads in the White House. First and Second Lady. I tell you, honey, there's no limit to what they can give us."

"All I want," Robin said, "is for Dip to get out."

"Get out? You mean quit?"

"That's right."

"Now that's the dumbest thing I ever heard. I know women who'd give their eyeteeth to be in your shoes."

"I don't doubt it," Robin said. "But I'm in them, and that's what I want."

"Well," Eva said, "you oughta think about it. There's a lot at stake."

The way Robin saw it, Eva Barone couldn't have been more obvious if she were a pane of glass. Still, she was curious about the woman. "Answer me something, Eva."

"Ah-ha," Eva said. "I see you're already thinking about it."

Robin said, "Aren't you worried? I mean, what they do, it's . . . Well, you know."

"Of course I worry," Eva said. "We're not married yet."

"What's that got to do with it?"

Eva smirked. "You *are* naive. Let me tell you how it works. Right now, you and me, we're nothing more to them than a steady piece of ass. Sure, we get gifts, and their people respect us. But it's only good while they're out on the street. If they get busted, it's all over. We either wait like good little girls, or we move on. But!" She raised her ring finger. "Put a gold band on this sucker, and everything's different. Once a month there'll be someone at your door with a nice healthy envelope. It's like alimony, for God's sake. Only it's bigger, fatter and, best of all, tax free. You getting the picture, hon?"

Robin said, "And what if it's even more serious than jail?"

Eva grinned. "You mean, bang-bang, you're dead?" Eva turned away from the mirror, looked up at Robin. "All the more reason to get that ring. And I'll tell you this. The way things are going, the sooner the better."

CHAPTER ELEVEN

Dip answered on the first ring. Snatching the receiver, he rolled over and tucked it between his face and the pillow.

"Hello."

"Wake up, you dumb shit!"

"Prize?" Dip whispered.

"Who'd you expect? How the hell are you?"

"Never mind that. Where you been?" Dip rubbed his face.

"Paradise," Prize said. "The land of milk and honeys. Except I'm running outta honeys. How are things in the Point of Green?"

It was the way he said it, his voice going soft, a slight crack at the end. Prize was hurting.

Dip said, "You shoulda waited, man. Talked to me first. You scared the shit out of me. I thought . . . you know."

"Yeah," Prize said. "I owe you fifteen large."

Dip said, "Forget it. So what's the story? You're not comin' in, are you?"

"You tell *me*," Prize said.

"Where are you?"

"Too far to walk, my man. Too far to tell."

"Don't give me that shit, Prize. I gotta see you."

"I'm hot, huh?"

"Whada *you* think?"

"Yeah," Prize said. He sounded dejected.

Dip said, "I know it's tough. But you gotta hang in there, wait for a break. Now tell me where you're at. I'll come the first chance I get."

"Cape May," Prize said.

"Where the fuck is that?"

"Just follow the map."

"What map?"

"The one I'm givin' you. Okay, here it is." He told Dip where he was, how to get there. It was tricky, but Dip recited it back.

"That's it," Prize said. There was silence. "Dip?"

"Yeah?"

"I was wrong, man. About leavin'. I mean, it wasn't much of a life, but it was all I had. All I know."

"We'll get you back, man."

"I want you to know, Dip. You and me. . . . Ah, shit. Just watch yourself, okay?"

The only graduation Dip had ever sat through was his own at P.S. 26, so many years ago he could hardly recall it. He tried to remember what his thoughts were that day, if he'd been proud, relieved, or just plain indifferent. He remembered his future being laid out for him, Nickie saying, "Just kill a year or two in high school, kid. Later on I'll bring you down the club. Time you're eighteen, you'll be on your way."

It seemed to Dip that he had never had a choice. Not that he would've wanted one had the choice been offered. He saw his brother and couldn't wait to join up. It made him think about Jimmy's future. What choice did *he* have? Nickie was only a soldier and Dip had followed him. Tony Montello ran the whole show.

Tony had made a big deal about Dip's coming along to dinner.

Also Jimmy had three tickets for the commencement and since Tony couldn't safely sit outside in public for two hours, who deserved to go more than Dip? Dip balked but Tony insisted: "You kiddin' or what? Wasn't for you, none of us would be celebratin'. Besides, Dip, you're almost family." So Dip stood in for Tony, and Diesel went along to cover him, in case.

The names were read and one by one the kids walked across the outdoor stage, shook hands and got their diplomas.

"Philip Mann," Dean Bell called out. "Colleen McGuire." Bell hesitated. He scanned the audience and Dip felt the man's eyes tracking him down. "James Montello."

Jimmy looked over. Dip raised a clenched fist and pumped it.

When the commencement was over Diesel went to get the car and Dip went outside to hook up with Jimmy. He found him off to one side with Henry Bell. Bell was doing the talking and Jimmy didn't seem thrilled about it.

Bell smiled and waved him on.

They shook hands. Bell said, "We were just talking about you. At least *I* was. I think your boy here is still in shock."

The kid definitely looked weird. "I ain't his boy," Jimmy mumbled. Then he looked out, saw his classmates huddled up with their parents. He shook his head. "But I might as well be."

Bell frowned.

Dip said, "He's all right. All this talk about college, it's got 'im nervous."

"Sure," Bell said. "But don't worry, he'll do fine. You'll see to that, won't you, Dip?"

"Ain't up to me," Dip said, then to Jimmy, "Your friends are waitin' for you. Better get over there."

Jimmy walked away.

"Good luck," Bell called after him. The kid never looked back.

"Well," said Henry Bell, "I've got things to do. Lot of paper work in this business." He held out his hand and once again Dip shook it.

"Listen," Dip said, "I wanna thank you for what you did. For both of us . . . me and Jimmy, I mean."

Bell said, "For a minute I thought you were talking about his father."

Dip shrugged. "He'd say it, too, if he was here."

"Too bad he isn't. Well, this is it, I guess. Keep in touch. Let me know how he makes out."

"Yeah, sure."

Bell turned to leave and Dip suddenly remembered the money. "Hold up a second." Bell came back. "Look," Dip said, "his old man gave me this to give you. I said you wouldn't take it but . . . well, you know how it is."

"You're right," Bell said. "I won't take it. But—just for the record—how much is it?"

"A grand."

Bell smiled. "And they say there's no money in education. Hey, is that Diesel back there?" He shaded his eyes.

"Yeah," Dip said. "You know 'im?"

"We were in grade school and junior high together. Smart kid. A real joker. He was the class clown."

"You're kiddin'."

"No," Bell said. "Maybe he's not so funny anymore." He squeezed Dip's arm. "Take care now. And stay out of trouble, will you?"

"I'll give it a shot," Dip said, and went to find Jimmy.

The crowd was breaking up, parents taking their kids home to private parties with family and friends. All except Jimmy, who stood there with Diesel, both of them gazing around like they had a thousand other places they'd rather be.

Dip joined them. "Why the long face?" he said to Jimmy, and the three of them walked slowly along the tree-lined street toward Dip's car.

"I don't know," Jimmy said.

Diesel said, "He's worried about his future. Not that I blame him. You get too smart it can fuck up your mind."

Jimmy yanked hard at his tie, pulled it off. "It ain't goin' like I thought."

"If it's college," Dip said, "don't worry about it. There's a lotta dummies go to college."

"And they come out the same way," Diesel said.

Jimmy paused, looked at him.

Diesel said, "I ain't shittin' ya. I mean, what the fuck they gonna teach ya? If your name was Albert Einstein, I'd say okay. But your name's Montello. You want the Law of Relativity? Just look in the fuckin' mirror."

Dip said, "You don't have to be Einstein. You got brains, kid. A lot more than me. More than your old man, too. Be a shame to waste 'em."

"Shit," Jimmy said. "You sound just like 'im."

"It's the one thing him and me agree on. But I'll tell you this. Don't go because *he* wants you to."

"Fuck, no," Diesel said. "Do it for the Dipper. Look where it got *him*."

Jimmy ignored Diesel. "What if I do go? What then?"

"That's up to you."

"Yeah," Jimmy said. "Come on, let's go. This sun's givin' me a headache."

"Hold up a second," Dip said. Diesel kept walking but Jimmy stopped. "Let 'im go," Dip said. He reached in his pocket, pulled out a small narrow box, gift wrapped in blue paper. "Here," he said. "A present."

"Ah, man," Jimmy said. He looked flustered. "Whadya do that for?"

"'Cause you're an asshole," Dip said. "Go on, open it."

Jimmy tore off the paper, opened the box. "It's a cross and chain," he said.

"No shit," Dip said. "How'd that happen? I asked for a basketball."

Jimmy examined the cross. "Eighteen karat."

Dip rubbed his cheek. "I figured you had more rings and watches than you got fingers and wrists. How many chains you got?"

"It don't matter," Jimmy said. "Thanks, Dip."

Dip shrugged. "Come on, let's go. You can tell me again what you're gonna do in Las Vegas." He started to walk.

"I ain't goin' to Vegas."

Dip stopped, looked at him. "You better get outta the sun. What the hell's wrong with you? For months that's all you been yappin' about: 'I can't wait, I can't wait.' What the fuck?"

"I changed my mind. I don't wanna go. Not with Eva, not for no weddin'."

"So that's it," Dip said. "Back on that again, eh? Look, get it through your head. They're gettin' married and that's all there is to it."

"Let 'em," Jimmy said. "Long as I don't have to see it happen. He wants a best man, let him use Trick. I got unfinished business."

"What the hell happened to you?" Dip said.

"I grew up," Jimmy said, and jogged ahead to catch Diesel.

The Sea Cliff was more like a garden apartment, a building that used to be classy when it was built; before the stink of chicken fat, pork roast, and cabbage filled the lobby, before the kids went ape shit with spray cans; when the elevators had music and didn't shake.

"Here it is," Dip said to himself, leaning over, checking the slots where the mail goes in. "Four B." He rode up.

It took a few bings and a half dozen hard raps on the door, but she finally answered.

"Whatever you're sellin'," Arlene Consolo said, "I ain't interested."

She was clutching a short cotton robe to her oversized breasts, and didn't seem to care about her lower half, naked under the robe, chunky thighs gaping at him.

But it wasn't her thighs Dip stared at. It was her face, bruised and swollen. He could see a pair of mean-looking shiners even though she was wearing dark glasses to conceal them.

Dip shook his head. "Did *he* do that?"

"Who?" she bristled.

"You know who," he said. "Louie Parisi."

She slammed the door but Dip jammed it with his foot, pushing his way in before she could stop him.

He was in the living room, or what was left of it. The sectional sofa had been cut to ribbons, its stuffing pulled out and scattered. A glass coffee table had been shattered, overturned. Curtains flew at half-mast from their rods; lamps were broken, pictures dangled off the walls.

Arlene said, "Pretty, ain't it?"

"Yeah," Dip said. "Real modern." He looked at her. "Are you okay?"

"Me? I'm great. Don't I look it?" She removed her glasses and squinted at him through slits that used to be big round eyes before Parisi laid his fists to them. "You're the guy from the other night," she said. "Dippolito."

"Yeah."

"You were lookin' for Boppy."

"Yeah."

"Charley Bop," she said with disgust. "That douche bag!"

Dip said, "That's why I'm here."

"Huh!" she said. "Whadaya gonna do, bounce me around? Go 'head. There ain't much left to bounce. How'd you know where I live, anyway?"

"Don't matter," Dip said. "Why'd he do it, smack you around?"

"*Why!*" she said. "Because Louie Parisi is a certified fuckin' low-life lunatic. He thinks *I* know where to find his fuckin' cousin. Two years I gave 'im bed, board, and all the snatch he wanted. Never charged 'im a friggin' nickel. And what do I get for being good-natured? A busted face and a—" She spun around, threw up her hands and bawled like a baby.

Dip took her arm and led her into the kitchen. On the counter was a liter of Absolut. He sat her down, poured her a tall glass and gave it over. She drank it, sobbing between gulps, while Dip doled out tissues from a half-empty box nearby.

It took about ten minutes of soft talk, but she finally quit crying.

"Thanks," she said, wiping the last tear off her cheek.

He allowed her a few more minutes, then he checked her out. She looked different. As if her tears had washed away the self-pity and what was left was an overpowering urge to get even, to hammer Mr. Louis Parisi right into the fucking ground.

"I got a friend in trouble," he said. "Big trouble. He's countin' on me to bail 'im out. That's why I looked you up in the first place, why I'm here now."

"I don't care about that," she said. "Just tell me where Louie fits in."

"It's complicated."

She smirked. "So's my life. This friend of yours, do I know 'im?"

"You told me you didn't. But I think you lied."

"Probably," she said. "It's a habit. The men I see don't like their names mentioned. Who is he?"

"Prize," Dip said. "Lenny?"

"Yeah, sure," she said. "I remember. Yeah, I know Prize. But he wasn't the guy in Rockaway. Me and Prize, we never got it on. It's too bad, though. He's a real fox. And he knows how to treat a girl. Not like Boppy. Or Louie, that scumbag! No. Prize, he'd come down the Polka Dot with Bop, buy me a drink, tell me how great I looked. Didn't matter to him I was a few pounds overweight. Boppy, he'd kid 'im along—'She's a pig,' all that shit. But Prize never cared. He was nice, you know."

"Did you ever see Prize alone with Louie Parisi?"

"No. Always with Bop. But he knows Louie, knows they're cousins."

Dip took a moment to think it over.

"So what is it?" she said. "Do I get Louie's nuts or don't I?"

Dip shrugged. "What I need to do, Arlene, is find Louie before he finds Prize or Boppy."

She said, "One thing I can tell you for sure. Louie wants them guys."

"Maybe," Dip said.

"Hey," she said. "You weren't here when he beat the shit outta me. Believe me, he wants 'em."

"I believe you," Dip said.

"There wasn't much Boppy did that Louie didn't know about. It's kinda weird when you think about it. I mean, here's Louie workin' for Joey Cara. And there's Boppy out in Greenpoint with a crew that hates his guts. I could never figure that out."

Dip said, "That's easy. Nobody gave a shit about Boppy. He was too low on the ladder for anybody to worry about. They figured, what the hell does *he* know? That's why whoever hired 'im wasn't worried. Give 'im a few bucks, let 'im do the job half-assed, then put 'im away for good. Who'd miss 'im? Nobody."

"I see what you mean," Arlene said. "But what's all this to me?"

Dip said, "You wanna get Louie or don'tcha?"

"Sure I do. But I wanna live more. I start pointin' fingers, what happens to me?"

"I know it's risky," Dip said.

"Risky? That what you call it?"

"Look," he said, "I'll hide you some place. No one's gonna know where, not even me if you don't want. I'll give you money, set you up until it's over. Whadaya say?"

Arlene took a long minute to think about it. "And what about after?" She got up and went to the door. "I say forget it. I say take a walk and don't come back."

181

CHAPTER TWELVE

Tony Montello didn't like the setup. He'd have an army of body-guards with him, but he still didn't like being in a public place, at a prearranged time.

Trick had agreed with Tony. But it didn't stop the man from saying what was on his mind: "Forget it's my daughter's weddin' day," he'd said. "Forget I own the hall and I got twenty guys to watch the place. There's gonna be a lotta guys there from outta town. Whada they gonna say when you don't show up?"

"I'll think about it," Tony had said.

As the wedding day drew closer, Tony was still thinking about it. Eva, too, pressed Tony for a "yes" answer. "I haven't been out in so long," she said, "I'm gonna smell like mothballs."

"We'll see," Tony said. But by then he knew he was going. He just wouldn't tell anyone. Let them think what they wanted. Then he'd show up unannounced, breeze in, give his gift, then blow the joint before word hit the street that Tony Montello was a sitting duck. As a show of confidence, he'd bring Jimmy along.

The catering hall was a swanky joint called *Casa de Oro,* out on Long Island, just off the expressway on the eastern border of Nassau County. Trick had taken over the place from its original owner, moving in when the guy had bellied up on the loans Trick had given him. Since then, Trick had been using the place to launder some of the family profits.

They arrived an hour late. Which was the way Tony had planned it. He'd split his forces, taking two men with him and Eva, sending Jimmy in a second car with three other men.

"Don't let those clowns near the car," Tony said as they pulled up under the awning at the front door, and the valets rushed to greet them. They were only kids, eager to serve, eager for tips.

"Welcome to the House of Gold," one of them said as he opened the rear door for Eva and was promptly shoved aside by Tony's men.

"Hmmm," Eva said, getting out, showing as much leg as she possibly could. She was wearing a Romeo Gigli original, black and clingy with a single shoulder strap and a thigh-high slit on the right side for flashing young valets. "House of Gold, eh? They giving away samples?" she said.

The kid wanted to park the car, but Tony wouldn't let him. "We'll do it ourselves," Tony said. "Johnny, you and Rocco stay with the cars. I'll send you out some prime rib and cherries jubilee."

"Yeah. And a pot'a demitasse," Rocco said. "I got a feelin' we're gonna need it."

They walked in and Eva immediately excused herself. "I have to tinkle," she announced. She gave Tony a peck on the cheek, and swished off to find the powder room.

Tony watched her go, then drifted toward a vine-covered archway of pure marble. From there he could see the entire layout.

There were several reception rooms in the hall, where any number of parties often took place simultaneously. Tonight it was different. Only one room was being used: The Venetian. It had marble floors, Ionic columns, chandeliers of Venetian crystal, and tapestries flanked by blue velvet drapes, and it was the largest of all the opulent rooms. It had to be to accommodate a guest list of five hundred, many of whom were wiseguys from affiliated families throughout the country.

Jimmy Montello ambled over and stood next to his father. Tony nudged him. "Some place, eh, kid?"

"It's okay." Jimmy dug his hands in his pockets.

"Okay?" Tony scowled. "Look around. This ain't your everyday catering joint."

"I know," Jimmy said. "Rocco called it 'a state'a-the-art launderette'."

"Yeah, yeah," Tony said. "But that ain't what I mean. Open your eyes, kid! Everything you see here's been imported from Italy. It's top'a the line, from ceiling to floor."

From a bandstand against the far wall, a quintet of overaged musicians began playing some bogus tune in three-quarter time.

Jimmy winced. "That band," he said. "They imported, too?"

"Yeah," Tony said. "Now shut up and listen. And keep your eyes open."

Eva returned, her lips flame red, her perfume competing with the vines overhead. She raised her chin toward the band, and elbowed Jimmy. "Where the hell they get that band from, the feast of San Gennaro?"

"Let's go," Tony said. He crooked his arm for Eva. She took it, and they walked in. Jimmy followed with the three men they'd come in with.

Trick was up on the dais, talking with the bride, and looking proud and elegant in a white dinner jacket and black bow tie. He spotted Tony, grinned, and hurried over.

They were halfway across the floor when Trick intercepted them. "Tony!" Trick barked, and applied a bear hug that took Tony's breath away.

"Easy," Tony said in Trick's ear.

Trick had had a few drinks, but he was sober enough to sense Tony's embarrassment. He let him go. "I knew you'd come," he said, looking around while he adjusted his bow tie.

Tony laughed. "*I'm* gonna miss your daughter's weddin'? You kiddin' me or what?"

Trick's face lit up. "I told 'em," he said. "I said, 'Don't worry

184

about Tony Montello. He'll be here with bells on his feet.'" He faced Eva and Jimmy. "I see you brought the family."

Eva extended her hand. "He'd have some case leaving *me* home," she said.

"Yeah," Trick said, and shook her hand. He reached out for Jimmy, squeezing his chin. "And you," he said. "Look at'cha! More like your old man every day. Come on," he said, gesturing, "there's plenty'a room at Diesel's table."

They followed Trick to a round table near the dais where five men were sitting, unescorted. Each was a ranking man in Tony's organization. They greeted him with lavish hugs, then rearranged themselves, putting Jimmy next to Diesel, and Tony beside Paulie Jr. Eva took the chair between her husband-to-be and her future stepson.

"This is lovely," she squealed.

"Yeah," Diesel said. "Lovely." He eyed Jimmy. "How about it, kid? You think this is lovely or just nouveau?"

Jimmy ignored him.

"You been readin' that magazine again," Paulie said, laughing.

Tony leaned over. "Who's here?"

"Everybody," Paulie said. "Except Vinnie Musto and old man Fresina."

"I didn't expect them," Tony said.

"Rippi's here from Phillie. So's Tomasino from Miami. They been askin' for you all night."

As the evening wore on, the out-of-town dons came over to pay their respects. They showered Eva with compliments before pulling Tony aside for some private talk. While they huddled, Eva took the opportunity to show off her new dress. She forced Paulie onto the dance floor, leaving Diesel and Jimmy by themselves.

Diesel said, "Where's your teacher tonight? Thought for sure he'd tag along."

"Better he didn't," Jimmy said.

"Yeah," said Diesel. "There's enough bums in this place."

"Speak for yourself," Jimmy said.

Diesel raised his eyebrows. "What'sa matter? You ain't fallin' for that guy, are ya?"

"Get real," Jimmy said.

Diesel chuckled. "I *am* real, kid. I just don't like the guy."

Jimmy lit a cigarette with his new gold lighter.

"You shoulda brought a date," Diesel said. "Show her what it's like bein' around the top guys and all."

"You mean like you?" Jimmy said. "Gimme a break."

"God forbid," Diesel snickered. "I was meanin' your old man."

"That's right," Jimmy said. "Who's bigger than him?"

Diesel nodded but didn't say anything.

Jimmy gave him a sour look, started to say something but held it in. The huddle was breaking up and Tony was coming back.

"We're leavin'," Tony said. "Jimmy, go get Eva. I wanna give the boost and get outta here. Deez, get the cars ready."

Ten minutes later, Tony, Eva and Jimmy were leaving The Venetian Room. The band was playing and they had to weave their way across the dance floor. Diesel and Paulie were ahead of them, clearing the way while the three-man escort brought up the rear.

They were approaching the vine-covered archway, just passing the drapes, when Eva said, "I have to tinkle."

"For Chrissake," Tony said. "It's only a half-hour drive. You can't hold it?"

Eva made a face. "It's bad enough your giving me the bum's rush, dragging me off the dance floor and all."

"All right," Tony said. "But make it fast, eh? All this tinklin'. Jesus."

Jimmy said, "I'm gonna wait outside."

"Go with 'im," Tony said to one of his men.

Eva said, "You gonna send somebody with me, too?" She chuckled and leaned over to give Tony a kiss. "Now you wait right here," she said, puckering. Tony leaned forward to meet her lips.

And the gun went off.

. . .

"I hear what you're sayin', Dominick," Tony Montello said. "Trouble is, you ain't hearing *me.*"

It had been a losing battle for Tony ever since he walked in, Dominick Fresina behind his desk, surprised when Tony barged in unannounced, shaking his head as if to say: You know better than this.

Dominick Fresina didn't use a clubhouse like every other boss. If his crew needed a hangout, they could damn well find their own place. Instead, what he had was a big paneled office on Lexington Avenue, high up in the Chrysler Building. Tony paced the carpeted floor, Fresina looking grim, wanting Tony out before some upstanding citizen dropped by to discuss community affairs. The don was big on community affairs.

Fresina got up from behind the desk. "You're overwrought," he said, throwing Tony a ten-dollar word like some hotshot Manhattan mouthpiece.

Tony said, "If you mean I'm pissed off, you're goddamn right."

Fresina motioned toward a long black leather couch on the opposite wall facing the window. "Why not sit a while? Cool down."

"What for?" Tony said. "It's gonna sound better sittin' down? She's in a coma, for Chrissake. The bullet's still in her head. They can't even operate. They don't know, will she walk again, see again. A blind cripple, that's what she's gonna be."

Fresina shuffled over, lost in a dark blue suit a mile big for him. "It happens," he said.

Tony said, "What happens are earthquakes and hurricanes."

Fresina shook his head. "You're not takin' this very well, Tony. You oughta look at the bright side."

"Bright side? Sure, Dominick, I'll look at the bright side. Show me where it is, I'll fuckin' look at it."

Fresina held up a finger to count Tony Montello's blessings. "For one thing," he said, "it ain't you in that hospital."

"Thanks," Tony bristled. "What the hell's it comin' to? Ain't nothin' sacred anymore? You can't take your family to a fuckin' wedding? I've been patient, Dominick, doin' like you say. But that's over. I don't give a shit anymore."

Dominick Fresina said nothing. He rubbed his chin and frowned. Tony stiffened, waited for the threat. What he heard was the telephone, a soft ring from one of those modern instruments that didn't look like a phone. Fresina gave it a glance, not sure if he wanted to take it.

He snatched it finally. "Yeah," he said and listened a moment while Tony watched his face go soft. Fresina was grinning.

"Commissioner," Fresina said. "Glad you called. Hold on a minute." He covered the receiver, gave Tony a look. Tony grunted and Fresina started in. "I know they want it, Commissioner. Twenty million, who wouldn't? That's why they shouldn't get it."

Tony could hear the Commissioner's voice crackling through the wires. He wondered which commissioner he was. Not that it mattered. Fresina had them all in his portfolio.

"I agree, it's a marvelous project," Fresina was saying. "A tremendous lift for the ghetto kids."

Tony drifted around the office, wound up by the window. He looked down at 42nd Street, the cross-town bus like a tinker toy. He pictured Fresina in a swan dive, a forty-story plunge and a big splash at the bottom. Let the Commissioner clean that one up.

"My advice, Commissioner. Don't let those guys bid the job. You need a company can do it right. Now these other guys, them I can vouch for."

Tony shook his head. Ever since it happened he'd been running it through his mind: the way Eva had caught the slug meant for him; the shooter jumping out from behind the drapes, so close to Jimmy the kid could've kissed him on the lips. And Jimmy walking by, not seeing.

Which bothered him more? Tony wondered. Eva going down? Or his son standing there like a fucking statue?

Fresina was wrapping up his good deed for the day. "Okay, Commissioner. We'll talk some more." He hung up.

Tony said, "I didn't know you cared about the ghetto kids, Dominick."

"We do what we can," Fresina said. "Now where were we?" He snapped his fingers. "Oh, yeah. Patience! I'm patient, too. So I'm listenin' to what you say. If it's just talk, okay. Talk is cheap and nobody dies from it, unless they're stupid enough to believe what they're sayin'. You wanna get even, that's up to you. I got nothin' to do with it."

"Since when?" Tony said. "You run the Council. Get me the okay and I'll end this thing."

"How?" Fresina said. "You don't even know who it is. Whackin' that shooter was a dumb move. You get 'im whole, you might'a learned somethin'."

"Yeah," Tony said. "And I'd be dead now. Diesel did what he had'a do. Guy shows a gun, you put 'im away. But I'm sick of sittin' around. You keep tellin' me to back off."

"I'm still tellin' you."

"What if I don't?" Tony said. "I'm already marked."

Fresina moved in close. "Not by me, you ain't," he said, his voice lowered. "And that's the difference."

Tony came home with a blinding headache, partly from rage, partly from weariness. Fresina had offered nothing. Okay, let him play his fucking games. He grabbed the phone. Trick answered.

"Do like I said," he told Trick, and clicked off.

Jimmy drifted in. "What's goin' on?"

Tony said, "I'm tired of lookin' over my shoulder. From now on, it's them gonna look."

"What can *I* do?"

"Nothin'."

"For Chrissake!" Jimmy groused. "I'm gonna be twenty years old. I ain't seen shit."

Tony looked at him. "Ain't seen shit, eh? There's been two attempts on my life and you been there for both'a them. What the fuck you call that?"

Jimmy said, "That ain't what I mean. I'm gonna tell you somethin', Dad. I ain't goin' to no fuckin' college. The way it's goin', by the time I get out there ain't gonna be nothin' left. So make up your mind. Am I in, or out?"

Tony's first reaction was to smack the kid. Put him in his place. But there was something different now. Tony couldn't put his finger on it, but one thing he knew for sure. It had nothing to do with college.

"What is it you want?" Tony said. "You want a gun? Blast a few guys? Any jerk can pull a trigger. You need more than that to run your own crew."

"Like what?" Jimmy said.

"You need somethin' that's gonna set you apart from the rest."

"Well, then, I got no problem, do I?" Jimmy said.

"How do you figure?" Tony said.

Jimmy smiled. "I got somethin' to set me apart, Dad," he said. "I got you."

Jimmy knew why he was there and what he was supposed to do. His father had already told him ten fuckin' times. Trick had gone over it, too. And now Diesel was running it by him one last time: "You put the gun behind his ear. See? Like this."

Jimmy and Diesel were in the back seat of a parked car, one of their guys up front, playing the mark so Diesel could show him exactly where behind the ear to stick the barrel.

"Now, the guy's gonna yap, see? He's gonna cry: 'I got kids, a pregnant wife, a sick canary, and a hundred-year-old fuckin' grandmother.' It don't mean shit. If you was up front and he was in the back, you'd be sayin' the same thing. You just lean over, say somethin' cute, like, 'Adios, Dickface.' And pop! One shot'll do it. And I'll add one more for good measure."

Diesel sat back and folded his arms, staring out at the blackness of Dead Horse Bay, Floyd Bennett Field off to the right.

"Who's the guy?" Jimmy said.

"Who knows? He's with DeMarco. That's all that counts. Trick worked it out. Paulie's gonna snatch the guy and turn 'im over to us." He slapped Jimmy on the shoulder. "Pretty good, eh?"

Jimmy said, "I still can't believe it."

"Why?" Diesel said. "It had'a happen. What better time than now, wid things heatin' up. You're the old man's social security."

"Guess so," Jimmy said.

"Fuckin' A," Diesel said. "Tell you what. Do this right and I got another job for ya."

"Whatever it takes," Jimmy said.

"My man," Diesel piped. "Hey, I bet you never learned any'a this from Jackie Dip, eh?"

"That's history," Jimmy said.

Diesel said, "Yeah. And I'm current events. You ready?"

"I'm ready."

Diesel chuckled. "Yeah, you're ready. Whadaya gonna hit him with, your fuckin' finger?" He reached under the seat and handed Jimmy a pistol with a very long barrel. Jimmy, wearing rubber gloves, took the gun and tucked it inside his belt.

Diesel scratched his chin. He wrinkled his brow like he was searching hard for more information. "Oh, yeah," he said. "After you hit 'im, don't breath in. The guy's gonna shit himself and you'll have that stink in your nose all fuckin' night."

Jimmy tried to swallow. But there was nothing in his mouth.

CHAPTER THIRTEEN

Dip had been casing Louis Parisi's Carwash for the past half hour, watching from across the street, checking out the workers. So far, all he'd seen were black guys: two at the entrance to vacuum, four at the exit to wipe and buff. If Ralphie Scimone *was* over there, he was inside Louie's office.

There was only one car left on the line. Dip watched them hook a chain to its undercarriage and pull it through. He drove in behind it, and waited.

One of the guys, a short Hispanic with a pencil mustache, came over. Dip lowered his window.

"Wha'ju want, man? Hot wax? Cold? Wha'ju want?"

"Just wash it," Dip said.

The guy reached for the door handle. Dip shook his head. The guy made a face. "Ju'gotta get out, man."

Dip sat there. "Tell Ralphie I got somethin' for 'im."

The guy squinted, swiveled his upraised chin in four different directions. "He ain't here, man."

"Tell 'im I got a package from Hack."

Again the guy looked around. This time he smiled. "Wait here," he said. "I tell him."

A moment later he was back. "Pull up," he said.

"Where's Ralphie Scimone?"

"Ju'want the wash? Pull up!"

Dip eased the car toward the conveyor. They hooked him up. The car lurched forward, plunging him into a wet, noisy darkness. It was eerie but nice; like he imagined John Glenn must have felt when he dropped out of orbit into the stormy sea.

He sat there hypnotized by the water cascading down the windshield, pelting the roof and hood. He could have stayed there forever. Then it stopped: the noise, the water, the dreamy feeling.

He heard a tap on the passenger window. A black dude in a bright yellow slicker was grinning at him. Big head, big white teeth, and a short stubbly beard dripping with water. Dip beckoned him in.

He slid onto the seat. "I'm Ralphie," he said in a bass voice.

Dip said, "Scimone?"

"What of it?"

"You're black."

"So's Roy Campanella. Look, man, I ain't got all day. Whatchya got and how much is it?"

Dip slid a hand toward his ankle. "I got this," he said, and pulled his gun. "And there's no charge."

Ralphie's eyes bulged. He threw his head back and groaned. "Oh, man! I knew I shoulda called in sick."

"Where's Parisi?" Dip said.

"He's outta town," Ralphie answered. He sounded depressed.

"I understand Louie talks a lot," Dip said, "doesn't worry who hears 'im."

Ralphie's eyes were fixed on the gun. "Yeah," he said. "Louie talks. You gonna shoot me? How you gonna do that and get out? You're hooked up underneath."

"Tell ya what," Dip said. "We'll try it and see how it works."

Ralphie nodded slowly, the slicker crinkling at the back of his broad neck. "I can't hold us here too long," he said.

Dip moved the gun toward Ralphie's chest. "This ain't gonna

take long," he said. "Louie's tight with Sonny DeMarco. That's right, ain't it?"

"He knows 'im."

"Louie's a shithead. So why the romance?"

"They like the same kinda food," Ralphie said.

"We could drive on outta here," Dip said. "Go some place else where it's quiet. You get my meaning?"

"I know it sounds nuts," Ralphie said. "But Louie's got a thing for Chinese. Sonny's hooked on Chinese. Everybody knows that."

"You're tellin' me they eat together? That's the connection?"

Ralphie shook his head. "They're workin' on somethin', man. Louie pulls it off, he gets hisself made."

"Workin' on what?"

"Yeah, sure," Ralphie said. "Like I'm gonna eat a boloney san'wich while Louie spells it out. Why'ntcha ask Louie?"

A car horn blared. Ralphie turned around, waved the guy off and turned back to Dip. "What's it gonna be, man?"

"Let's move," Dip said.

Ralphie opened the door, stuck his head out. "Okay, Jose," he shouted. "Start it up!"

Once again Dip's car was submerged in water, inching forward. He watched Ralphie all the way through it, Ralphie watching back until they reached the outside and Dip put the gun away.

Dip said, "When you see Louie, tell 'im his cousin Boppy sends his regards."

Ralphie said, "That mean you comin' back?"

"I'll be around."

"Listen, man," Ralphie Scimone said. "Next time you come, you think you can bring me some shit?"

So far as Dip was concerned, Cape May was the ass end of the world.

He'd followed his map the whole way and he'd still gotten lost, making several wrong turns before he finally found the right road. Good thing, too. It was almost nightfall and in the dark he would have missed it—Lani's camper, sitting fifteen feet from the water-line on the inland side of the Cape.

He parked at the end of the road and got out. No sign of Prize. Dip wondered if Lani was with him, how they were making it. The nearest town was miles away and he didn't see Lani's yellow Toyota.

He looked out at the water, teeny wavelets lapping the shore, pushing empty shells in and out. Horseshoe crabs scuttled along the narrow beach close to the camper.

Why here? Dip thought, walking slowly toward the camper. There was no back way out. Was Prize trying to tell him something? Like he was guilty and didn't give a shit anymore what happened to him? Maybe so. Though Dip still didn't know what Prize had actually done to make him feel that way.

"Yo!" Dip called. "Yo, Prize!"

Nothing. Only his own echo.

Moving cautiously, he approached the camper door. He tried it. Locked. Out back, he thought, Prize walking the shoreline, gazing out at the bay. He headed for the water.

It was getting darker. The moon had just broken some clouds and was cutting a milky path of light for Dip to follow. The beach felt gooey under his feet, but he kept going.

His feet were sinking deeper in the muck. He kept going, indifferent to the water seeping into his shoes. Then he stopped. Something on the shoreline, part of it wedged in the silt, part of it floating in the shallows like thick seaweed. But what he had thought was seaweed, were arms and legs, bloated and buoyant, rocking with the tide.

The man was wearing the shredded remnants of blue jeans, and nothing else. His hair was long, but only the lower half of the skull was visible. The back of the head at the top was missing.

Dip tried to move, but his feet were stuck in the mud. He forced himself out, losing both shoes, not caring, wanting only to see the face. He turned the corpse over, and wished he hadn't. Dip heard himself moan.

Whoever killed Prize had shot out both of his eyes.

CHAPTER FOURTEEN

"It's so hard to believe," Robin said. "He had so many friends and no one came but us."

They were standing at the side of Lenny's grave, Robin, Dip, and the Fish Lady, Angie Parisi. Angie had shown up as they were leaving the funeral home. She'd given Dip a cortege sign, and the three of them formed a two-car procession to Calvary Cemetery. Now, the priest and the undertaker were heading back to Brooklyn, and Dip was lighting a cigarette for Angie.

"If Prize had that many friends," Angie said, exhaling smoke, "he wouldn't be where he is."

"That's not fair," Robin said. She was thinking of Dip, the one friend Lenny could always count on. Dip, blaming himself for what had happened.

Angie gazed at Dip with a sardonic grin. "Fair? Is she kiddin'?" Then to Robin: "The only one who really cared about Prize is your boyfriend here."

"Then why did you come?" Robin said.

Angie shrugged. "What can I say? I'm just a sentimental old broad."

Dip said, "He ain't gonna like bein' buried with his mother. He hated his mother."

"What better place?" Angie said, looking around at the other gravestones. It was a warm day and the sun was an orange smudge in a hazy blue sky, the Brooklyn-Queens Expressway off in the distance, heavy with mid-morning traffic. "Now that he's here, they'll have forever to work out their differences."

Dip shook his head.

"This going to funerals can get to be habit formin'," Angie said. Dip blinked at her. "Case you ain't heard," she said, "we're plantin' Louie Parisi tomorrow morning."

Robin said, "Who's Louie?"

"My nephew. Another winner."

"When?" Dip said, his forehead wrinkling over.

"When did it happen? Or when did they find 'im?"

"You know what I mean."

"Yeah. At first I thought you and him had had your little chat. But I still have some friends in Greenpoint. If it was you, they'd'a told me."

"I don't think I like this," Robin said. "In fact, I know I don't."

"I don't blame you." Angie smiled sympathetically. She looked up at the sky. "I wonder where Charley is right now?" she said. She looked at Dip.

"I'm still gonna find out," Dip said.

"My God," Robin said. "Haven't you had enough? You want to end up like Prize?"

Dip didn't answer.

Angie said, "It's none'a my business, but if I was you, Dip, I'd listen to her. She's wrong about Prize, but she's right about you. You see, it don't matter anymore." She bowed her head toward Lenny's grave. "Not for him it don't. And my Charley neither. So forget about it."

"Sure," Dip said. "I'll close my eyes and forget the whole thing."

"I know how you feel," Angie said. "Look, I don't know what they did, or who they pissed off. But the chances are they got what

197

they asked for. So don't yap. And don't hate anybody, either. Cut your losses. Take what you got left and go on home."

"That's just what he's going to do," Robin said. She reached out for Dip's hand. Dip took it, held it a moment, then let it go when they heard a car approaching.

It was a white sports car, brand-new, with oversized racing tires, slate black windows, and a low-slung body that hugged the ground like a metal mantis. It rolled down from a nearby knoll, and stopped in the shadow of the BQE. The engine purred for a moment, roared once, then went silent. No one got out.

Dip squinted at the car. "Wait here," he said.

He loped down the hill expecting to see one of Lenny's girlfriends behind the wheel: her hair in curlers and a kerchief, shades for weepy eyes, lips quivering while she tried to tell him what a terrific guy Lenny had been, how he'd loved life, and that he was the greatest lay she'd ever had. The window slid down.

"Figured I'd find you here," Jimmy Montello said. He poked his head out the window, followed by his hand, which Dip considered for a second, then shook.

"Yeah," Dip said. He lifted his face toward Lenny's grave, Robin and Angie Parisi looking down at him. "Me, and a cast of thousands. Prize had a million friends. Where the hell are they?"

"I know," Jimmy said. "But whadya expect? The word's all over Brooklyn."

"What word?" Dip said. "Whadaya talkin' about?"

"Rat," Jimmy said. "They're callin' him a rat."

Dip didn't say anything. He glared at Jimmy for a second, and turned away.

"Hey," Jimmy called out, "*I* ain't the one sayin' it. Besides, I'm here, ain't I? Better late than never."

Dip looked at him. The kid showed a hurt expression. "You're right," Dip said. "Thanks."

"No big deal." Jimmy held up his hand as if warding off the gratitude. "I know how you felt about the guy—your best friend and all. Least I could do was check you out, see how you're takin' it."

"I'm okay."

"Yeah. Sure."

There was an awkward silence. Dip figured Jimmy had more to say. He rubbed his hand across the roof of the car. "Nice set'a wheels."

Jimmy nodded. "We didn't go to Vegas." He tapped the steering wheel with the inside edge of a new ruby ring he was wearing on his middle finger. "So I got this instead."

"I heard what happened," Dip said. "How's Eva doin'?"

Jimmy shrugged. "I don't ask."

"That's beautiful," Dip said.

"Why should I care? I hated the bitch."

Dip shook his head. He said, "You're some piece'a work, you know that?" Jimmy said nothing, merely grinned at him. "You look different," Dip said. "Whad you, cut your hair?"

"Yeah. Whadaya think? I look older, or what?"

"At least twenty-one." Dip looked up, saw Robin beckoning impatiently. "Listen, we're gettin' ready to leave. Why don'tcha come with us? Have a drink or somethin'."

Jimmy flushed. "Jeez, Dip, I'd like to. But I ain't got the time. You know how it is."

"Yeah," Dip said. "I know."

"The main thing is you're okay," Jimmy said. "I was worried you might flip out, do somethin' stupid."

"Like what?"

"I don't know. I know what *I'd* do."

"I'll bet you do," Dip said. There was another awkward pause. "So tell me, what's happenin' with college?"

"Nothin'. I ain't goin'. I guess Tony realized I wasn't cut out for it."

"Are you shittin' me?" Dip said. "After all we went through? I don't believe it."

Jimmy half-smiled. "You ain't been around lately, Dip. There's been a lotta changes you wouldn't believe."

Dip smirked. "I've been livin' in Brooklyn my whole life. There

199

might be a different face here and there, but lemme tell you, nothing ever changes."

"You'd be surprised," Jimmy said, a little too coy to suit Dip.

"What's that supposed to mean?"

"I'm workin' for 'im now, Dip. That's right. My old man finally caved in."

Dip shook his head. "That's great. Whadaya do for 'im?"

"Odds and ends."

"You mean you run errands. That's why you're here, ain't it? Your father sent you: 'Tell Dip to bury his friend and get back on the job'? Well, go on home. Tell 'im I got the message."

"Nobody sent me," Jimmy snapped. "I'm here on my own."

"I can see that. What I don't see is why."

Jimmy laced his fingers around the wheel. "I don't know either. Maybe I thought we were friends."

"That's good," Dip said. "I like that."

"Come on, man."

Dip said, "Remember that day you met Prize? He told me I was nuts. Told me I was kiddin' myself about you, that one day you'd run the show and I'd get a kick in the ass for my trouble. Friends. How the fuck can we ever be friends? Even *you* said it. Remember? You said, 'You and me are miles apart.'"

"I remember." Jimmy nodded. "But it don't have to be that way."

"No. But it is."

"Now, maybe. In a couple 'a years . . . who knows? I'll be the one givin' out jobs."

"Is that what your father says?"

"Stop bein' a jerk. I'm tryin' to help you out."

"Forget it. I'm in for the small change and that's how it is."

"That's a crock!" Jimmy said. "All you gotta do is get closer to the top."

"Thanks, but I'm close enough. I get any higher, my nose'll bleed."

Jimmy's face went dark, he seemed to age ten years, right there in the sunlight, in his new Corvette, a gift for not going to Vegas.

"You shouldn't joke about it," Jimmy said, soft, serious. "I mean, look what happened to your buddy."

"I saw. I don't need you to remind me."

"Then smarten up, for fucksake. This thing with Prize— whadaya gonna do about it?"

"Nothin'," Dip said. "Not a fuckin' thing. I tried to help the guy. It didn't work out. That's how it goes sometimes."

Jimmy shook his head. "I'm supposed to believe that?"

"I don't give a shit what you believe!" Dip was hot, ready to yank Jimmy Montello out from the leather seat.

But Jimmy stayed cool. "Chill out, man. All I'm sayin' is nobody's safe."

"Sounds like a warning."

Jimmy shrugged, pursed his lips. They stared at each other for several seconds. Their eyes were still locked when Jimmy hit the ignition. The Corvette roared to life. Dip backed away.

"Hey," Jimmy said. He had to shout over the rumbling engine. "That's what friends are for. To give advice. Right, Dipster?"

Dip started to answer, but the kid smiled and took off, skidding on the gravel, stones flying in his wake.

CHAPTER
FIFTEEN

Before Sonny became boss of the late Joey Cara's organization, nobody had ever cared where he was spending his nights. He could slip away any time he wanted, eat in his favorite restaurants, and gamble in any one of a dozen private clubs. He could pick whichever lady he wanted, take her wherever he pleased, and satisfy every fucking fantasy he'd ever dreamed of.

He'd been thinking about this lately, and wondering if it was worth all the trouble he'd gone through.

Sure, there were up sides, things he really liked about running the show. Like the block party his neighbors had thrown for him when they learned it was him taking over. He had liked that. And the way the wiseguys were treating him: two hundred guys kissing his ass, and a hundred more on their knees, waiting their turn. He liked that, too.

What he didn't like was that he was never alone anymore. No matter where he went there were people breathing down his neck. He couldn't even get laid, for Chrissake, without a dozen *gabrones* hanging around outside, sticking their ugly faces in the door, checking up on him: "How you doin', Sonny?" "You okay, Sonny?"

It didn't matter that the ugly faces were there to protect him. He'd rather they disappeared for a while. Which was why, like today, Sonny would lie to his own men just to get away for a few hours. Yeah, it was risky. And if his boys ever found out, they'd have a shit fit. But Sonny had it all figured out. If his guys couldn't find him, neither could his enemies. Besides, he'd recently discovered that the added risk was turning him on.

Like now. He knew Tony Montello was hitting back: two of the men had already been popped, and two more were reported missing. Yet here he was, all by himself at the Golden Dragon, scoffing dim sum in broad daylight, and nursing a hardon that wouldn't go down if Montello himself came through the front door toting a fucking Uzi.

Sure it was scary. But it felt good, too. Like being a kid again, so worked up that he couldn't stand it another minute. He had to find a girl and get his rocks off. Not just any girl, but the hottest one in Chinatown.

Sonny had had a special thing for Orientals ever since he'd returned from Korea, so many years ago he'd lost count. But he hadn't forgotten the R&R's, those long, sweet nights in Seoul where he'd learned some special tricks, the kind he could find only here in the Lower East Side, between Canal Street and Park Row.

The boys in Brooklyn would have thought he was some kind of sicko if they ever caught wind of what he was into. They hated the Chinese to begin with, the way the slanty-eyed little fuckers were moving into Little Italy had them all talking to themselves. But not Sonny. He didn't mind at all. He was the only wiseguy in New York City who wasn't worried about the "Chink invasion." Let them have downtown, he thought. At least he had a place to go when he needed refuge. And when he wanted his ass whipped by some cute little Suzie Wong.

Pushing aside the piled up little dishes that served as a running tally, he dropped a fifty on the table and sauntered out.

The sidewalks were crowded and noisy, the air thick with a

thousand heady smells from a hundred different restaurants and produce stands. He had a good idea where he was going and he headed there without so much as a glance over his shoulder, flowing through the crush of people who were making their way among the outdoor markets. Fresh vegetables were piled high in wooden crates stacked from doorway to curb. Fast against the building squatted a man with a box of live turtles, hawking them to the locals for their evening soup pots.

Delivery trucks were double-parked on the narrow side streets, their drivers cursing the store owners, the owners cursing back in Chinese, Korean, or Vietnamese. It all sounded the same to Sonny.

On Bayard Street Sonny noticed a huge fish tank behind a plate glass window. Some weird-looking fish were swimming around, and he moseyed over for a closer look. As he was gazing at the fish, his eyes involuntarily switched focus and he found himself looking *at* the glass instead of through it. Seeing his own image, he stepped back to admire it, and the plain black satin warm-up jacket and cotton pullover shirt he was wearing today.

Not bad, he thought, smiling at himself, doing a half-turn as if he were buying a new jacket, looking it over. In Brooklyn he always wore suits and ties. Here it was casual clothes— inconspicuous.

He took a deep breath and checked himself out. He'd always had the lean, solid build of an athlete. Even now at fifty-seven his chest was still firm. He still had a flat gut and his waistline measured thirty-three inches, no different than twenty years ago. His black hair was as thick as ever, and the grey flecks he saw were not signs of age, but intelligence. His friends had all told him so. He agreed.

He could have admired himself a while longer, but a reflection in the window caught his eye. A wino was standing behind him, staring him down.

Sonny stiffened for a moment, then relaxed, letting his right hand drop casually toward the .32-caliber snubnose inside his jacket. Gripping the gun, he sidestepped before the window, wagging his head as if admiring the fish. Then he whirled.

What the fuck? Where'd he go? Was he seeing things, or what?

No, the guy had been there. He was sure of it. A tall, down-and-out looking white guy with a hard look on his face, sizing him up like he wasn't too impressed with what he was seeing. It pissed Sonny off. Nobody threw him hard looks and got away with it.

He stood there, glaring at each passer-by as though they had helped the guy disappear. He was angry, but he wasn't worried. The guy was no button or Sonny would be on the ground right now, a swarm of soup turtles crawling all over his dead ass. Forget it, he told himself. It's nothing, some hophead, probably.

He put the thought out of his mind and hurried along Bayard to a cobblestone alleyway. Stopping at the corner, Sonny waited, looked in every direction until he was sure he hadn't been followed, then scooted over the cobblestones toward a small souvenir shop. He peered through the front window and went in.

The shop was dim and dreary, a long, narrow room with rows of display cases under a low-hung ceiling. He scanned the place until his eyes got accustomed to the darkness. Then he headed for the back.

The owner, a skinny Asian named Loy, was in his usual place, deep inside the room, on a high stool behind one of the glass counters. Wedged in the corner of Loy's mouth was an unfiltered cigarette with a long ash that drooped. A plume of blue smoke spiraled up his cheek into his squinting eye. He smiled when he saw Sonny DeMarco, and the ash fell.

"Ah, Mr. Dee," Loy said. "You back see Loy. Always good see."

"Yeah," Sonny said. He cast his eyes on the trinkets Loy had on display. Mostly ivory and cut glass figurines. Miniature dragons and pagodas. Fans, kites, artificial flowers, and Buddhas of all different weights and sizes.

Raising his eyebrows, Sonny said, "Tell me, Loy. You ever sell any'a this shit?"

"Sometimes sell," Loy said. He smiled broadly, the cigarette wobbling in his mouth. "If sell, fine. No sell . . ." He shrugged.

Sonny chuckled. He knew Loy wasn't here to hawk tourists. "That's right, Loy," he said. "Who cares about this shit when you got a piece'a the house." In fact, Loy had a piece of two houses: the gambling parlor in the basement, and the house of pleasure upstairs. Smart Chinaman, this Loy, Sonny thought.

"What you rike today?" Loy asked. He made a fist and shook it alongside his ear. "Dice? You rike'a dice?"

"I *rike'a* pussy," Sonny said. "The dice'll come later."

Loy closed his eyes and put his head back like he was thinking it over. It was a game Loy liked to play: did he have the right girl for Sonny? He knew damn well he did.

"C'mon, Loy, you know what I like."

"Ah, yes. Know exact'ary." He opened his eyes and grinned. "But today . . . today special. Two gi'ls, one plice. Big noise, no matte'."

"A double-header, eh?" Sonny winked at him. "Loy, you're a giant in the industry. Same room?"

Loy nodded. "You find," he said, and turned his bony face toward a silk screen that concealed a door on the opposite wall. He reached under the counter. The door clicked open.

Sonny threw him a C-note. Loy mumbled something in Chinese, but Sonny was already behind the screen, slipping quietly through the open door into a poorly lit stairwell.

He closed the door and stood on the landing for a moment. From below, muffled voices rose from the basement casino like the hum of machines in a boiler room. A sudden shout broke the drone. Men cheered, others cursed. Someone had scored big, and for a second or two Sonny considered going downstairs to check out the action. He'd been feeling lucky all day, and the two-fer Loy had offered was a good sign. But the thought didn't last. What he really wanted was upstairs, not down.

His room was two flights up, first door on the right. He'd been there many times. It was a windowless cube with special features, like suspended leather harnesses, retractable mirrors, a rotating waterbed, with shimmering silk sheets, and pink padded walls that made the whole thing soundproof. Sonny liked that it was soundproof. He could step inside, close the door, and shut himself off from the outside world. Very important for what he had in mind.

The door was unlocked and the girls were waiting for him.

They were just sitting there: two sloe-eyed beauties with jet black hair and smooth, ivory skin that looked pink in the soft lighting. They were stark naked and they both uncrossed their legs and smiled at him as he approached.

The smaller one had a huge tattoo on her shoulder. She stood up and turned slowly, giving Sonny a good look at the entire package. Her compact little body had orange-sized breasts, narrow hips, a slim waist, and a tight, round ass coated with baby oil.

"My name is Kim," she said. Her voice was soft and had no trace of an accent. She motioned toward her playmate. "My sister Ming."

Sonny chuckled. "Ming the Merciless. That's good."

Ming stood up and fondled her sister's breast. "Don't let the dragon scare you," she said.

She meant Kim's tattoo. Which Sonny had just noticed was a blue, fire-breathing dragon whose gaping mouth was pointing downward, blowing red flames over the breast Ming was holding out for him.

He reached for it, but Kim pulled away.

"Uh-uh," she said, wagging her finger at him. "That's hot stuff. Mustn't touch or you'll get singed."

"I'll chance it," he said and threw them both on the bed with a howl.

Sonny couldn't believe his luck. He would have settled for either one. But this—what a parlay!

They worked him over for a good twenty minutes before Ming got out of bed. Sonny watched, admiring the way her ass twitched as she padded across the room to a small tin closet.

"I think it's time for his lesson," she said over her shoulder.

Sonny smiled. Directly over the bed, suspended from the ceiling, was a nylon strap with a metal loop attached to it. Ming returned with satin cords and an oversized Ping-Pong paddle. "You've been a bad boy!" she scolded. "You know what happens to bad boys?"

Sonny was so worked up he couldn't even talk. He shook no.

"We tie them up," Kim said.

"And play bed tennis with his tushie," Ming added, slapping her own with the paddle.

Sonny didn't wait to be told. He held out his hands and Kim quickly bound his wrists while Ming did the same to his ankles.

"Now the blindfold," Ming said.

"Hey!" Sonny said playfully. "How'm I gonna see?"

"You're not!" Ming said, gleeful and menacing.

The bed rocked beneath him as they pulled him up onto his knees.

"Raise your arms." They were getting rougher, the way he liked.

Obediently, he lifted his arms high over his head. "Make it tight," he said as they lashed him to the metal ring. They had secured him to the strap which was attached to a small winch alongside the bed. A few easy turns and up he'd go, until he was hanging in mid-air like a smoked salami—vulnerable, exposed to whatever they devised.

They hauled him up. It hurt his arms, but he didn't mind. He could feel himself getting hard and that was the whole idea.

"Hey!" Sonny said, squirming to make it look good. "Whadaya think you're doin'? Cut me loose!"

"Give him the paddle, Kim," Ming said.

"No! Not the paddle!" God, how he loved this. He wished he could see himself, hanging there with his ass out and his dick hard as a rock.

"Now you be good," Ming said. She whacked him hard on the ass. "We're going to dress up. Stay quiet until we come back."

"Wait! Don't leave me like this."

They giggled. "Quiet," one of them said. She was moving away. The door opened and closed.

He was alone, but he didn't care. They wouldn't be gone more than a few minutes. How long could it take to slip on fish net stockings, spiked patent leather heels, and matching garter belts? Last time he had been spreadeagled on the bed, his wrists and ankles tied down, and the girl had suspended herself in the harness just above him and spun, with him as her axis. There was nothing like that in Brooklyn.

What would the boys from Bensonhurst say if they could see him now? Sonny wondered. It was a comical notion that made him laugh. The more he laughed the more he had to laugh. He couldn't stop himself. Sonny DeMarco, tied up by a couple of Chinese broads who couldn't weigh more than a hundred pounds apiece.

He was still laughing when he heard the door creak. He cocked his head toward the sound. "That you girls?"

The door closed gently.

"Kim? Ming?"

Nothing.

"Stop playin' around!" Sonny demanded. They would know by his tone that he was serious. They'd apologize and get on with the game. But all he heard was a scratching sound that seemed to be moving away from him, as if someone was dragging a wooden chair across the floor.

He twisted and turned, tugged violently at the cords. No effect. This wasn't entirely titillating anymore.

Footsteps. The little shits were doing a number on him. Somebody shifted. One person or two? Man, woman? He couldn't tell. But inside his head an alarm sounded.

"Who are you?" Sonny said. "Whadaya want?" His throat had dried up and his voice cracked when he hollered, "Who the fuck *are* you?"

Whoever it was, was standing right in front of him on the chair. Sonny tried to pick up a scent—perfume, aftershave—but the incense was too strong and he was too scared now, close to panic. It was the blindfold. Not being able to see had him crazy with fear.

His chest had already tightened and now his lungs were closing down. He opened his mouth, took a deep breath, and felt the muzzle of a gun slide past his lips.

"Say when it hurts."

"I just want you to know, I ain't had a decent night's sleep since my daughter's weddin'."

"Neither has Eva," Tony Montello said flatly.

Trick nodded, and the two of them went back to sipping their coffee.

They were in Huntington, Long Island, on a screened porch facing a well-groomed backyard and a modest inground swimming pool glistening in the afternoon sunlight. It was all part of the house Trick's new son-in-law had just bought for his bride. They had gone away for the weekend and Trick had invited Tony out for "an afternoon in the country."

It was supposed to be quiet, and it was. Nothing but crickets and an occasional squawk from a soaring blue jay. He couldn't tell how Trick was doing, but so much quiet was getting on Tony's nerves.

"Your son-in-law," Tony said, waving his arm nonchalantly around the porch. "What's he do?"

"He sells firewood and packaged ice," Trick said. "Not a bad little business. You know, wood in the winter, ice in the summer?"

Tony pursed his lips. Amazing how many ways there were to make a legitimate living.

Trick said, "I'm real glad you came out here today. The way it's been lately. . . ." He shrugged. "We haven't been alone much. I mean, I don't know who you're talkin' to, but it ain't me."

"You know how it is," Tony said.

Tricari frowned. He had a meaty face with loose skin. When he wrinkled it up, like he was doing now, he reminded Tony of a bulldog with a bad toothache.

"Sure. I do," Trick said. "We got a rat and you think maybe it's me. I understand. But understandin' don't make it any easier."

"That shooter was waitin' for me behind the curtain, Trick. I been thinkin' . . . about who might've put 'im there."

Trick's face went red. "What the fuck!"

Tony raised his hands. "Take it easy. I know how it sounds, and I don't blame you for gettin' pissed off. But it wasn't you. I know you too long. First of all, you wouldn't pull a stunt like that at your own daughter's weddin'. Secondly, you didn't even know for sure that I'd be there."

Trick sulked. "Nobody did."

"Yeah. That's what I keep tellin' myself."

"Well, somebody tried to nail you and it wasn't Sonny De-Marco. He could never've planted a button that close without one of our guys spottin' 'im."

"He could," Tony said, "if one of our guys helped 'im."

"And you thought. . . ." Trick lowered his head.

"What choice did I have? Look, forget about it, eh? I know where you stand." He waited for Trick to look at him again. "So? Whadaya think? Any ideas?"

"Yeah," Trick said. "But you ain't gonna like it. I think it's that dumb fuck you hired to help your son with school."

"Dippolito? C'mon, you can do better than that. What's he got to gain?"

"I ain't sayin' he's the brains," Trick said. "But he's right there in your house, for Chrissake. You know what that's worth to a guy like Sonny?"

"Of course I do," Tony said. "That's why I used 'im in the first place. Dip's the kinda guy I don't have to worry about. He'll break a few arms and legs for ya. But don't expect 'im to whack nobody. He ain't the type. Besides that, he's lookin' to quit. Told me himself."

"Told me, too," Trick said. "But I don't believe it. I mean, who the fuck quits? I never seen anybody quit. You? We love this shit, every one of us."

"Not him," Tony said.

"Maybe so. But I still don't trust 'im."

Trick's face went dark. Tony let him stew. He'd told him too much as it was.

Chimes went off inside the house—a sudden burst of *Winchester Cathedral* that jarred Tony and got Trick off his chair in a big rush.

"Who the hell is that?" Trick said as he hurried inside the house.

Tony stayed where he was. He wasn't concerned. He had two of his men in the backyard and he called them over. They were standing beside him when Trick came back with Paulie Jr. in tow.

"You ain't gonna believe this," Trick said. "Go on, Paulie, tell 'im."

"It's Sonny," Paulie said. His face was flushed and he was breathing hard. "They found him bare-ass naked in some alley in Chinatown. Somebody strangled the sonofabitch."

"Strangled? You sure you heard right?"

"Absolutely," Paulie said. He paused to fill his lungs with a mixture of country air and cigarette smoke. "A friend of ours called direct from the morgue."

"That's a fucked-up way to kill a guy," Tony said.

Trick said, "Unless they used a garrote on 'im."

"The cops don't think so," Paulie said. "More like a rope. He's still in the morgue, but they're sayin' he coulda been strung up by his neck."

"You mean somebody hung the cocksucker?"

"Looks like it," Paulie said. "There's a Chinese whorehouse nearby. Sonny went there a lot, had the hots for slopes. They think he was offed there and then dumped in the alley outside."

"I love it," Trick said.

"So do I." Tony allowed himself a slight grin. Listening to Paulie had been like his doctor telling him he didn't have a brain tumor after all, just a common headache. But it wasn't all good news. He still had the Council to deal with. "Fresina ain't gonna like this," he said.

"That's tough," Trick said and Paulie's head bobbed in agreement.

212

Tony ordered his bodyguards off the porch.

As soon as they walked out, Trick said, "Sonny DeMarco got what he deserved. Everybody on the Council will know that. Talk to 'em, Tony. Make 'em understand. A guy hits you, you gotta hit 'im back."

"Sure, Trick. Except Sonny didn't hit us first. He might've started the whole thing by whackin' Joey Cara. But we took the rap because I couldn't prove it. It's the same thing now. We gotta find who did it. The way I figure, we got less than twenty-four hours to turn 'im over."

CHAPTER SIXTEEN

"Know what I think?" Diesel said. "I think this is fuckin' ridiculous."

"I think so, too," said Paulie Jr. "I mean whada we doin' out here in the middle'a the fuckin' woods?"

"I already told you," said Trick. "The man said we should meet 'im here. Besides, we ain't in the fuckin' woods. My son-in-law owns this place."

"Owns what? All I see is trees and piles'a wood."

"It's a woodcuttin' yard," Trick said. "They chop the trees into small logs and cut 'em up for firewood."

"And what's that?" Diesel said, pointing to a white boxlike structure in the farthest corner of the yard.

"What's it look like?"

Diesel cocked his head and squinted in the fading daylight. "Like a Mr. Softee truck without wheels."

"Close. It's a freezer."

"What's he do, freeze the wood so it burns longer?"

Paulie laughed, but Diesel remained straight-faced, like he wasn't kidding about frozen wood.

He said, "I don't like this, Trick. What's so special we gotta come all the way out here? We coulda seen Montello in Brooklyn."

"What's the difference?" Trick tugged at his tie. "If he told us Alaska, we'd be there."

"Alaska's a whole lot better than this," Paulie said. He brought a meaty hand up and whacked himself on the back of the neck. "At least there ain't no fuckin' mosquitoes in Alaska."

Trick said, "What's the matter with you guys? All you been doin' lately is bitch and moan."

"It's what happened to Sonny," Paulie said. "Somebody does you a favor, you oughta know who he is so you can thank 'im."

"What favor?" Diesel said. "You ask me, we were better off when Sonny was alive. Don Fresina wants our heads 'cause of this."

"The only guy Fresina wants," Trick said, "is the one who started all'a this."

They stood quietly for a moment, except Paulie Jr., who was beating up on himself, trying to knock off a few more mosquitoes. He threw a thumb in the general direction of the shack Trick's son-in-law used for an office. "Let's go inside, eh? These little fuckers are eatin' me alive."

They started toward the shack but were stopped by two short honks from a car horn.

"That's him," Trick said as Tony Montello's Cadillac appeared on top of the hill about fifty yards away.

The car hesitated, then rolled awkwardly down the narrow dirt lane toward the three men clustered in front of the squat building.

The car hadn't come to a complete stop and Tony's foot was already hitting the ground. "Get back to the gate!" Tony told his driver, and got out.

The car slammed into reverse, leaving Tony in a cloud of dust. He waited for the dust to blow away, then looked around.

Trick had described the place to Tony as a one-acre lot a half mile off the main road, with lots of trees, and a high wooden fence to keep out the kids.

Tony gave it a long look and nodded as if he liked what he saw. He was smiling when the three men greeted him.

Dip packed his bags with what he thought Robin would expect him to take if he really believed he was going somewhere. They were booked on a flight to Raleigh, North Carolina, departing LaGuardia Airport at 11:38 P.M. That was four hours from now. But Dip knew, he'd never make the plane.

"I don't understand," Robin was saying from the bedroom chair directly behind him. "He's got a telephone. Why do you have to *see* him to say goodbye?"

Dip closed his suitcase, pulled it off the bed and placed it on the floor next to Robin's. "I gotta give 'im somethin'," he said, putting on the act so she wouldn't worry. "It's only gonna take a few minutes."

He'd been lying to her a lot lately, going along with whatever she wanted. Like leaving town. It was part of what she'd called her "three-phased plan." She'd explained it by holding out three fingers: "One," she said, folding one of the fingers, "quit Montello. Two, put the house up for sale. Three, leave New York and get married."

She had believed him when he told her he wasn't working for Montello anymore, that he'd talked to the man and everything was okay. Which was why phases two and three were moving along so nicely.

Well, Dip told himself, that's the last lie I'll ever have to tell her about Tony Montello.

He'd worked it out very carefully. They would meet tonight. Someone would pick him up and deliver him to Montello at around 8:30 P.M. Dip had no idea where he'd be delivered, but that was part of the arrangement. Dip's only demand was that Tony have his top three guys with him.

And now, right on schedule, here was Tony's man at the front door.

"I'll get it," Robin said, beating Dip by a half step. She opened the door and fell back in surprise. "For heaven's sake," she said. "I almost didn't recognize you."

"Hello," said Jimmy Montello. He glanced over Robin's shoulder and fixed his gaze on Dip. "How's it goin', Dip?"

Jimmy was wearing a light blue, double-breasted suit, a maroon tie, and a dark blue shirt with white collar and cuffs. Dip might have been impressed if he wasn't so disgusted with the whole damn show. He could still see the kid on that outdoor stage, James Montello getting his diploma, shaking hands with Bell while he scanned the audience for the only person out there who cared about him.

"Would you like to come in?" Robin said.

"No thanks." Jimmy smiled. "We gotta go. You ready, Dip?"

"I'm ready," Dip said. He kissed Robin, forcing himself to make it short, like everything was cool and he'd be back in less than an hour.

"Don't get lost," she called after him as they were heading for the car. "We've got a plane to catch."

They pulled away in Jimmy's new Corvette, Dip low to the ground in the passenger seat, feeling small and cramped.

"You and Robin takin' a trip?" Jimmy said.

"That's up to your old man."

Jimmy nodded and headed east on the Long Island Expressway. "You didn't look surprised to see me," he said.

"I wasn't."

Dip threw him a look but the kid kept his eyes on the road, driving casual with his right hand on the wheel and his left arm half out the open window. He was beating rhythms on the outside roof, and for a moment Dip pictured Prize alongside him. He shook his head and the image fell away.

"Did you volunteer?" Dip said. "Or'd your old man send you?"

"What's the difference? I'm here."

"I heard he put you in Diesel's crew. I woulda thought Paulie Jr. But I guess it don't matter. They're both dummies."

Jimmy blinked and the rhythms stopped for a moment. Dip watched him, saw his ear getting red, his hand squeezing the wheel. Whatever the kid felt, he was holding it back. He'd come a long way since graduation.

"So how does it feel to be a made guy?" Dip said.

"I dunno. They didn't make me yet."

"That ain't what I heard. I heard you popped somebody."

"Then you heard wrong. I was *supposed* to whack some guy, but I fucked it up." He glanced over at Dip. "Yeah, you believe that? I wait all this time for my chance and when it comes I blow it."

"What happened?"

"I ain't sure. It was all set up for me. I mean like we're all there, right? Me, Diesel, Paulie Jr. The mark's in the front seat. All I gotta do is put the gun behind his ear and pop 'im. But I hesitate. The guy freaks and I wind up droppin' the gun. Diesel had to shoot the guy in the face. Got blood all over our suits."

"Why'd you hesitate?"

Jimmy shook his head. "I wish I knew. Been kickin' myself in the ass ever since."

"Maybe you're not cut out for that kinda work," Dip said. "Maybe your old man was right, you shoulda went to college."

"Don't rub it in," Jimmy said. "I feel bad enough as it is."

"I can understand that," Dip said. "You had the chance to whack a guy and you couldn't do it. That's somethin' to feel bad about."

Jimmy didn't answer. Instead, he hit the gas and the Corvette swerved with a jolt that pushed Dip back in his seat.

Dip let him have his way; Jimmy, with his foot heavy on the pedal, passing cars along the expressway as if they weren't even moving. They'd reached ninety miles an hour before Dip slowed him down.

"Very impressive," he said. "But you better lay off. We ain't got time for a ticket."

"Fuck it!" Jimmy snapped. But he eased off. "You shouldn't do that, Dip," he said when he'd reached a safe speed. "You shouldn't piss me off. It ain't like it was before, you know what I mean?"

"Yeah," Dip said sadly. "I know *just* what you mean."

They got there right on time. It was almost dark. Jimmy had his headlamps on, but the place was hidden by a tall fence and Dip didn't see any signs on it to tell him where he was. About all he'd been able to figure was that they were somewhere out on Long Island.

Tony's man was at the front gate. He unlocked it and waved them on.

Jimmy eased the Corvette through the open gate and onto a bumpy lane that funneled downhill for about fifty yards toward an open lot. Across the way was an old shack with a rickety porch and a tar paper roof. Jimmy pulled up to the porch and stopped.

"Nice place," Dip said.

Jimmy shrugged and turned off the motor.

"Where are they?"

"Must be inside," Jimmy said. He turned to Dip. "I'm gonna have to pat you down. You know how it is."

"Yeah, I know."

Dip got out, went to the front of the car and leaned on the hood, spreading his legs in the standard frisk position. Jimmy patted him down, paying close attention to Dip's ankles.

"Okay," Jimmy said.

From behind them came the sound of a closing door. Footsteps on the porch, then Tony Montello saying, "You'll find out in a few minutes."

They came down off the porch. "He's clean," Jimmy told his father, and backed away, leaving Dip in the center of a tight circle comprised of Tony, Trick, Diesel, and Paulie Jr. There were no handshakes.

Tony said, "Okay, Dip. You called this, so let's hear it."

"Whadaya mean *he* called this?" Trick said. "Who the fuck is this guy, anyway?"

"Dipsy Doodle, that's who," said Diesel, laughing.

"I'll tell you who I am," Dip said. "I'm the guy who's gonna nail one'a you pricks to the wall."

The circle tightened—all but Montello, who stayed back, a slight smile on his lips. The son of a bitch is enjoying it, Dip thought.

"Back off," Tony said. "Let's hear 'im out."

Dip said, "You told me to find your rat, Tony. You said if I found 'im, I could have anything I want."

"That's why we're here in this shit hole," Tony said. "You said you had 'im. So get on with it. I'm gettin' dust all over my suit."

"What I'm gonna tell you," Dip said, "comes right from the horse's mouth."

"Horse?" said Diesel. "What the fuck's he talkin' about? What horse?"

Dip glared at him. "A dyin' horse, Deez. A horse that ain't gonna lie when he's takin' his last breath. You hear what I'm sayin'?"

"So far you ain't said nuthin'. Horse! Horseshit's more like it."

"Let him talk," Tony said.

Dip let his glare fall on each of them in turn before it came to rest on Tony Montello. "After I found Prize," Dip said, "I wanted to come back here and kill all'a you. Especially *you,* Tony."

Tony started to speak. Dip cut him off. "Yeah, I know. You didn't know anything about Prize. It wasn't you had 'im zonked. No. But you would have if you coulda found 'im. That's why he was hidin' out. He was more afraid of *you* than the no-good sonofabitch who was really after 'im."

It was Tony's turn to glare. "I was you, Dip, I'd be careful what I say."

"Why? Whadaya gonna do? Kill me? 'Anything I want,' ain't that what you said? You goin' back on your word?"

"Stop fuckin' around," Tony said. "Who is it? I want that ratfink low-life bastard burned at the stake."

"It's him!" Dip said, pointing his finger.

Diesel went bug-eyed. He sputtered and stammered and tried to smile at the same time. But it wasn't working.

"Get real!" he finally said. Then he lunged at Dip.

Dip was ready for him. He hit him hard with a straight right hand. Diesel dropped to one knee, dazed, but still sharp enough to try for his gun.

"Grab him, Paulie!" Tony said.

Paulie moved fast. He jumped Diesel before the guy's hand ever reached his holster. Within seconds Paulie had him wrapped up in his short, pudgy arms, pinning Diesel's arms to his sides.

Diesel struggled for a moment, then quit. "Hold it here!" he said. "Whadaya gettin' on *me* for? The guy points a finger and all of a sudden I'm a rat bastard! *He's* the rat, not me."

Tony raised his hand. "Shut up, Diesel! Don't say another fuckin' word!"

It was much darker now, but the moon was bright and Dip could see Tony Montello clearly. His mouth was tight and straight, and frown lines were trenched deep in his forehead. Dip recognized the signs. The man was doing some heavy thinking.

Stepping closer to Dip, Tony said, "Tell me about this dyin' horse."

"You know who I'm talkin' about," Dip said. "I followed 'im all afternoon. Saw 'im head for this Chinese whorehouse some snitch told me about. I waited outside, then went in after 'im. It cost me five hundred bucks to get past the little Chink that runs the place."

"You're talkin' about Sonny DeMarco," Tony said. "You sayin' it was *you* clipped Sonny? *You?*"

"That's a crock!" Diesel shouted. "He'd never get *near* Sonny. No fuckin' way!"

Dip ignored him. "It was easy," he said. "Sonny was upstairs with a coupla bimbos. I waited outside the door. They left and I went in."

"He's *lyin'!*"

"I don't think he is," Tony said.

Dip said, "He was tied up nice'n pretty, playin' leather games with the fluff. They had him danglin' by his wrists from a nylon cord. We talked for a while. Then I hung 'im by his fuckin' neck."

Diesel squirmed but he wasn't going anywhere, not with Paulie Jr. on his back.

"He died with his tongue hangin' out, Deez." Dip stared at Diesel. "But not before he told me a few things. Like who it was got Joey Cara. And who paid Charley Bop to start the whole thing."

Dip made a half turn toward Tony Montello. "He's your rat, Tony. He put Eva in the hospital . . . and he killed Lenny."

"That's why you did Sonny DeMarco," Tony said. "To get even for Prize. That's good, that's good." He jabbed a thumb toward Diesel, who's face was twisting with anger and fear. "You can do this bag'a shit the same way."

"Whadaya sayin'?" Diesel whined. "I been a made guy for fifteen fuckin' years. I got my own crew, for Chrissake. You can't take his word over mine."

"He's got a point," Trick said.

Tony thrust his hand straight out. "Look at 'im! Look at 'em both! Who do you think's lyin'? I don't give a shit who he is. A rat's a rat. He's gotta—Give Dip your piece. He's gonna make his bones right here, right now. And when he's done killin' 'im, I'm gonna kill 'im again."

Trick pulled an automatic from inside his jacket. He gave it to Dip.

"Move away, Paulie," Dip said and released the safety.

Paulie stripped Diesel of his weapon, and stood to one side. Arm extended, Dip sighted the automatic directly at Diesel's forehead. Diesel covered his face and fell to his knees.

"I didn't do nothin'," he cried. "I swear to God!"

"*Do* it!" Montello said. "Do it and you can step right in. You can have his crew and everything with it. Go on, shoot!"

Dip's finger tightened on the trigger. Diesel groaned with each quick breath. Jackie Dippolito wanted Diesel even more than he had wanted Sonny. It was Diesel who had tortured Prize and then killed him. If anyone deserved to die it was this son of a bitch. But it wouldn't stop with Diesel. It couldn't. There was someone else he'd have to kill, too. He lowered the gun.

"Whadaya doin'?" Montello said. "He's a fuckin' traitor. He's lower than scum. I want 'im cut in little pieces like all this fuckin' wood you see layin' here. Then I'm gonna toss the pieces in that freezer over there. You hear what I'm sayin', Dip?"

"Yeah. I hear you."

"Then what the fuck are you waitin' for?"

"There's somebody else," Dip said.

"Whadaya mean, 'somebody else'? Who?" Tony bellowed, his voice bouncing off the shack and up the hill toward the front gate. "Tell me and I'll kill 'im myself!"

Dip didn't answer.

Jimmy Montello was standing alongside his car, taking it all in. He'd removed his necktie and had opened the top four buttons of his shirt. Dip walked over to him.

Jimmy's eyes were almost as wide as Diesel's. He tensed when Dip stopped in front of him. The kid was sweating, but he didn't move.

Dip looked back at Jimmy's father. Tony Montello was chalk white, dumb silent for the first time in his life.

"Here," Dip said, offering Jimmy the automatic. "I'm givin' you another chance to make your bones."

Jimmy shook him off. "I didn't want 'im to do Prize," he said. There were tears in his eyes and Dip had to fight the urge to cry along with him. "I didn't want that," Jimmy said. "But I'll tell you. He had class. He checked out . . . like a man."

Dip was silent. He noticed the gold chain and cross on Jimmy's neck. It glinted in the moonlight. He took it in his hand and let the chain hang loosely over his fingers.

"You want it back?" Jimmy said.

Dip lowered his hand. He shook his head. "You're gonna need it."

SOHO CRIME

Other Titles in this Series